8/9/08

Dear

GW00864961

,

I wish you swift recoveries
and wonderful journeys ahead.

With all my love,

BEHIND THE MIRROR

Short Stories and Reflections

by

Nicolas D. Sampson

authorHOUSE®

AuthorHouse™ UK Ltd.
500 Avebury Boulevard
Central Milton Keynes, MK9 2BE
www.authorhouse.co.uk
Phone: 08001974150

First published by AuthorHouse   1/14/2008

ISBN: 978-1-4343-2514-3 (sc)

Printed in the United States of America
Bloomington, Indiana

This book is printed on acid-free paper.

Dedicated to Rica and Dimitris,
loving parents, brave warriors, good people.
Your love illuminates the way.
May you rest in peace.

"He was a part of my dream, of course – but then I was a part of his dream too"
–Lewis Carroll

Introduction

This is the odyssey of Victor Gente Delespejo, and these are some of the letters and essays and stories that he exchanged with his friend, Xavier Thorntrail.

A brother in arms and warrior soul, Xavier was there when Victor needed him, if not in person then in spirit, spurring him on in his endeavours, holding him up when he would falter, inspiring him to continue and never give up. A friend in need. A friend among the countless self-involved faces. An ally.

Truthfully, this is not any one's story. This is their story. Or, to be more precise, these are their stories — at least some of them, for not all of them survive. These are the stories they exchanged about friendships and connections, about hypocrisy and deceit, about greed and taking, contentment and giving; these are stories about unhealthy dependencies, about false promises and failed attempts, about letting one's guard down and taking things for granted; stories about various disturbing behaviours and attitudes that are being handed down to the next generation without much thought; stories that seek to gaze into these unsettling reflections — into them, around them, through them, and even behind them — in order to rediscover the gems of our existence buried underneath the glacier of consuming and confounding impulse.

These are the stories they exchanged while fighting for what they believed in, defending their homes and loved ones. They are the oxygen that fed their blood, their hearts and their minds. They are medicine. For that's exactly what stories are. Medicine… Medicine for the soul.

The Writings of Victor and Xavier

"Philosophy cannot soothe your soul, but in the mirror the truth will be known"
Sanctuary – Into the Mirror Black (1991)

Warrior Butterflies

Dear Xavier,

Thanks for your previous letter. You know, being in a foreign land far away from anything remotely familiar, can be very lonely. Extremely lonely. There are times here when even the simplest things acquire a most impossible nature. Food shopping becomes a test in language and communications skills. Posting and receiving mail is like working with the Bureau of Bureaucracy during the administration of an obsessive-compulsive director. Walking the streets is far from leisurely... Birds begin to sound annoying... The sunsets appear sinister... These are not good signs!

But then a letter like yours makes it through the stamp and red tape, and if it hasn't been rained upon, or gnawed upon by some wild animal, I read it with the outmost satisfaction and begin to ground myself in the warm assurance of a familiar voice that is speaking wonders through a modest piece of paper.

You know, I'd like to come back home for Christmas for as many days as I can scrounge up. I love being home during the Christmas period. I just love it because people let go of their everyday masks and reveal a more human, less pretentious and less rigid aspect of themselves.

I haven't of course forgotten that there is always a sort of tension back home, an underlying menace floating in the air, lingering between the words, beneath the expressions, behind the movements and interactions. I know very well that it's there. And truth be said, while this tension rarely becomes apparent – not directly anyway – it is definitely there; one must simply focus on the switch-around the Christmas holidays bring about in order to see it; one must pitch the transient mood of celebration against the steady flow of the mundane in order to sense the disparity between the normal and the festive.

Most people, though, don't pay attention to these things at all, I guess mainly because the transformation I am talking about has been taken for granted; all the focus falls on the holidays and none goes to the imperative that rises out of relativity and comparison, the imperative that demands more than one perspective.

In other words, my dear friend, while being happier during

2

the holidays is a tacit and foregone conclusion to most, it also reveals something else: not how happy holidays make you, but how repressed everyday life can make you if you begin to take it for granted.

Like I said, more than one perspective. And from this angle, one can challenge the pervasiveness of anxiety, stress and general restlessness in the modern world. We have lived so long in such dreary states of mind that we have started believing and accepting that an adult life is synonymous to them. An adult life is not considered seriously adult anymore unless it contains anxiety, stress and general restlessness (if not all three, then at least one of the three). We not only believe it and accept it but have also begun to expect it. We prepare ourselves for it as we are about to enter the adult arena, ready to engage in what is consensually considered a gruelling and exhausting marathon that shall drain all traces of wellbeing from our… being! Well, we believe it, and have even begun to teach it to our children too, just as we were taught it when we were young.

If only adults reflected for a moment on the things they tell children in order to prepare them for the cynical realities of the "real" world, they would remember that they are just recycling the things they were taught by adults when they were kids themselves. Only then would they begin to understand why the cynical world is not only actively created but also passively perpetuated. They would realise how they play a part in the continuation of cynicism without actually meaning to.

Where have the days of wellbeing gone? Where have the cynics buried them? Where are the dreamers that have always spoken of loving what you do and doing what you love? Where have they gone and why have they left the world to the sordid and nearsighted visions of the Robotons? Robots don't dream. They just execute. So why leave the world in their hands?

You know, as I write this I can see the automatic melding and welding begin to take over the argument, pinning such questions on utopian New Age labels, leaving us rats (all of us, cynics, dreamers, utopians etc) racing for the cheese on the trap while our lease on the map expires slowly. Mind you, in a race of rats, who will bear notice of the cat? More importantly, who will heed the warning call? I shudder to think of the answer when I see the callers being drowned like rats in barrels of indifference and in rivers of similitude that flow towards the sea, towards the Promised Land, towards the Watery Graves.

Rats, mice, lemmings – in this case are they not all rodents? Are we not all rodents bearing the plague of our demise on our backs, as it too bears us in its infectious network? I wonder if another deluge is the only way to eradicate this plague that has hooked itself onto our skin. Or can we perhaps shake it off by drowning the cynics in deep waters while the rest of us reverse our course, and in literal back-to-front fashion transform each of the 'rats' to a 'star' of revelation? Talk about utopia now!

It's a nice thought but let's not get ahead of ourselves. I think that avoiding getting trampled by the stampeding rodents is a good first goal, and steering their flow back towards green pastures is a good second goal. Little steps for small feet.

And that's just one perspective. From another perspective, I consider myself no more a rat or a rodent than you do. We are just humble, yet, noble creatures in search of the dreamers, those tigers who once roamed the jungles of harsh life… those pioneers in search of new lands… those martyrs and rebels and visionaries… those warrior butterflies gliding their way through endless rugged fields, never allowing their sensitivities to become their Achilles' heel – nor letting their fears and apprehensions turn them back into caterpillars. They just become what they need to become…

Be well and stay in touch. There are many stories to tell and many sunsets to survive.

Warm regards to you and Sandra,
Keep the Faith,

Victor Gente Delespejo.

Strangers

Dear Victor,

Let me tell you something man. You talk about the harshness of life faraway, about being a stranger in a strange land, about the time when even the simplest things acquire a most impossible nature. And you know what? I understand you, man. I've been there, as you very well know. It's tough. It's harsh. It's lonely and dangerous out there. I struggled with the food and wrestled with the languages many times. I heard the annoying birds and seen the sinister sunsets. I been the foreigner too, man. So let me tell you something that I think will help you through those times when the sunset seems like the end of the world. Let me tell you about another set of rodents that mauls the incoming mail. Let me talk to you about another stampede, about another flood that rushes through the fields, about another end of days. It starts somewhere around the attack on wellness…

With the drudge and chore becoming the predominant characteristics of an adult's life, the cynics are taking over and their insidious principles are spreading like the plague, infecting the good health of a once aspiring society. Gone are the days when I married my Sandra in the garden of our family's country house under the blessings of a family that had travelled through the dire straits of inconvenience to be right there with us on that most joyous of occasions. They are gone but not forgotten.

I remember that day very clearly. Everybody came bearing kids and smiles, leaving their troubles and miseries behind. They just came together, like drops of water, uniting under a scorching sun, gaining strength in numbers, man, strength in mass. Unwilling to evaporate in the heat, they came together and offered us their honest blessings during our rite of passage. They offered us their joy. They offered us love.

And when the occasion was over, in the violet twilight of a mild Sunday evening, the voices began to fade away, giving way to a pervading silence that was advancing steadily towards our home. Everyone was saying goodbye to each other, slowly receding in the background of a long distance relationship, and we began to feel alone. It was a sad moment, melancholy. Goodness knew when we would all get together again. Yet, for all its sadness, this goodbye could not eclipse, not even for one second, the warmth of that weekend-long get together that had reinvigorated the greater bonds of our circle, tempering my wedlock to Sandra in a field of loving fire.

We had been blessed. We knew it, and we were grateful for it.

As we watched our loved ones venture back into the depths of our horizons, out of sight but not out of mind, we thanked our lucky stars for long-distance phone communications. No more waiting for the mail to dodge its way through the fangs and claws of a wild stamp-and-toss procedure. No more delayed gratification. This was a new era man, the era of Now, and we were grateful for it.

But most of all, we were grateful for the warm spirit that burned in each and every one of us, kindling our relationships and warming up our hearts, providing wellness to our lives and tending to our wellbeing. Mail or no mail, phones or no phones, we knew we would always be together, in spirit. And that was a comforting notion.

Nowadays, well what can I say? I see people coming to weddings and to other such glorious occasions for the free food and drinks! I see guys coming to meet chicks... to dip their yardsticks in a well oiled machine... to wet their dry appendages and suck a little spice up. And I see chicks coming to hook up with some hot doctor, or to dabble in the forbidden loins of a wealthy married man who is turning crusty from the sex deprivation that his trophy wife is subjecting him to. They come, they toss around, and then they leave like parasites that have descended from planet Cynic for a quick raid-and-feast, for a little snack attack, for a Taker expedition in the grounds of heart and soul.

Unfortunately, it seems to me that it's become more about the meet-and-greet rather than anything else. Meet-and-greet, wine-and-dine, talk-and-walk, take-and-take, then take some more while giving a generous amount of bull-and-crap to the one with whom you've met-and-greeted, wined-and-dined, talked-and-walked and taken to the privacy of a well designed bull-and-crap room that you have equipped with all sorts of fancy toys and arguments, praying that your bull-and-crap room is better equipped than their bull-and-crap room – for after all, in a gathering of Takers, one person's target is a cynic on the move, a counteracting Taker, a bull-and-crap counter-host, and no one knows who will prevail until the snout locks in and starts sucking the other's vital force till it drains it all out.

Now, at the end of such jolly encounters there is usually only one winner: the one who's still standing. As for the losers, they are usually flat and devoid of all energy, lying on the ground, beneath the sucker's feet.

But truth be told, and unbeknownst to all Cynics and Takers and loudmouthed Gurus, there is never a real winner. They all lose – even those who have sucked the others completely dry. They lose big time, for nothing can fill the wide gaping hole that cuts across their suffering soul. Nothing can ease their needs. They just end up craving for more and more, and their greed begins to get the better of them, taking over their minds, seeping through their dreams at night, tying them up in little knots while they sleep, nibbling away at their soul; the wide and gaping hole inside them keeps expanding, sending them further and deeper into their own personal hell, and they gradually perish inside the vortex of their obsessions.

Their only hope is to be spirited away by a caring loving creature. Sadly, there are none to be found, for they have been sucked dry a long time ago by other Takers. And those few who did manage to survive the bull-and-crap desiccations, well man, they took off for new and promising lands, in search of their dreams, in search of Givers – not Gurus… in search for a place – a long-forgotten place – where people help each other to live instead of die; where in order to be great, individuals make those around them great too by providing them with what is asked for and not with what they presume they should offer; where Taking is considered ugly. They took off in search of that place long ago and never looked back, leaving behind the desert of humanity, that most horrifying of places where the Takers are drying up like bones in the wasteland, cracking slowly under the scorching sun of their greed.

You see, man, what I'm talking about is something worse than being a stranger in a strange land, far worse. This is the gruesome tale of men and women who are being infiltrated gradually and agonizingly – in the sacred grounds of their homes – by Cynics, by Takers, and by meddling and imposing Gurus. This is the tragedy of a home suffused by greed and invaded by rodents. This is the prelude to a flood that is threatening to drown everything out in slush and mud. And as the birds start to sound annoying and the sunsets begin to appear sinister to me, too, my world has evidently become the morbid scenario of men and women who are slowly becoming strangers in their homeland, strangers in their domain, strangers in their own home.

So hang in there man. Out there, in the faraway loneliness, you are a migratory soul who may have taken one of the few ships out of a festering mess. Remember that, man! Remember it well. And bear in mind that in order to deal with a mess of this calibre effectively, one has to detach oneself from it for a while, looking at it from the outside, seeing things for what they are and analysing them without involvement, without bias, without the shortcomings of skewed perspectives and vested interest… analysing them critically and with discernment, only as a fresh eye can register. It's the only way to aid the healing process – a process that may be now ripe for deriving. Not a happy task, I agree, but it is necessary. Very necessary.

And when things get rough and seem totally unbearable, remember what the alternative is. Remember that there's nothing more unbearable than being harmed by your own close environment; than seeing your own homeland being overrun by ugliness and greed; than sensing that the vice has started infecting your own wellbeing, your dreams, your life… and doing nothing about it – as if everything is normal and ok. For this is what happens when you stay put and comfortable – you get trapped in the vortex of a mess that keeps getting more and more vicious, spinning down to the depths of an abyss in oblivious delight. And then you wake up dead. Or worse, you wake up living dead.

Hang in there, man, hang in there and fight. It's the only way to go. And who knows, you may not be in strange lands for long. Sooner or later you will become part of the bigger world you have migrated to. The strange will become familiar and you will no longer be a stranger. And before that happens, who knows, we may even join you – if not in body, then in spirit… not just me and Sandra, mind you, but the whole circle, family and friends. Coz that's what we must do if we are to survive the competition. We must choose our battlefields carefully, now more than ever – especially if we want to win more than just a battle here and there; if we want to win the whole war; if we want to protect our home.

Home. It's where the heart is, a principle worth leading a good life and fighting the good fight for. It is where the noble principles of respect, love and sacrifice reside. It is where the locusts have not landed, where the rodents have not infiltrated, and where the warrior butterflies are on the lookout, guarding our spirit with their lives and keeping the infection at bay.

So hang in there man. Hang in there and fight hard! Your home is at stake. Your spiritual home. Our spiritual home. This is not just any fight. This is a fight we must win, so we must fight as if our lives depended on it. If we don't, we will perish – to a very ugly adversary.

But to be quite frank with you man, and without beating about the bush, I just don't feel like perishing. I feel more like flourishing. Don't you?

Dream man,
Dream,

Your friend,
Xavier

Erasing the Taker

Dear Xavier,

There's a reason why all things happen, I guess, whatever it may be. There's a reason – good or bad – behind everything, just like there's a reason for falling in love or for falling off a bike on a smooth straight road despite the odd thirty years of biking experience. It happens. For some reason it does. For some undeniable, but nevertheless, unknown reason the world just falls in love with a sideshow and then loses focus and falls off its bike. And when it finally gets up, it realises that it has been surrounded and overrun by parasites, Takers that are spreading like the plague.

There's a reason why all this happens. But that's not all. There's also a question behind this, a very important question, and it goes something like this: what are we going to do about it?

...

Here's something I wrote.

As a man meets his woman
On the bridge of a fleeting moment,
Love is kindled from the embers
Of a life immersed in expectations,

And the lips of a lover begin to seek the pulsating skin,
Radiating heat and moisture,
Bearing promise of a thousand passions
Concentrated into a single touch, a single solitary kiss,

And the pores of the skin tremble to the soft caress,
Sending chills across the spine,
Spreading warm and blissful pain,

And the bodies writhe in ecstasy and heat,
Melting in the seeping waves of each other's stormy desire…
As a woman meets her man

On the bridge of a fleeting moment,
A wedge… a wedge is trying to cram its way between them,
Harassing the union,
Hovering around them like a greedy rodent,
Gnawing and nibbling, shrieking, and shredding,
Jealous and greedy,
Born of dejection, bred in isolation,
Festering, dying, mad…
A Taker…
The dark and lonely soul that has been
Littering the clefts of history throughout time,
An emotional vermin…
The scum of used up and long gone relationships
That has accumulated on the brim of harmony's tracts,
Bitter and grey and foul as excretion,
Foul as a rapist,
A burglar,
A thief,
Taking – with force – that which can only be offered and given,
Taking – without remorse – to fulfil its fetid needs,
Its vices and greed, sucking vitality out, feeding off the rest,
A parasite, deadly, horrible, insatiable,
Taking,
Taking,
Just taking…

The man and woman turn around
And face the taunting vermin,
Which hisses with malice
Through matte, yellow incisors…

They turn around and face the spectre of greed,
The Taker,
Pointing their indexes towards it,
And summon from the dungeons of their psyche
The memories and recollections
Of what the Taker took, of what the Taker's done,

Dredging up the maladies and woes it has inflicted upon them,
Bringing them out in the open and
Shooting them back inside the Taker's greedy and compulsive core,
Smiling behind their aiming hands,
Smiling, glaring and singing…

'Take abhorrent Taker, take without reprieve,
Take our grief and sorrows now,
Take them back, they're yours to keep,
Taker is your name and rank, and taking is your game,
So take the misery you caused
And relish in its wake;
And bear in mind that it will stick,
That it will stay with you until you learn,
Until you learn to earn what you now yearn for;
It's time to earn, rapacious Taker,
It's time to earn,
To earn, not take!'

With the last smidgeon of strife
Consumed by the undiscerning Taker,
Their souls sucked clean from
The filth that was clogging them up,
They tear the barriers apart
And start melting into one another,
Combining their love,
Creating a sun,
Calling from the lifelit towers of their psyche
The effervescent spirit that inhabits their domain,
Summoning all their dreams and inspirations
From the fibres of their being
And infusing all their substance with a zesty, flowing stream…

As man and woman meet each other
On the bridge of a fleeting moment,
Their love begins to pulsate through them stronger than ever
While the Taker's wedge has been destroyed,

Reduced to nothing but a smudge,
A dark mark, a heavy stain,
A stark reminder
Of the horror inherent in feeding off others' lives,
In gnawing away at their souls,
In shredding their dreams,
Stealthily and bit by bit,
With force and greed and sullen parasitic need…

As man and woman join their lives
On the bridge of a fleeting moment,
In the wake of the Taker's demise,
They share their love with each other
And shine together like the mighty sun
Across the bleak and frozen plains,
Melting away the millennia-old grey
Accumulated layer of rotten snow,
Allowing the land to finally show,
Allowing the land to finally breathe.

Victor Gente Delespejo

Keep the faith, my friend. I am finding it increasingly hard to do so.
Don't let it happen to you too. Keep breathing. Just keep breathing.

Peace

Dear Victor,

I bid you peace,
And I bid myself peace,
For it is then that we
Find what we need;
Only then;
Not before;
Just like this.
I bid you peace.
I bid you peace.
I bid you effervescent peace
As I bid all those who stand before me,
Eager to see,
Eager to be,
Eager to follow their destiny.
I bid you... peace.

Be strong my friend and remember... if it's not worth dying for it's not worth having. Before we find peace we must always fight the good fight. Such is the way of the Warrior Butterfly. Such is the way of transformation. This is where the future will be born. So prepare to face the Taker and the Cynic in a battle that will shape the days to come. Prepare to stand and fight for everything you believe in. Prepare to smite the ones who kill.

I bid you strength in all of this. I bid you strength. I bid you bliss. I bid you unrelenting force of will. And in the end, when all is said and done again, I bid you everlasting peace.

Xavier

Jungles

From: victorgente@yahoo.com
To: thorntrailxavier@yahoo.com
Subject: The Advantage of Cities

Dear Xavier Thorntrail (hehe:),

I have decided to take your old advice and write an email. But getting access to the web is no easy task where I am right now. Over there it may as simple as getting out of bed, walking to your desk, and switching your terminal on. One, two, three, done. But not here. Here you have to toss a blanket of thorny ferns away, get up, duck from mosquitoes the size of hummingbirds, jump onto the nearest rock, avoid falling in the sludgy river currents, juggle yourself towards land, jump over the snarling caiman and onto the shore, slap the howler monkey that gets in your way, dash through the trees, turn right on the dirt road, run like hell for three hours, turn left at the village with the thatched malocas, find the one with the sign that says 'Internet' on it, go through the door, ask for a terminal, and then wait for countless hours until everyone who was there ahead of you gets their turn. And once they're all done, you sit down full of excitement, ready to start surfing like a stuntman on crack, ready to ride those crazy cyber waves, and suddenly your excitement is punched out of your body as if you had taken off on a monster wave and landed straight onto a rude piece of rock, chest first, your breath completely knocked out of you from the blow, hanging limp, watching the webpage trying to load... slowly... steadily... loading... loading... loading... still loading... almost a quarter way there... loading... loading... growing a beard while you wait... loading... loading... going to the bathroom three times already... waiting... loading... almost half way through now... dodging curses... dodging spells... dodging the poisonous darts shot from angry proprietors who have been travelling three days upstream to use the internet and who are not impressed by your short stroll over a measly couple of caimans to get there... three quarters almost loaded now... solving two Sudoku sets, hard level... finishing the bottle of firewater you'd brought with you... watching the barren field across the street grow into a forest... waiting... almost there... that's right... there we go... come on now... YES! Finally!! The page is loaded! The cursor flashes beautifully on the Yahoo page, simply awaiting your command. All you have to do now is type in your details... log in... and wait for your mail page to load up!! So you put your caiman skins on, buckle up, and prepare to fight off some seriously pissed off locals while it loads slowly... If I don't write you again, then it means I have probably been dipped in honey and thrown to the fire ants.

All this does not apply to urban reality, of course. In the cities here things are easy. You don't have to travel over great distances to get to where you're going. Everything is in close proximity. Everything is readily available. To find an internet café you only have to cut across a few streets, walk a little while, dodge the hysterical cars and buses and motorcycles that are dashing at you from every direction with no regard for traffic signals whatsoever... pay off a cop so that he doesn't arrest you coz you're a foreigner... shake and salsa your way through the street-dancing... push your way through the demonstrations demanding wages of $2 an hour instead of $1... dodge the bullets from the riot police... dodge the bullets from the gangs that have descended upon the city from the renegade outskirts to raid, pillage, and plunder... negotiate your way out of a kidnapping... marry a landowner's daughter... enter the family business, set up your office, install an ADSL line and get connected in no time! Simple as that. One two three! See?

Take care of yourself and don't blame me for not sending any more emails! The truth of the matter is that I like the feel of pen on paper. You just can't beat it.

Be well,

Victor Gente Delespejo

Genevironmental Blvd

"With the birth of every child a reflection becomes a projection"
–Croshi Ganaig

For Every Action...

Like father like son. He preferred the feel of more familiar things to the restless nature of technology, your father, didn't he? I remember you telling me once how he scorned cars with automatic gear shifts and cruise control facilities, longing for the days when people operated the machines, instead of the other way around, and insisting that one day technology would inevitably erase the need for humans to exist at all. "The price to pay for technological convenience is that one day we will disappear into the technology we create." Isn't that what he wrote on a piece of yellow paper that he stuck on his bathroom mirror to see first thing in the morning? Isn't that what you had secretly copied on a piece of paper, which you always carried around in your schoolbag, reading it over and over again during class, reminding yourself that you must always be in control of your projects and creations? Isn't that what you were thinking of when you one day realised that children are creations too, and that we cannot be in control of their lives forever? That we must let them spread their wings and fly away to new skies in search for their calling if we want them to truly become what they need to become? Isn't that what you were thinking of when your parents came one day and gave you their blessing for the path you would follow in life, no matter how far away from them it would lead you? The price to pay for technological convenience is that one day we will disappear into the technology we create, and so as the years went by, like all children, you saw your parents slowly fade and disappear into you as you took hold of the flame and set off for the adventure of your life on the evolutionary highway they had paved for you, creating the path in which one day you, too, will disappear in favour of your offspring.

Yes, like father like son. So the saying goes. Contrived in those gender-biased ages, it of course reeks of discrimination these days, for it does not cover the whole range of the biological spectrum. One can easily say that fathers and sons are not the 'be all end all' of society anymore, and that there is a host of mothers and daughters out there who are being greatly offended by such discriminatory adages. Then again, one can also see through the adage without getting stuck in mist engendered by those before us, absolving oneself from excess tribulations and cutting through to the core of the matter; the chromosome minefield is avoided altogether by taking the short route to meaning, and the journey is marked with neither perceived insult nor perverse injury.

Apart from revealing a more agreeable route to the essence of an adage or a statement, of course, this smooth approach to meaning also reveals how we may have become a little oversensitive and touchy lately, not to mention disoriented and very confused. A brand nowadays seems more prominent than the contents of what it represents, and that says a lot about our way of life; essence has given way to pretence and the fabric of our relations has been thrown against the prickly egos of the insecure, the easily-offended and the image-aspiring. Tremendous amounts of caution are necessary in our day-to-day routine, lest our opinions get snagged on the thorns of political correctness. So let's be correct. Let's be politically correct and join the prickly party.

Not 'like father like son.' No! We don't want to offend people, do we? Certainly not, so let's be nice and proper. Ahem… 'Like parent like child.' Ah, there you go! After all, daughters resemble their mothers too, don't they? So why omit that? Are we discriminatory? No! So…

'Like parent like child.' Hmm… Doesn't quite have the same ring to it. Not that I want to offend anyone – or imply anything against any organisation or group, all of which I deeply respect – but I kind of think that maybe this comment does not hit the spot, sort of.

There, I said it. Hope everyone is cool with what I've just said. I didn't mean any disrespect. But you already know that, right? So, let's move on, shall we? – if you want to, that is! I don't want to pressure anyone, you know. I just get carried away sometimes. It's just so exciting to exchange views and ideas freely, without offending anyone… I think! Well, maybe. I'm not certain of it, to be honest. After all, there is a certain charm in speaking out without thinking ten times about it, isn't there? So I would say that it, too, has its merits – speaking without over-thinking, that is. Don't get me wrong though, I don't want to offend those who believe that people should mind their tongue lest they offend anyone. Then again, I don't want to offend those who like to talk from their heart now either, do I?

Hmm… let me rephrase. 'Like parent like child?' Don't like it, don't like it at all. In fact, it sounds like shit!

Yeah, that's better! Free expression, truly free expression; a thought spoken in its raw unfiltered form without worrying about conventions and faux-pas.

'Like father like son,' alright! Like father like son, and let the discerning and clear-minded see through the labels, past discrimination and across to the blooming field that unfolds far behind. How? There's nothing to it. All one has to do is focus on the road and not on the asphalt, and the way ahead unfolds like a red carpet. It's as simple as that. After all, when you travel, you want to learn the territory, not the map.

Yep, like father like son alright! It's a wonderful feeling. I know it well. I've known it ever since I was old enough to realise that one day I could have my own son. What a wonder that would be, daddying away at a little me! Wonderful!

Years later, I realised that my son could only be a little partial me. Yet, this did not diminish the experience at all. That little 'partial me' provided a newfound purpose to my whole existence. And as if that wasn't magnificent enough, I also appreciated the parallel joy of having a little partial 'reciprocal' me. You see, I had a daughter too.

What a blessing. A son and a daughter. Beats the hell out of having a single hermaphrodite child. Not very politically correct, but hey… that's life man! That's life! Like father like daughter, like father like son!

Xavier Thorntrail

I said, for every action...

Like mother like son. So the saying could go. It doesn't, but it could – and it should. After all, sons are the offspring of their mothers too, aren't they? It's not as if they spring out of their father's penis straight into adulthood. On the contrary, they have to spend nine odd months inside their mother's body before they can be ready for this part of the world.

During these nine months, and before their dramatic exodus, offspring grow from morula to foetus to embryo. From one cell they become two, from two they become four, eight, sixteen, thirty two whole cells... sixty four, one hundred twenty eight... and nine months later they are an organism. Rudimentary, but an organism nonetheless, made up of billions of cells. From one to one billion and rising. Now that's a miracle!

But aren't we forgetting something? We don't go from one to one billion. No, we go from two to one to one billion; we start with two cells – sperm and egg – two gametes – two wonderfully reciprocal and complementary organelles, which join their forces in wholly matrimony to create one single new lifeforce. Their fusion is the greatest wedlock of all time and one of the grand mysteries of this universe. The two become one. Now that's a miracle!

Mind you, this is one union that cannot be undone. It can be terminated but not undone. The morula, the foetus, the embryo can die; they can be deformed or grow incomplete; they are an aggregate of cells that can suffer countless forms of harm or damage... but they can never be split back into a sperm and an egg! That union is permanent and irreversible. The two become one till death does them part!

Now, when death arrives what happens? Does it actually part them? Does consciousness actually dissolve into its sperm and egg counterparts? Or does it remain as one – a new composite – separate, unique and individual?

Who knows, you might ask? No one really understands what happens after death anyway. For all we know, we may not even live after death; we may just be disintegrating into nothingness. What we do know though – with considerable certainty – is what happens before birth, upon conception: the two become one. $1+1=1$!

Aren't we forgetting something else though? We don't go from two to one to one billion, you know. We go from one billion to two to one to one billion! Millions and millions of sperm cells are racing doggedly to get to the egg first, fighting and dying to enter it, but, at the end of the day, every single one of them shall wither away and die. All except one. The champion. His victory is his survival, and his real life begins upon conception, where the two cells fuse into one and then grow into billions.

So we have come full circle. From millions of cells to two to one to two to millions and millions again. A fascinating spiral. And as these cells grow around each other, they develop into shape, growing straight into form and back into gender. The primordial morula turns into a human foetus turns into a male or female embryo. And the future offspring assumes solid gender, creating not only a man or a woman but also a future father or mother.

Parenthood, though, is a long way off. An embryo has to be born first, let alone grow, before it can consider rearing its own children, so its parental attributes aren't pertinent just yet. For now, it still has a number of months to enjoy in the incubated hospice of gestation, where it will experience whatever mother does, all while suspended in fluids, weightless, and temporarily amphibious. Mind-bending, isn't it?

When the waters finally break, the ground gives way and the baby passes through the tunnel into the light, into the dry world, the world of oxygenated air. And there it is greeted by its parents, mother and father, progenitors and creators, who will rear it and prepare it for the harsh realities of the dry world.

Now, if it's a boy it will be reared differently than if it's a girl. From the onset. And it will never be treated as an 'it.' But it will be referred to as an 'it' in discussions that deal with the more abstract and neutral nature of 'the baby,' whatever that means. After all, how can a gender-defined entity – and a human entity at that – ever be referred to as an 'it?' Well, over the years this is how it has come to be! Makes no sense, but neither do a great number of things in the dry world, so go figure.

With the waters mopped away, the baby son or baby daughter is now ready to face the challenges of light, gravity, oxygenated air and gender divisions. Sons resemble their fathers, daughters resemble their

males are not 100% males; they have female qualities and needs within them, just as females have many male qualities and needs – for females are not 100% females either! So...

Like father like son? Surely, but not absolutely.

Like mother like daughter? Again, surely... but not absolutely! The gender similarity just can't carry an absolute parallel all the way.

Which of course takes us to the next question:

Like mother like son? Like father like daughter? Well, yes... yes indeed... surely... but not absolutely! After all, we do not want to exchange the extremes of the scripture-minded for the extremes of the homogenisers. Certain gender distinctions are there – unambiguously clear – and just cannot be done away with no matter how hard we try to relativise them together. Gender remains, and it is tangible...

Which of course brings us right back where we started: to the world of the plural parents, where the temporarily neutral child is growing.

Funny how things come full circle, isn't it?

Xavier Thorntrail

An Equal and Opposite Reaction!

Speaking of circles, let me tell you a story. My son and daughter looked exactly like me. They had the same eyes, the same forehead and the same facial structure as me. This upset the hell out of their mother, and consequently me, for I never heard the end of that story. She was always jealous and bitter about it, bearing it wherever we went, like a personal cross. Her life became a Golgotha. Consequently, so did mine. The weight of her obsessions was too much for her to bear, and so it became too burdensome for me as well. Family life was under the shadow of the huge chip on her shoulder. All because of a whim of nature and a little gene splashing that just hadn't gone her way. Was it my fault that the kids looked like me?

Apparently so, and I was punished for it every day, severely. She made sure of it.

Part of her problem was that she was extremely good looking and I wasn't. Not that I'm all that bad. But she was simply exquisite. And she knew it. So when both our children appeared to have fallen from the Y end of the helix, she was livid.

At first she didn't show it. She pretended not to mind at all. And if I hadn't known her well enough, I would have believed her nonchalant act. But that's all it was, an act. Deep down, she was fuming.

Good as it was, though, her act didn't help at all. It made things easy at first, but only by bottling up a host of bitter feelings and other nasty ghouls inside her. With the venting valves tightly shut the pressure was just building up. One could see it in her eyes, clear as day – when a friend or relative would comment on one of the children's looks, she would smile and joke around while her eyeballs appeared to be ready to pop out, fall on the floor and roll out the door. It was extremely awkward. And it was only getting worse.

Then she started saying things… throwing little jabs at me here and there… mucking the atmosphere.

"Well, apparently there can be too much of a good thing, but if it were up to me the children would have been stunning."

"With these looks, one would expect them to be smarter."

"Well, so much for modelling school!"

Horrible little comments, they were. Absolutely horrible. Yet, I used to take them in my stride, not paying too much attention to them. After all, she was joking, wasn't she? – at least that's what she would always claim whenever I confronted her.

And so it went for quite a while, behind the curtains of our private dialogue. Comment, comment, comment, tension, confrontation, evasion, and back to square one we came. Comment, comment, comment…

Then it got worse. I could see that she wanted to say things in the presence of others and not just in private anymore. She was just bursting at the seams. For some reason, though, she was holding back. She would just smile wide at everyone, revealing her perfectly aligned shiny white teeth while trying to contain her impulses, holding everything in and pretending that she was just fine. Yet, nothing about her eyes was smiling. They would simply assume a disconcerting gleam that bore warning of severe internal turmoil, giving her thoughts away. With time, people began to notice the disparity between her inner and outer worlds with more and more ease, and her obsession became a very public secret.

Then one day she lost her composure in public, at a pre-new year's eve party, in front of thirty two other people – without counting their babies and toddlers. She just blew her top off right in front of everyone, joking on about how her nose was like a button, how my nose was like a potato, and how all my family would have been the rave at the National Portrait Gallery should the theme be "Facial Vegetables and Other Juicy Features!"

It would have been a hilarious burn, if only it had stemmed from humour. But the bitterness could not be missed. And when no one laughed at her joke, she knew that things had just taken an ugly turn – the really ugly turn that goes beyond looks and reaches straight into the nature of the inner world.

She tried to save face and started smiling, but her charming looks could not hide the spitefulness that had surfaced from deep within. And now all her perfectly chiselled nooks and crannies dissolved like make up in a sauna, revealing a face I had never seen before. Neither had anyone else, from the looks of things. Everyone was just sitting there dumbfounded, unsure of how to deal with what they were witnessing – my wife, dripping with spite.

Then my daughter, Cindy, turned around and blurted out

something in the inimitable way kids just blurt out things. 'Am I a potato nose, mommy? That's an ugly thing, isn't it? Am I ugly too, mommy?'

'No, no, honey,' she answered back. 'Mommy was just making a joke about daddy's nose.'

'But everyone says that I have daddy's nose. Everyone says that I look like daddy!'

Thirty two pairs of adult eyes glared at my wife. They glared mercilessly, heckling her in silent accord. She tried to say something but then changed her mind and focused on our little girl, who had now started crying.

'No honey. Don't cry. You're beautiful. The most beautiful girl in the world,' she assured her. But Cindy was not convinced. She just kept crying and crying.

I was absolutely furious with my wife, but I contained myself because the last thing I wanted to do was to put on another show in front of everyone, especially the kids.

Then my son, Tommy, turned around and blurted something out too. 'Better to be like daddy than you, mommy. At least people will like us.'

Then he walked towards his crying sister and pulled her gently by the hand. She turned around and looked at him curiously. The crying had subsided. He made a silly face at her and then smiled widely while still holding her hand.

'Look Cindy, I'm Mr Potato,' he said and started jumping around. 'I don't want to become French fries… no, I don't like the hot oil… you're not gonna catch me… you're not gonna catch me…'

Some people started laughing out loud; Cindy watched her big brother jump around in joyous racket and smiled; Tommy saw her smile and got excited, jumping even higher; everyone saw Tommy respond to his sister and they laughed and cheered on; Cindy heard the laughter and sensed the good mood rising, so she cracked a little giggle.

Half a minute later, there was a huge party in the room. Cindy was having the time of her life jumping around with Tommy, and the adults were dancing with their children, singing, laughing and enjoying themselves. The ugly episode had been cast away and everyone was now celebrating in every sense of the word. Well, not everyone. Mommy was alone in the bathroom, crying.

You see... some things you must pay the price for. There's no other way.

One year later I filed for divorce. It took six months to complete. Then I became a free man with two little me's in my custody. And my ex-wife got married again. She married a male model. And I married my Sandra.

And we lived happily ever after.

Xavier Thorntrail

The Shadow of Shades

"A photograph is usually looked at – seldom looked into"
–Ansel Adams

How Shall I Put It?

I saw S.W.A.T. the other night. Great movie! There's nothing like a good punch-up, a booming shootout and lots of explosions to make someone feel better. Yeah, S.W.A.T. is that kind of a movie – boom, bang, caplang. Brilliant. Just brilliant! But you know what? It also got me thinking. The following morning I got up and just couldn't stop pondering over a simple, incontrovertible fact:

A typical movie for guys involves fights, shoot ups, explosions, fighting enemies, and getting the girl in a happy ending. A typical chick flick, on the other hand, involves fights, arguments, revelations, fighting hormones, and getting in touch with one's feelings in a happy ending...

Now, are we talking about two essentially different processes that involve totally different factors, totally different worlds... or could one say the opposite? Could we say that they are two basically similar processes that involve basically similar factors, basically similar worlds?

Victor Gente Delespejo

The Colour of Coffee

A man makes his fortune again after being bankrupt, down and out. A woman can love again after having her heart broken by her terrible husband. Or vice versa. Typical examples of themes in guy movies and chick flicks.

"Such stereotypes," some may think. Man and business, woman and love. Is this what men and women are all about? 'Man = cold and practical' and 'woman = emotionally complex?'

Ok, let's play. Suppose the examples were reversed. Imagine the following examples appearing on first instance instead of the previous ones. Pretend that you haven't read the above and focus on the following.

"A man can love again after having his heart broken by his terrible wife. A woman makes her fortune again after being bankrupt, down and out."

Can of Worms A, may I introduce you to Can of Worms B. We move from gender stereotypes to the next level: gender complications! For example: if a man had his heart broken by his wife, then she must truly be a terrible person, and he, he must be a sissy, a pushover, a totally whipped specimen; and if a woman can make a fortune again, after being bankrupt, down and out, she must be one hell of a person, yet, not so ladylike. Right?

These are just some of the undercurrent complications that may be operating in the above statements. You get the gist though: gender complications!

Let's look at a two more permutations. Let's see what else lies at the bottom of a can of worms. But let's reverse the order in which the genders are mentioned this time. So... Just pretend that you haven't read the above – and beware; we are now moving into the realm of the Great Chip-on-the-Shoulder!

"A woman makes her fortune again after being bankrupt, down and out. A man can love again after having his heart broken by his terrible wife."

It sounds different to the previous ones, doesn't it? Woman first, man second. Exudes a different vibe!

Here's another permutation.

"A woman can love again after having her heart broken by her terrible husband. A man makes his fortune again after being bankrupt, down and out."

Again, it sounds different. Love first, fortune second. When the order of presentation is changed and the sequence altered, the whole meaning changes too!

Now, why mention this? To some it makes no difference. Mention the man or woman first, big deal. Refer to stereotypes, yeah, ok. Yadda yadda yadda. Who cares?

Well, some do, and very much so! They insist that order and sequence make a huge difference by carving up impressions that determine the whole interpretation of a text, even if counterbalancing terms are inserted – terms which seek to nullify any discrimination.

Observe.

a) "A man makes his fortune again after being bankrupt, down and out. A woman can love again after having her heart broken by her terrible husband. Or vice versa."

The "vice versa" tries to restore balance by providing a two-way direction to the statement, but it still falls within the sequence with which things were originally presented. In this case: man first, woman second, *then* vice versa.

Furthermore, if the statement were reversed and the stereotypes crossed over, its apperception would still be different despite the equilibrating "vice versa." Behold.

b) "A man can love again after having his heart broken by his terrible wife. A woman makes her fortune again after being bankrupt, down and out. Or vice versa."

Again, the statement falls within the given sequence, and so do the respective attributes. In this case: love first, fortune second, then vice versa.

And when compared to each other, 'a' is clearly not the same as 'b.' Each has a different tinge to it, not to mention that only *one* of the two can come *first* in a text. After all, you have to mention something first, something second, something next and something last. There's no other way about it.

So... why mention all this?

34

Simple! To show that if someone wants to find a problem somewhere and make an issue out of nothing, he or she will predominantly succeed.

But where there's smoke there's fire, right? The above examples deal with the gender issue and are meant to grab the lens and focus it on that smoke. They can't really point out with certainty who started it, true, but their initial purpose is to sensitise awareness to the presence of smoke and fire.

Let's symbolise.

Say a man or a woman has some attitude issues regarding the other gender…

Oops, did it again! Why mention the man and not the woman first? It must be a subtle sign of "Chauvinism," of "the order of things that needs to be changed," of "a de facto phallocracy," of "the seemingly innocent comments that modern women should no longer tolerate…" The list of remarks could go on. It's as big as the chip on the fair shoulder.

Scratch that paragraph completely. Here's another one.

Say a person of either gender has some attitude problem regarding the other gender at work. This person seems to be overreacting to certain situations and appears very sensitive to comments about his or her (or vice versa) performance in relation to gender issues. He or she doesn't take jokes lightly and tries to make a point out of every situation. When asked about his or her behaviour, he or she says that the persons of the opposite sex are complacent about their standing. Our person claims that those persons are distorting certain facts and skewing normal affairs into a gender agenda, which they, of course, deny with surprise. As far as they are concerned, they are being very normal. But where there's smoke there's fire. Our imaginary person must have a chip on his or her shoulder, otherwise he or she wouldn't be reacting to his or her colleagues in this way… or, on the other hand, his or her colleagues may indeed be ganging up on him or her – and on the opposite gender in general – spreading tension in the office and causing rifts between the genders. But one thing is for sure. Every incident starts from our symbolic person – who is the common denominator to all the rising divisions – and from a specific group that meets him or her at the water cooler.

For example, the other day, while our person was having a glass of water, his or her colleagues started teasing him or her. He or she reacted and posited that their jokes were indirectly assaulting him or her. They denied his or her accusations, to which he or she answered...

Pretty shitty writing, don't you think? Politically Correct and boring as snails! And annoying, very annoying! You don't get anywhere with this kind of his or her expression. Sure, you can always get around it and find ways to construct text while showing a sensitivity and appreciation for delicate issues such as gender, religion and colour, but that's called functional adjustment, and it's different to blind overcompensation.

- Can I have a dark coffee please?

- You mean a black coffee, don't you lady?

- No, goodness no! I could never say that! I mean a dark coffee.

...

What is this?! Ridiculous! But it happens. Just open your ears and you'll hear it.

By this token of perceived insult, of course, 'dark' coffee sounds like something that is brewed by the Blair Witch, or by the Church in the Middle Ages, and this could pose some other serious problems.

Let's listen in.

- Hey you, what did you order?

- A dark coffee.

- I find that extremely derogatory. I belong to the FMW, the Foundation of Misunderstood Witches, and I do not tolerate the utterance of the term 'dark,' nor do I appreciate the casual way in which you use it. We are not dark. We are just misunderstood. So stop stereotyping us. And don't use the term 'dark' like that. It's a taboo term. Didn't you know that?

- Ok... I'm sorry. Good to meet you by the way. Now please excuse me. Ahem... please, yeah... em... waiter... waiter! Can I have a coffee with milk, please?

- You mean a white coffee, don't you lady?

- Wait a minute you two, what do you mean 'a white coffee?'

- Oh dear God, here we go again. Will you just let me have my coffee?

- Let me tell you that I will have none of this attitude, you hear? You will respect my democratic rights and sensitivities like every modern day citizen should or I will slap the blood out of you. Now,

I will have you know that I belong to the OLW, the Organization of Liberal Witches, and we don't like our capacity to be stereotyped as white. We are not constrained by the white colour. Not only are there various colours in our midst but we also possess different shades of each and every colour. So don't go around using the word 'white' with such arrogant ease. If you can't say 'black coffee' or 'dark coffee,' then you shouldn't say 'white coffee' either.

- But I didn't say 'white coffee.' I asked for a coffee with milk. It was the waiter who said 'white coffee.'

- Don't you yell at me like that! I have rights, you know. I have rights. You better respect them if you know what's good for you! I shall have you reported if you raise your voice at me again, do you understand me?

- Ok, ok! Whatever you say. Now, if you don't mind. Waiter... waiter! Can I have a coffee without milk?

- Listen lady... first you want 'dark' coffee, then you want coffee 'with milk,' and now you want coffee 'without milk.' Make up your mind, will ya? Milk or no milk? Black or white?

- Just a coffee without milk, thank you!

- A coffee without milk for the lady, coming right up!

- Wo, wo, wait a second sister! What did you say to the waiter? A coffee 'without milk...?'

Shazam. There goes all reason, drowned in a cup of lousy coffee that hasn't even been served yet.

"Wait a minute! Did you just say 'lousy' coffee...?"

Xavier Thorntrail

A Colourful Week

Where there's smoke there's fire. Our person at the water cooler seems to be the cause for the gender row at the office, and the people at the cafeteria across the street seem to be fuming, especially a black man who just walked in, straight into an order for a 'coffee without milk.' Not a black coffee. A coffee without milk.

What if we trace this man's path to the cafeteria by taking a peek into his week? Perhaps we will get to see why he is so furious and thereby gain an insight on why everyone seems to be so high-strung lately.

Day 1.

He sees a KKK Grand Flying Tyrannosaur on TV, who claims he doesn't drink coffee without milk because he hates everything black.

Day 2.

He asks for a black coffee at a diner, and the pink-skinned waitress is slightly embarrassed at having to repeat his order. 'One black, um, coffee for the, um, for the gentleman,' she garbles. Then she turns away and rattles to the kitchen on the double, where she finds three empty coffee pots, so she shouts, 'No more coffee left!' The tanned WASP chef jumps up startled and tells his café au lait non-Caucasian white Italian-American apprentice to brew some fresh stuff. After a few minutes, the apprentice jokes to the waitress, 'Fresh coffee, black like molasses,' which the black man overhears and doesn't appreciate at all. The waitress notices his frustration while serving him and becomes even more embarrassed by his agitated look, eventually fumbling the pot and spilling some coffee on his lap. He screams, 'Not the equipment, you skinny bitch,' and rushes out the door towards the city fountain.

Day 3.

He overhears two non-black kids talking on the subway. One is telling the other a joke.

- What do you call a black man in Texas digging and striking oil?

- Dunno. What?

- Black humour.

Now, was this joke making fun of the white Texans or the black ones? Or maybe both! Whatever the case, he didn't find it funny. But the kids did. They were cracked up. He was furious.

Let us take a small detour and follow the kids for a while.

They get off at the next stop and find their friends at a nearby park. They play ball for 45 minutes, then they take a ten-minute break, joking and trash-talking on full throttle. The competition hasn't paused, only the sport has.

The kid tells them the joke about the black man in Texas digging and striking oil. They all burst out laughing. Then the kid who laughed the most comes up with a counterjoke.

- Yo, what did the people in Harlem call Vanilla Ice's tour?

- ...

- White trash.

- Ok, so what do you call rap music?

- ...

- Black trash.

- Yo, what do you call it when the black man in Texas gives some of his oil money to charity?

- ...

- White humour.

- ...

- ...

- Time to play ball.

- Wait. One last one. How else do you call the 'black and white cookie?'

- Wait, I know this one... Martin Luther King Jr.'s Dream Recipe AKA Shot in the Dark! Now let's play!

The kids play some more ball, drink some more Powerade, and then renew their meeting for 10 that night at the "Amistad Pearl" – their favourite hangout bar – where their fake ID's go the distance.

Our two kids arrive there early, around 9:45, and find 'Uncle Ben' – a local neighbourhood character they got to know over the past few months – sitting at the bar, swinging and gulping them bourbons down like cough syrup. Gulp. Aaah!

Some people prefer drowning their troubles in alcoholic solitude rather than in merry company. One of the biggest giveaways is a stubborn reluctance to any form of casual conversation; talking becomes like pulling teeth. So as the conversation with Uncle Ben begins to become more and more painful, they get the hint and turn around, leaving him be. A couple of buddies of theirs bump into them just then and they forget all about him. They order a few drinks and begin to catch up. After a couple of generous swigs, the jokes begin to roll.

- Hey, what do you call a black man in Texas digging and striking oil?

- Dunno. What?

- Black humour.

Uncle Ben turns around and taps one of them on the shoulder.

- Hey! What do you call a garbage can full of rice?

- Dunno. What?

- Chinatown.

- Wait, that's not very funny...

Crack, slash... the bourbon short glass splinters on the kid's face, tearing through his cheek, right into his cheekbone and jaws.

One ambulance and a police car later Uncle Ben is shouting maniacally as the police officers haul him in:

- What my cousin do to deserve getting shot? He been driving on the interstate yesterday, outside our hometown. The police pulled him over. And he moved in his seat while they was coming to check him out. People not supposed to move when they stopped by the police over there. It's "potentially hostile action." So he fiddles his hands in his ride and they shoot 'im. They shoot 'im dead! Then they find his driver's licence in his hand. They said they sorry. They on paid leave right now. What the hell is the matter with this place?

A bystander asks one of the kids where Uncle Ben is from.

- I don't remember. From somewhere in the Bible Belt, I think.

Meanwhile, in another part of town...

The black man is watching the movie 'The Animal,' a comedy about a man who's sown up with animal parts after an accident and a side story of a black man who is treated very nice, almost too nice, by every single person in the vicinity. In fact, when he publicly confesses to a crime, nobody believes him. Funny!

When the movie's over, he tries to decide where the weight of the joke falls:

- Racism on the whole.
- High crime rates among the black population.
- Satire on minority people who commit crimes and deny responsibility for their actions. It's always the society's or someone else's fault.
- Satire on majority people who deny the existence and effect of a skewed society that may promote a disproportionate rate of crime among minorities. It's solely and always the perpetrator's fault.
- Reverse satire on criminals. They never did the crime. Something else less serious, yes, but never the crime.
- Extreme Affirmative Action, which even the beneficiary doesn't appreciate or affirm.

After a while he doesn't care. Whichever of the above issues the joke may have been about, it still points to a great problem that is in a flux. The rest are just feathers on a falling bird.

Day 4

The news show covers the story of a man known as Uncle Ben who slashed the face of an Asian kid in a bar. Amateur footage by a group of tourists reveals the scuffle after the assault, as well as the whole takedown by the police. Some channels show Uncle Ben's farewell proclamations while others just show the scuffle and the takedown. It is reported that the incident had something to do with either a racial joke or with a police shooting in another state, where Uncle Ben's reported cousin has been allegedly shot during a standard 'stop and search' procedure. An investigation is underway in both states.

In other news, earlier today, two people were shot outside a Korean restaurant in broad daylight by two Asian youths. The victims were brothers Jamal and Kobe Latrell, both of them social workers. Police are speculating random gang activity but they don't preclude more sinister possibilities such as honour killings or racial retaliation.

Also, two people were severely beaten up downtown and a few cars were torched in the suburbs, while in global news a cat was rescued by the National Guard in Hawaii and the Air Force has carpeted another insurgent area in… Breaking news, a police officer was just shot and killed moments ago and another was seriously injured… We are now going to a live report from…

He switches the TV off and goes to bed, drifting into a battery of nightmares. So do the two kids across town, along with the slashed kid, his best friend, and our not-to-be-forgotten genderless PC person at the office. Yeah, I know, it's an easy person to forget, the genderless one. But guess what! Tomorrow 'it' will wake up with a vagina and develop into a veritable 'she,' setting the text free and allowing it to finally flow without any type of PC pretence whatsoever.

Day 5

The black man walks into a café, where he finds our woman from the office. Freshly born and oozing with purpose, she has stepped out for a quiet little break at the cafeteria across the street – having had enough of the water cooler conspiracies for the day. So as the black man walks in, simmering and ready to blow his top off at the slightest sign of discrimination, he stumbles upon our woman who is fighting two witches and a waiter over a confounded cup of coffee. He can't help but overhear.

- Can I have a coffee without milk?

- First you want 'dark' coffee, then you want coffee 'with milk,' and now you want coffee 'without milk.' Make up your mind, will ya? Milk or no milk? Black or white?

- Just a coffee without milk, thank you!

- A coffee without milk for the lady, coming right up!

- Wo, wo, wait a second sister! What did you say to the waiter? A coffee 'without milk…?' Yo, why don't you ask for a black coffee? Because I'm black? Is that it? Are you embarrassed to say the word 'black' in front of a black person? Think you're better than me?

- No, not at all, I…

- You think that asking for coffee 'without milk' changes much? Do you? It don't change nothing! Ask for fair attitude, not for coffee without milk. Ask for company that's less fair-skinned and more fair-minded!

- But many of my friends are African-American and Jamaican!

- So what? That don't mean nothing to me bitch. You think that by having black friends you're gonna erase the damage your people inflicted on my people?"

Now this person may have a point, but he also has a great chip on his shoulder. Massive. The kind that crushes bones and sanity…

And what about our newly-born woman ordering coffee? She may indeed be a PC language freak; or she may be hanging out with his people because she wants to be PC by having the right percentage of colour in her relation spectrum. Conversely, she may indeed have good and genuine relationships with some of his people; she may be just defending herself from his aggressive accusations and his counter-racism; or she may be just a timid and non-confrontational person who, nevertheless, has honest multiethnic relations.

She may be just ordering coffee.

- Can I have a coffee please, just any coffee?
- Any sugar with it lady?
- Yes please.
- Brown or white sugar?

Clearly, there's no end to this mess. And there's no pleasing the critics and the pissed off ones. The only solution to this shit is to exercise constructive criticism, all-around constructive criticism on the inflated idiocy that is circulating around totally unchecked.

Enter Dick and Earl.

- Shut yer mouth you monkey.
- A white coffee for the lady. White sugar. On the double.
- Was he bothering you ma'am?
- We can take care of animals with nasty attitude.
- Yep, we sure can.
- And we all take our coffee pure white. Our cousin even said so on TV the other day. He don't drink it without milk. No, sir, it's white coffee for him and our clan. Pure coffee. Always!

She sighs.

- Pure coffee is without milk or sugar, you idiots! Pure *milk* is pure white!
- Hey Dick, she's right!
- Well, I'll be damned, she *is* right. Hey buddy, got milk? Four glasses please. Yeah, four. He's gonna have one too. We're gonna shower him with it! He's gonna look like a black and white cookie when we're done withim.
- Aw, shoot, Dick! How many times do I have to tell you, dawg? It's 'white and black' damn it! *White* and black. Don't let the propaganda get to you. 'Black and white' cookies, 'black and white' clothes, 'black

and white' TV… It's a conspiracy, dawg. They're trying to take over the country.

    - They're trying to take over the world!

    - Now you're talking, Dick. Now you're talking!

The woman takes off. No need for coffee anymore, it's just not worth it.

She cuts across the two witches – who have been cursing each other without pause from the moment they met each other – and heads for the door, stepping on a sachet of sugar of unverified colour on her way out. The sugar crunches loudly beneath her shoe and she mumbles something between her teeth. Then she dashes outside, cutting through the cars without looking, and storms into her office building. Frazzled, she has only one image in mind – the emergency brandy reserve.

Those close to her know that she is peculiar with words because she has a passion for describing things literally. Coffee with milk is not white in her eyes – it is a shade of brown. But more accurately and above all it is 'with milk.' It is 'coffee with milk.' Black coffee, on the other hand, is more dark-brown than black. Very dark-brown indeed. To be precise, it is just coffee, pure coffee, or 'coffee without milk' – if she wants to be redundant and very very clear.

Yes, she's kind of quirky in some respect and has gotten into trouble many times because of her unequivocal eccentricity to describe things exactly as they are. Her friends know it very well. They also know, though, that she is great at her job. In the past year she secured employment for 8,000 minority citizens and won a court case against a large company which was conducting systematic racial discrimination.

If only those fools at the cafeteria knew.

Then again, what difference would it make to them even if they did? Their minds had been set supersolid a very long time ago. There was no chance of changing them whatsoever.

Day 6

The recent racial incidents at the Amistad Pearl and the Korean restaurant are received less than well. Plucking abruptly an already tense situation, they send a huge wave of demonstrations across the city. The steam is suddenly blowing its tops off, one by one. The black man joins the angry crowd that is marching through the streets and begins to yell. The slogans are short and simple. End discrimination; raise cooperation; take affirmative action.

The crowd advances. They seem to mean business. Some are wielding baseball bats, crowbars and rocks. Their ferocity increases as more people join them, armed like lobsters. Emotions take over and the crowd degenerates into a mob; some shop windows are smashed; the sound of shattering glass electrifies the instincts and disarms the inhibitions; fires spring everywhere, smoke fills the streets, and guns make their appearance in the hands of the mob... amidst the mayhem, some shots are heard.

Choppers suddenly circle the sky and command the mob to disperse. The police and army descend on the scene and a battle begins. Chaos ensues – a chaos aiming to restore order.

The black man is dumbfounded. Consumed by discrimination and carried by the tide, he had marched mindlessly into the frenzy, but now everything seems to be getting out of hand. Is all this necessary? Is it? Well, yes, perhaps it is! Perhaps this is the only manner to turn the tables, the only means to mean business, the only way to make headway.

He looks around and begins to frown. His muscles tense up and his voice starts to rise once again, merging with the crowd's. He is ready to go ballistic. Then he sees a few kids beat up an elderly shopkeeper to a pulp and stops cold. In dread, he watches them beat him, loot him and then shoot him in the head, and he zaps out of the red mist. The next thing he knows, he is falling to the ground with a bullet in his chest.

Where did it come from? Does it matter? No, not really. The ethnicity of a bullet doesn't really matter to the victim. It won't matter to him at all in a few moments or hours. He'll be dead and he knows it.

As his soul is vacuumed out of his body agonisingly slow, he wonders whether he will RIP. Suddenly, he has a flashback of the woman at the cafeteria ordering her coffee. He sees himself going behind her. He orders an OJ, then cancels it and orders a super Sundae. He pays for the whole lot and invites her to sit with him at the table by the window screen, where they end up enjoying their sweets and concoctions over a laugh and a cheer – after they have torched the witches and restored order to the establishment, of course.

Something itches. He doesn't like his flashback. He doesn't like it at all, for behind every witch who burns at the stake he sees an arsonist wielding the gift of the gods.

Day 7

He rests. The city rests. The woman rests. Everybody rests. Tomorrow sets off another week.

Xavier Thorntrail

Welcome to the Closed Loop

"Mirror, mirror in the eye, who will laugh and who will cry?"
-Unknown

The Story of the Storyteller

There was once a boy who was very good at school. He always studied hard and aced his classes. His dream was to go to university and become an economic analyst, which he did. In fact, he became one of the best analysts in the country. Firms would call him up for consultations and universities would ask him to give lectures. Even the government would call upon him, seeking his advice on national economic policies.

He was so busy he naturally saw very little of his friends. In fact, he had practically no social life at all. His friends urged him to take a break and come out with them, even for an hour or so, but to no avail.

One night, after six whole months of not meeting with them at all, they finally convinced him to go out and spend some time together, like the good old carefree days, sitting around a table and having fun together.

'Now that you are the top dog in economics,' said one of his friends to him after a couple of drinks, 'we don't get to see you.'

'Well, you know what it's like,' he replied. 'A constant battle. To know your stuff and climb to the top you must go at it day and night.'

'So come on then,' said another, 'give us an economic analysis of the energy industry.'

The man thought for a moment. He didn't know how to start. He realised he couldn't give an analysis on command. He would have to give a plasmatic one, a forced one, one that would have to be squeezed into this thin and rarely experienced R&R slot. But he wasn't up for that, especially not when the request was more of a jab rather than a query. Especially when it was coming from a friend who, a few hours ago, had asked him to take a complete break from work and come out with them strictly for drinks and laughs.

He turned to the other side of the table.

'You're a writer, right?' he asked one of them.

'Yeah…'

'I'll make that analysis after you tell us a story,' he stated.

'What?' replied the writer.

'Tell us a story and I'll make the analysis,' declared the economist. 'It's only fair. I scratch your backs if you scratch mine.'

'But I...'

'Oh come on, just tell us a story,' interjected the salesman. 'Or are you too shy?'

'Shut up and let 'im get on with the bloody story, will you?' snapped the accountant.

'Look who's suddenly developed a conscience. The numberer!' heckled the lawyer.

'That's funny, especially when coming from a lawyer!' interjected the software developer.

'Say, are you all eager to hear the story or just in a hurry to get it over and done with?' asked the professor with a wry smile.

'Shut up!' shouted the CEO.

'Yeah, let the man speak,' said the physiotherapist.

'Go on, we're listening,' stated the teacher as a matter of fact.

'Yes, Seattle, we're listening,' the mechanic chortled.

'Stop it!' yelled the nurse. 'Let him speak. Come on, what are you waiting for?'

'Yeah, what are you waiting for?' asked the economist. 'Speak. Say something, will you?'

The writer coughed to clear his throat and looked at each person on the table intently, biting his tongue until there was silence – no whispers, no sniggers, no fuss and distractions; just total, undivided attention and silence. Then he began to tell his story.

When he was done, the economist was nowhere to be seen. In fact, everyone at the table had gone. In their place sat a bunch of noisy girls and boys, having the time of their life. The writer smiled. His story had once again done the trick, stripping the adult spikes off everyone's mind and allowing their deeply-contained souls to emerge from their jaded cells and fraternise instead of socialise – fraternise like the good old days.

He sighed, and then whispered a small word between his lips. And in the blink of an eye he, too, turned into a child, ready to have some genuine fun just as they used to, before the weight of adulthood came crashing down on their youthfulness.

And the story he told? Well… You've just finished it.

Victor Gente Delespejo

Friendship

"The best mirror is an old friend"
–Peter Nivio Zarlenga

"And you are an old friend's best mirror"
–Unknown

Armstrong's Visa

Lance Armstrong used to get on his bike and ride the hell out of highways, hills and treacherous mountains, with his friends or alone, come rain or shine, despite his cancer condition. Completely cured now, he probably still does, well after his newfound purpose for life had spurred him on to claim seven record-breaking Tour de France victories. His books "It's Not About the Bike" and "Every Second Counts" are inspiring odes to perseverance and conviction that could raise the dead from the grave. Sadly, the dead don't rise – not so easily anyway. But the living dead do; they rise from their deathbeds, and Armstrong has certainly helped raise many of them en masse, rejuvenating their spirits and giving them a reason to fight for their lives.

The cynics that branded him "Lance Inc." say otherwise; they claim that he wrote his books only to gloat and make more bucks. A shocking allegation, it says more about the ones who came up with it rather than about Armstrong himself. As for his books, they have inspired a great deal of individuals, rejuvenating them and reminding them that life has horns that must be grabbed before they gore you through and through.

Armstrong exercised Utilisation. He grabbed whatever situation was facing him and utilised it to produce a positive and desired outcome. Even negative situations were utilised. In fact, they are the cornerstone of classic utilisation. Once you learn how to effectively revolve around a negative circumstance and resolve it by bringing its positive aspect to light, then the sky is the limit.

He did it, so why can't others do it?

The question has two faces. The one addresses the fact that "If he did it, so can others." It raises a question of potential; of circumstances; of intention; of the capacity in everyone to overcome any and every obstacle, given the right attitude. By utilising properly all the resources available, by putting every earned insight to effect accordingly, by using fear to wake up from the slumber – and love to keep priorities clear – he has become a symbol of victory and survival. Furthermore, he has also become a source of inspiration for a life of quality, a quality that can be achieved through the exercise of an attitude that he refers to as

"Survivorship."

He did it, so why can't others do it? If he did it, so can others. Everybody can do it. Everybody.

Yet, they don't. Why not?

Welcome to the dark side of a promising question, a very promising question now turning pale and sick – much like how Armstrong used to be when he was ill. Depleted of any vitality, this suffering face reflects the hardships of a gruelling fight against unrelenting enemies that batter and ram ceaselessly until all is reduced to derelict ruins, unless you're Armstrong. But not everyone can be Armstrong!

He did it, so why can't others do it? This is a very central question. Why do they lack the ability when they don't lack the capability? Why do some lose the battle with death and never even have the chance to fight for a life of quality in the first place? And why do those who do manage to win the battle with death end up subsequently losing the battle of life and any quality therein? Why?

Because the sky is very high and you need long strong arms to reach it. Because the way to the sky is obstructed by thick layers of suffering that only a sharp and sturdy lance can penetrate, that's why. Because you need to possess the mind that drives you to climb Mount Hautacam twice on the same stormy day without a break just because you didn't think you mastered the climb on the first training try.

Because you need to be more unrelenting than the enemy.

After Armstrong bike-climbed Mount Hautacam twice on the same day, Johan Bruyneel, Armstrong's team tactician, told him that he didn't believe what he'd just seen, while Chris Carmichael, Armstrong's coach, called him a "sick fuck."

The truth is that the road to success is paved with all sorts of suffering and can only be understood by the one willing to traverse it. Everyone else, even friends and family who support the contender, fail to fully grasp the nature of such a steep climb and the essence that's behind a successful accomplishment.

The Armstrongs of the world are sick fucks indeed. If only there were more of them around.

The symbol of Armstrong shines brightly in our skies because of the balance he strives to maintain in his life. His inimitable accomplishments on the bike circuit alone do not and cannot account for his quality "Survivorship." His inspiring triumph is founded on accomplishments that reach far beyond the bike circuit. Success is entailed in keeping a wide number of potentially conflicting priorities in equilibrium – such as family, relationships and professional life – without compromising any of them in particular. It is a legendary effort, larger than life, large enough to capture the attention of a whole world. Not without a price, and a heavy one at times, it seems to be well worth it at the end of the day.

Armstrong didn't do it alone though. He not only admits that behind any champion lies a team of colleagues and supporters, he proves it too. He corroborates that to reach his victorious culmination he received help from those select few who were there on both good days and bad; those who stuck with him through the grit and pain; those who understood and tolerated his incessant drive; who gave him slack when he needed it; who pulled him back when he was straying without assigning burden of blame to him; who didn't envy him or try to compete with him in order to assuage their own insecurities; who pushed him up the mountain when he was riding his bike – full of cancer and oozing chemo after-effects – despite the fact that when he was healthy he would toy with them and leave them trailing behind in a cloud of dust.

He couldn't have made it without those people, either friends or family, who were truly connected to him. But with their invaluable help he regained his colours and illuminated the paths of many ashen souls, bringing warm comfort to their hearts and hope to their lives.

Armstrong made it because he had a valid ticket for the greatest ship of them all, friendship, the vehicle that helps you get wherever you want to go however remote and dangerous the destination may be. Through the power of true and selfless friendship, Armstrong was helped back into the circuit, and when he cut through the Parisian finish line for the 7th consecutive time he created an inspirational modern-day legend, giving new meaning to the colour yellow.

Victor Gente Delespejo

Some Things Are Sacred

Understanding individuals as they are, and accepting them for what they are, can be described as the cornerstone of true and substantial friendship. Yet, as people grow, as lives change, so does the pyramid of their relationship, which means that the cornerstone is suffering constant, incessant shifts in relation to the structure it supports. It cannot be taken for granted, lest one day people turn around and realise that their pyramids have engulfed the cornerstone deep inside the catacombs, where it will hang out with the mummies of time, buried deep within the past and never to be seen again, save through the lens of recollection.

The price to pay for such complacency is to reduce the once crucial cornerstone to just another cobble in the maze, rob it of its essence and, maybe, catch a glimpse of it during the occasional tour where the ghosts of the past come to life for fleeting moments before they are shot back into the depths of historic oblivion. What a tragic dull fate for a once salient component; from the glory of foundation to the ignominy of the catacombs to the forgotten pits of history to the deserted tracts of inconsequential memories.

Sure, deep down in the catacombs lie mummified bodies that are far from forgotten. They may not be revered as monarchs or gods anymore, but they are prominent historical figures, preserved immaculate, which have spawned stories, myths, arts, and even sciences.

Most historical constituents, though, cannot claim such temporal glory and are reduced to the state of "immaterial" relic, if they are lucky. If they are not, they simply don't exist anymore, and for all we care they never existed at all.

Kind of sad, really, to know that you only live as much as the memory that holds you.

Some would say that it's far from sad, that it's magnificent. A person, an idea, a culture can outlast death, living on for as long as the fire is tended. Behold the mummies of the pyramids in their sarcophagi. Three millennia have passed them by and they lie there still, ossified but proud.

Yet, here is the other perspective: Their time is over and they only live as figments in our imagination because we still feed that fire.

But one day, when that fire is gone for good, it's going to be gone forever and ever. Poof, over, finished, gone, done, out, never existed.

Have you ever heard of the Dorranthean Civilisation? That's right, who? The Dorrantheans, have you ever heard of them? Well, neither have I, but who's to say they did or didn't exist?

Sad, isn't it?

So, why do I trace the sad aspect of this coin with my analytical finger?

The principle is that once something is thrown into the dungeons of history, it rarely emerges back out from them – and if it does, it rarely comes out unscathed. Most of the time, though, things just disappear. Such is the process of life as we know it, and new things come to replace the old in a cycle that guarantees progression and innovation.

Yet, some things are irreplaceable. Some principles are too valuable to throw away. And if their time has indeed come, then so be it and never mind the nostalgia, but at least let them go naturally… gracefully… smoothly… immersed in the shine of their own past brilliance. It would be wasteful and mean to let them fade under mindless and habitual complacency.

Ah, complacency, the evil cousin of familiarity. The latter incubates and protects us like a cocoon, but the former incarcerates and punishes us like a prison, calcifying our shell while dosing us with a mist of… what… who… where… huh…?

Things may be lost in the background and still be alive in memory or principle, but they are more substantial and throbbing with vitality when they are fully present in the forefront, when they are not allowed to pass away. A cornerstone is a cornerstone is a cornerstone. Once removed, it can be anything from another piece of brick to an integral component of the edifice, but it is definitely not a cornerstone anymore.

Now, the question is – if I can perform a number of activities that will allow my cornerstone to stay intact and solid, shouldn't I do so? Isn't it plain moronic to just let it slip away and be replaced by God knows what?

Not necessarily. Not if the replacement has been thought out and planned through. Some choose to consciously adjust the structure of their lives as they grow. Shapes change, sizes are altered, functions are modified, old building materials are upgraded and apparatus are decommissioned in favour of new ones, and the face of reality morphs endlessly.

It turns out that some new structures work better than others. Some work better than their predecessors while others don't. And some make no difference at all. Obviously, sometimes it's better to keep the cornerstone intact while at other times an overhaul may actually be necessary.

So where does that lead us?

To the calculation – and in the existence of one in the first place – whatever it may be. You see, in order to discover and explore the New World one must first dare to dream it, and the same holds for the calculation behind the shift; before you focus on the quality of your calculation, you must first establish the need to actually make one.

If a calculation is absent altogether and everything is being replaced through mindless misdemeanour, then 'Houston... we have a problem. We're either going to crash into someone's trailer-home, or we're going to become a high-tech sarcophagus and probably end up as a treat for some hungry and curious space amoeba. And we don't fancy becoming intergalactic toffee. We're coming back to Earth no matter what. No matter what! Help us out.'

Sick fucks!

Xavier Thorntrail

When the Ground Begins to Crack

"What can I do for you, my friend?"

How many times do we hear the word "friend" being used with merciless casualty? This sacred word is so overused it ends up lying on the sidewalk abused and battered. Rivers of blood flow from its ears and spread slowly onto the grey slabs of cement like seal-wax tributaries, steaming and thick, trickling into the gutter and out of the way.

"What are friends for?" he said as he pulled on the invisible strings that were tying her up, the ones he had casually wrapped around her one year ago with a smile.

"Take it from a friend, when X says Y, then you know that blah blah blah…"

"Here's a friendly piece of advice…"

"Keep your friends close and your enemies closer." Now here's a hidden meaning begging to come out. Sure, the traditional standpoint chimes the bells of caution and suggests that the way to keep your enemies in check is to keep them under close scrutiny, but what more does it say? What does having enemies closer than friends necessitate? What does it drive a person to do and think about?

For starters, it can fill one's immediate circle with people one doesn't like. And that's just a single possibility out of many. No need to list them all. You get the gist.

Keep your friends close and your enemies closer, eh? Forget those you know and like. Spend your time around those you don't like, watching over them, just in case! Right?

Hmm. By this token, you would need to have strangers close too, those you don't know. After all, they can be potentially threatening as well.

Hmmm… "Keep your friends close and strangers closer." I can argue that keeping strangers close to me serves to keep an eye on them, much like I would do with my enemies.

But I could also argue that keeping any unfriendly subjects close to me taints the whole concept of friendship altogether. Then again, maybe it doesn't taint it so much as re-examine and reframe it. After all, the worst kind of damage is the one which comes from a friend – a cursed possibility – and maybe the message is not to keep our enemies closer than our friends. Maybe the point is to watch our friends as we would watch our enemies, for if they decide to inflict damage on us it would be devastating.

Victor Gente Delespejo

Balancing on a Ledge
(A short story)

Many centuries ago a man was walking near his home, high up on the mountains. He loved to take a walk just before dawn every day, witnessing the wonder of nature's awakening. Glorious!

The rugged terrain was flanked by steep and unwelcoming cliffs, not fit for the easiest of strolls or the inexperienced hiker. But he, he knew his way around like the back of his hand. He'd been born there. Once a child of the Mountain, now he was her sentinel and friend.

They used to talk every day. He would ask her things and she would answer in her own unique way. He would tell her his innermost thoughts and she would tell no one else. The Mountain could keep a secret for eternity. He knew. He had tested her many times.

One day, he asked her to show him who his true friends were.

She was quiet. No reply.

He asked again, but the Mountain fell silent. Dead silent. No movement, no sound.

Surprised at her mute response, he thought perhaps to abandon his question and enjoy the hike. He looked up and saw a small trail leading to a plateau with a magnificent spherical view. Then he paused. His mind was itching.

'Who are my true friends?' he bellowed out, his question echoing through the cliffs, bouncing off the mountainsides, fading into the far distance until there was silence.

No response. Nothing.

Annoyed, he took the small trail and began ascending towards the plateau. 'Perhaps I should ask the question from up there,' he thought, 'where I can be seen and heard.'

The sun was about to rise over the horizon. The timing was just right.

He started hopping up the trail while replaying the question in his mind over and over again. But all of a sudden, the ground beneath his feet moved, giving way under his weight. He fell flat on his face with a mighty thump, his body slipping on the gravel, and skidded over the side. Before he knew it he was falling over the cliff, plunging to his death.

Fortunately, a sturdy old root and a protruding set of rocks offered him salvation a couple of seconds later.

He was hanging on. But for how long could he do so? The thought ignited every neuron in his body into action.

He looked around and assessed the situation. There was a small ledge below his feet, and ample places around him to lean on. In fact, he had landed in what seemed like a comfortable cliffside niche, a throne engraved in a vertical wall of stone, hovering high above the world. He smiled and blinked. Then gravity pulled on his gaze with unmitigated force, forcing him to look down. He adjusted his eyes and focused his sight beyond his feet – which had been firmly planted in the ledge – and saw the Salty River below, cutting through the rock and shining like a silver strand of hair in the deep shadowy ravine, flowing towards the Ocean, far away into the distance, over and beyond the world. He had never seen the Ocean, only heard the stories from sun-trodden travellers. But his mind would take him there every time he gazed in its direction. The Ocean… The Ocean… The majestic mystical Ocean…

He came back from his reverie a few moments later. He shook his head for a couple of seconds, clearing his mind, and then focused on the opposite side of the river strand, across to the other side. The neighbouring rock-face, high and steep, was standing right across him, leaning into his vision. He locked in on its rock bottom and began to slowly climb it with his eyes – ascending vertically and smoothly all the way to his level – then rising even higher – penetrating the cirrus clouds – tearing into the magenta-blue sky.

The sun pierced the horizon just then and a ray of warm light bounced off the glossy cliff across him, bathing him in the comfort of a freshly born day. He closed his eyes for a while and just sat there, immersed in its vibrant reflection.

A few precious moments later he opened his eyes and turned towards the trail above him, examining it from the point he had fallen to the point he had landed on. A smile appeared on his face. He stretched out his ears. The sun began to climb the sky slowly and the Mountain was beginning to jostle with diurnal life – timid movements, tepid sounds, silent noises in the dawn. They sounded a little crispier than usual this morning. Crispier, deeper and more meaningful than ever.

Soon, he heard the rustling of footsteps and a cheerful tune. A few small stones trickled down from his left hand side above, falling into the ravine. Somebody was on the trail.

'Hey,' he shouted. The tune snapped out cold.

'Who's there? Where are you?' asked a voice from above. 'Where are you?'

'Down here, over the side!'

'What the... I'll be damned! What are you doing down there, my friend?'

The stroller's head appeared. The voice had sounded familiar, and the face was more than recognisable. One of his best buddies!

'I just slipped and fell over. Luckily, I landed on a ledge. I'm hanging on, for now.'

'Are you ok? Anything broken or twisted?'

'No, nothing like that.'

'Do you need anything?'

'Now what kind of a question is this?' he thought to himself. 'Do I need anything?! Is he kidding me?'

He said nothing for a while, trying to understand the rationale behind the question.

'Do you need anything now?' his buddy hollered from above.

'Well, what do you think?' he replied.

'Do you need some warm tea?'

'No!'

'Some bread with hot soup, maybe? I made a lovely batch this morning.'

'No. No bread or soup, thank you!'

'How about a blanket?'

'No blanket, thanks.'

'Do you want to hear a joke? I heard a couple of good ones last night.'

'No, I don't want to hear any bloody jokes!'

'Well, ok. No need to be rude now. Anyway, if you need anything, just sound the bugle. All right my friend? You know that I'm here for you, whatever you need. All you have to do is ask. Better be on my way now. See you later my friend.'

'...'

The rustling started again and a wave of small stones started trickling down the path. A few fell on his head, while the rest fell into the steep drop on his right hand side under the sound of a cheerful tune slowly fading away into the woods. A few moments later, there was complete silence once again.

He sat there, on his cliffside chair, dumbfounded, staring into thin air and trying to comprehend what had just taken place, what he'd just heard. Had he been actually abandoned by one of his best friends? He couldn't believe it. Impossible! Simply impossible! Or had he just imagined it? Perhaps he had. Perhaps his mind was playing mean tricks on him.

He got lost in deep thought. Time rolled on. The morning began to mature.

Gradually, his mind returned behind his eyes and he began to look around again. There was no movement at all. Everything was still and quiet, gilded by the rays of a cold rising sun. A resounding serenity had settled all around, shrouding the land in the glaze of a chilly noon. He sighed. The day was moving sideways and the standstill was beginning to feel like a standoff. A terribly ominous standoff.

Soon enough, though, with the advent of the afternoon, the sounds of life re-emerged. Voices began to make their way through the woods, familiar voices, and a few more of his friends appeared on the small trail. He was relieved. Funny though! He didn't remember this part of the woods being so popular.

Most of his friends were worried sick upon seeing him hanging over his doom. They worried and stressed out, distraught by his deadly predicament, and offered to help him up, but they didn't have a rope to send down to him. They'd have to go and get one from somewhere. It would be many hours before they could find one – and as many to return – so he would probably have to spend the night there. They asked him if he needed some warm tea and some hot soup with bread, and he gladly accepted, ready to now put all those hours of throwing and catching pinecones to the test. They threw him some bread, which he snatched out of the air. Then they threw him a couple of flasks. He had no trouble with those; they landed heavily within his grasp.

He bid them farewell and began to nibble hungrily on a piece of bread. His mind wandered off once more. The afternoon began to advance fast. Dusk was not far away...

A little later, two more friends of his passed by. Horrified by his plight, they offered to climb down and help him back up on flat ground. He refused.

'It's too dangerous,' he insisted. 'No sense in risking your life when there's a safer, more practical option.'

'What... bring a rope? But you'll have to stay here all night. You'll freeze to death!'

'Don't worry, I'll make it,' he assuaged them.

'Well, at least here's a blanket, some warm tea, hot soup and bread. And one of us can stay with you and keep you company through the long cold darkness. Hey, I heard a few good jokes last night...'

'It's ok, there's no need to stay out here with me. You've done more than enough to keep me warm throughout the night. So go. See you tomorrow.'

'You sure? One of us can stay here and the other can go to get help from...'

'I'm sure. Don't worry about it.'

'Well, ok... is there anything else you think you might need before we go?'

'All I ask for is your swift return. Now beat it. And bless your hearts!'

'See you tomorrow amigo. You better not be an ice cube when we return!'

And off they went.

He laughed and sat back into his seat comfortably, gazing into the ravine, listening, processing.

Not before long a couple more friends of his passed by. They tried to climb down too and the story was repeated.

'One of us will stay here,' they shouted. 'It's ok... we're not first timers... we've camped out before...'

They had a number of good arguments, but he dissuaded them – or so he thought. They headed off into the forest, but only one of them took the trail back; the other hid in a cove nearby. They'd decided that one of them would stay behind and keep a lookout, just in case. You never knew what could happen in the wilderness, especially after dark…

The sun was descending fast, inviting darkness over from the other side of the horizon. Eventually, it slid behind a mountain peak, and a little while later it must have dived in the ocean, for the day went out like a candle. Darkness engulfed the Mountain swiftly and a biting breeze started flowing through the pitch-black ravine. The diurnal had given way to the nocturnal, and a host of very different movements and sounds emerged from the twilight to roam the dark moonless night.

Well into the night, he heard a scraping in the far distance, faint and intermittent. It was slowly coming nearer, getting clearer. Laughter slit the air, followed by thuds, bumps and slaps. He couldn't see the stones trickling down from the frail trail fringe, but he could certainly hear them falling in numbers.

Whoever these people were, they hadn't brought caution with them that night.

When they got nearer, he wasn't surprised at all. The noise was all too familiar. It was a parade of the Toper brothers, friends of the nighttime, old escapade buddies of his.

He waited…

They were now right above him, stumbling and mumbling. Suddenly, one of them stopped.

'Wait, I heard that a certain someone is clinging on to dear life… by the skin of his teeth,' one of them said, and they all burst out laughing.

'No,' added another. 'He'sz hanging from a root'sz tree… a, a, a tree'sz root… wait, a tree… um… he'sz hanging from the hanging tree! Or szhould I szay: the barely-hanging tree! Har!' More chuckles.

'Hang on, my man. We'll save you.'

'Yeah, we'll save you alright.'

'Are you thirsty my friend? You must be. Word on the trail is you've been here all day and night. Are you cold? Sure you are, balancing on a ledge, over the mighty river. Hic! Well, worry not. I have the solution for both your problems. A cistern filled with warm liquid. Two birds with one birdie… my birdie! Boys, anyone else for bladder release?'

They chuckled worryingly and seemed to huddle in a row…

When they were done, a pungent fume had covered the area.

They scampered on, doubled up with laughter.

'Don't worry my friend. They'll find you sooner or later, alive or dead,' one of them shouted.

'Yeah, they'll find you alright,' cackled another. 'They'll find you coz we'll tell them where you are, if we remember that we saw you, that is. But don't worry, we remember everything. We always do! Right guys? So… um… what was I saying?'

They all chortled like crazy, paralysing themselves with laughter.

'Good luck my friend,' said one of them. 'If you survive, we'll see you at the tavern for a ton of drinks, good food and fine women. Like the good old times. Come on guys, let's go.' And they staggered off, wobbling their way through the dark trail.

He sat there, drenched and livid, biting the back of his hand. The taste of iron suddenly struck his tongue – overwhelming the stench of fresh urine – and he felt a thick drop of blood running down his arm. Red mist engulfed him and he recoiled, ready to climb the treacherous cliff like a spider.

He froze. A scream pierced his ears, a scream that was fading fast, downwards! Somebody had fallen in the ravine. Distressed voices followed from the direction of the Toper parade.

Suddenly, a menacing yell swamped every sound. There was ruckus and mayhem, cracks, thuds, grovelling. It sounded as if rocks were being hurled amidst a battery of horrifying yells, sowing panic in the dark. Then a series of paralysing screams followed, echoing in the dark, fading fast downwards, down into the great ravine. And then there was silence! Complete silence.

He looked towards the source of the ominous incident. Nothing. Pitch black.

Suddenly, the clouds broke open and a storm of warm rain gushed across the cliffside for a while, washing everything clean. A warm breeze followed. It came from above and embraced him like a loving mother. His attention shifted to brighter moments. Gradually, he stopped shivering. His eyelids grew heavy and he drifted into a restful sleep…

When he awoke, the sky was flickering with tinges of deep violet. Night was rising away. Day was approaching. The world was going through its diurnal transformation once again. From night to day through the crack of dawn. Glorious!

It was that time of year when twilight was short but dawn was protracted. Night would drift slowly away, giving way to the advancing day at dawn. But at dusk, day would simply pick up and leave without hesitation, and night would have to take over immediately. There was no time to enjoy the nocturnal transformation. Only during a specific and brief time of the year could the mystery of dusk be observed in its freely unfolding glory... only when the sun would set in the gap between two towering mountainsides, behind which one could see the vapour of the fabled Ocean. During that short season, night would seem less dark and a little more welcoming as the sun would sink ever so slowly between the intermont frame, allowing the twilight to live out its full evanescing potential.

He gazed upon the gently unfolding dawn with eyes drenched in twilight memories. And for a fleeting moment he gazed into the heart of the world, witnessing reality through the crack of time, and could not tell whether he was watching a sunrise or a sunset...

When the shadow of night was driven away completely by the shine of a blue early morning, people started making their appearance once again. This time, he knew none of them.

Some of those strangers passed by without even bothering to answer his calls. Then again, he hadn't seen their faces or heard their voices. So why did he regard them as strangers? They hadn't peered over the side, and he'd never know for sure who and what they'd been. Based on yesterday's experiences, though, they could have very well been friends and acquaintances gone awry.

A few of the passers by did show their faces, though, and they proved to be total strangers, people he'd never seen before. Surprisingly, though, some of them offered to get some rope while others proceeded to climb down and offer a helping hand, which he refused. He kindly told them that help was already on the way and bid them all off with a smile...

As morning grew old a young noon emerged, and with it came his tunnel-visioned friend who had found him first, straight out of the path on the right where he had faded away the day before, singing a cheerful tune.

Upon hearing the familiar tune, he sighed and looked out towards the ocean, his ears still fixed on the approaching song. It was drawing nearer, slowly and leisurely, almost on top of him now.

'Hey,' he shouted out, still gazing out into the distance.

'Who's there? Where are you? Oh... oh yeah, it's you buddy! Still hanging on I see. How are you?'

'Not so good,' he replied, turning his head half way towards him. 'I'm freezing.'

He was lying. The warm breeze and the blanket his friends had given him had kept him out of harm's way all night.

'Well, strong men don't whine. I didn't know you were a whiner man!'

'You're right, I'm not.'

'So, do you need anything? Anything? Whatever you want! Just ask, or I'll be on my way.'

'How about a blanket please?' The tension in his voice had risen.

'Well, when I offered it to you yesterday you didn't want it! Now you're freezing. No wonder! And I don't have one on me today. I left it at my girlfriend's last night. Oh dear, what are we going to do now?'

'Do you have some tea or hot soup?'

'No, I'm sorry. I finished it off a while ago. Didn't think you'd still be here. Oh my! How about a joke though? Want to hear a joke to cheer you up?'

'No, thank you!'

'You're certainly too demanding for a guy in dire straits. Too demanding for your own good! Take it from a friend. You should chill out. Excuse the pun. Now, is there anything else I can get you? All you have to do is ask and I'll do my best to make it happen for you. Otherwise I'll be on my way. There's a convention a couple of hamlets down, you see, where I can make good business. And they're throwing a great party later at night! You should come too. No use hanging from a cliff, you know.'

'Well, how about a rope to pull me up?'

'Oh, come on buddy. You should have asked me yesterday! I don't have one on me now. Ok, listen, I have a couple of errands to run tomorrow morning, for my wife and all. I'll be back here some time tomorrow afternoon with a rope. If I can't make it, I'll send a couple of my best friends. You know them well. So… Anything else before I go?'

'Nope!'

'Say, wait a minute, wait just a minute… I'm way ahead of schedule! Damn, I forgot that the convention's been delayed for a whole hour. My girlfriend told me so last night after a fantastic dinner. Marinated venison, oven potatoes, full-bodied red wine by the fireplace, crème fraîche on fruits from these forests here… yeah, it was good… then we cuddled under the blanket and started fooling around… the fire roared… it got too hot… had to open the windows to get some fresh cool air in… Are you listening? Yeah, so we're fooling around… and she spurts this out: 'Honey, did I tell you that the convention's been rolled over a full hour? My daddy told me just before you came.' I mean, what was she thinking, telling me all this?! There we are, in the middle of a situation, if you get my point, and she just opens her mouth and out comes the only thing that should stay in… her daddy… what's her daddy doin' in her head while she's havin' sex with me…? Well, anyway, I could stay here for a while and keep you company for an hour!'

'What? No, no, I wouldn't want you to risk being late. I'll be fine!'

'No my friend, I insist. It's the least I can do for you. Keep you some good friendly company.'

'No, honestly. I'll be ok here. I'm asking you to go! Go away!'

'Oh, don't be a jerk! Asking me! It'll be my pleasure to stay. I won't be late for the convention. Here, look… I've set my stopwatch. I'm leaving in 59 minutes, wait… to the second, starting now! Now, where was I…? Oh yeah, last night…'

By the time the chatter was over he'd seriously considered flinging himself off the cliff. Twice! But now there was silence again. Much needed silence. The longest hour of his life had finally passed. And his old friend was gone, singing his way to the convention.

'Remember, all you have to do is ask, and I shall try my best,' echoed the fading voice of his old buddy. 'What are friends for… for… or…?'

He moved around in the ledge, shaking the disgust off him, making himself comfortable again. His mind began to process the information given to him. He had been shattered by some of his latest experiences and wonderfully surprised by others. All he had to do was integrate the various events into threads, and then weave those threads into a tapestry.

The spectacular vista zapped him into appreciating his newfound perspective. From his throne, he could see into the once invisible, the once imperceptible, the once concealed from eye and purview. It wasn't all roses. But it was real. Raw and very real indeed.

His lips moved inconspicuously, and he began to speak to the Mountain. His whispers were picked up by the turbulent winds and were carried to the four corners of the rugged land, where their contents would be vaulted inside the heart of a trusted confidante, safe from the vices of the well-disguised takers. In her heart they would stay, bearing truth and all its aspects, from the rosy to the raw, and everything that's in between…

He turned to the sound of solid feet. It was one of his friends who'd gone for the rope the day before – or so he'd thought.

'Hey there stranger, back already?' he joked.

'I have to tell you, these roads aren't getting any easier,' replied his friend. 'They get rougher over the years. You'd think we'd be used to them by now, but the more we traverse them the more perilous they get.'

'You got that right!' he chuckled. 'And here I am, dangling over a big rift in the earth!'

They laughed.

'Say, want something to eat?' his friend asked. 'I have a little soup and bread, and a drop of firewater.'

'You betcha! I'd love some.'

His friend threw him a piece of bread and a gourd of soup, which he ravaged. For a while the cliffs were echoing faintly with the clatter of frantic jaws munching away at the food. Occasionally, a grunt of content would ripple through the air, carried by the wind.

When he was done he felt rejuvenated.

'Thank you my friend,' he said. 'This was delicious. And just what I needed.'

'I know what you mean,' his friend replied. 'Hunger makes the taste grow sharper.'

'Can't argue with that!'

'Feels great when you fill up, doesn't it?'

'Feels magnificent…'

They sat there and talked for a while, sipping their firewater, exchanging opinions and stories. Soon, the ravines and crevices were echoing with joyous discussion and laughter. Only a bird's-eye view could reveal the economy of this dynamic; two people on a huge mountain range filling the place up, nature resonating with their vibrations and life clustering around them. Birds, insects, and animals of all sorts were approaching through the dense mountainside forest, gathering around the plateau, slowly and quietly, watching the two friends talk… Watching and listening…

A little later, the sound of steady footsteps announced the arrival of someone.

'One rope coming up. Or, in your case down,' stated a voice as a matter of fact. It was his friend's wife – the one who'd actually gone for the rope.

'Well, it better do both,' he chuckled at her. 'And not in that order!'

'One rope coming down, and then up. With its noose full!'

'Amen!'

As they tied the knots, a faint rustling was heard. More footsteps. A few birds slapped their wings and took off.

It was another couple, with a rope of their own.

They all greeted each other with kisses, smiles, handshakes and slaps on the back. It was a meeting of mutual friends.

More rustling. Somebody else was approaching. The animals scattered around and hid behind the trees. Some hid within them. The birds hovered a little further away. The insects stopped buzzing.

More people with ropes were coming their way. They were engaged in loud and heated debate.

'I'm telling you, if he fell over the cliff, then he's to blame. Whose fault is it? Mine?'

'I didn't say it's yours, but you can't hold someone's stray step, or his bad luck, against him.'

'How convenient for you! Mr Jinks himself has spoken.'

'Why, you no good…'

'Oh, forget it now. We can have our usual banter over warm dinner and plenty of alcohol. We're having roast tonight. You're all

invited by the way, did I tell you that? No?! Well, I'm telling you now…
Who the hell cares about the other party! Come over and we'll take it
from there…'

'Wait a minute. Did you say roast? I just love roast.'

'I know you do. Unlike our cliffhanging friend, who never liked it!
But now… now I bet he'll eat it and love it too. Hanging from the top of
a cliff for a day and night must have changed his appetite and attitude…
Hey ladies and gentlemen… Hey… Over here! We have arrived!'

People greeted each other with laughs and cheers. The event was
turning into a reunion.

'Came to help our buddy, huh? Hey buddy, better watch your
step next time, or we're leaving you here.'

Chuckles all around. Birds started flying away. The animals
began to backtrack from the scene.

Then, a booming voice broke through the trees.

'I'll be damned if there'll be another convention as big as this
one during the next month. Not in these parts. But I heard that they're
hosting something over the Range, in the land of Indulgion. My girlfriend
mentioned it the other night. Tell you all about it later… Hey buddy, look
who's back! It's me! I bumped into these crazy fellas and these beautiful
girls here, and we decided that we should all come over here and fetch
you. It'd be a shame for you to miss the party. Wouldn't be the same
without you, you know!'

All of a sudden, the birds took off in their thousands, cutting
through the sunny blue; large and small, predatory and prey, they swung
and flapped their wings strenuously, flying far away… the insects took
off in their millions with a deafening buzz, clouding the sky and bearing
shadow over the whole area… animals were dashing away, jumping off
the trees, skidding through the trails and bushes… Everything was just
rushing away. Only a bird's-eye view could reveal the dynamic of this
economy. Life just got up and took off in a hurry.

Soon, there was silence again. This time, though, it was a hollow
silence.

It didn't last long. The reunion's noises rose high once again and
infiltrated the forest.

'Well, I'll be damned buddy! What the hell is going on up here?
Talk about a serious animal party!' said the booming voice.

'Nope, that one's tonight, and you're not invited!' declared someone in a matter-of-fact tone.

'Nice try, birdbrain!' sniggered the booming voice.

'Shut up dickhead!' cackled the other, half-joking, half-not. 'Shut up or you ain't getting any of my roast. Now, let's get our friend out of the mess he got himself into. Ropes away!'

A dozen ropes fell towards him. He passed all of them over and around his waist, and a second later he was lifted from his cliff throne like a feather in an updraft. He landed among them and they all started hugging him and slapping him on the back, elated at being together again. Then they made a toast.

'To friendship!'

They all drank from copper gourds. The clear spirit inside was strong. It burned their throats. Many of them coughed.

Then he stood high and caught their attention, proposing another toast.

'To true and substantial friendship!'

'To true and substantial friendship,' they repeated, and they all drank again under the mass clanging of gourds, which sparked a short but potent festivity. They began slapping each other on the back, singing, kissing, clasping hands and arms into a merry chain. The booze was flowing and their voices were rising. They were having a great time. In fact, they were having such a great time that no one noticed that the circulating echoes were behaving strangely. The cheers and celebrations were hitting the mountainsides and echoing back stronger, reverberating through the air, drowning out the voices that were feeding them. They were growing louder with every toast. Unnaturally and disturbingly louder.

No one noticed, except him.

He also registered a few select meaningful glances being exchanged, gestures that spoke of triumph, not fanfare; gestures surreptitiously relayed amidst the carnival; gestures of friends, true and substantial friends.

He registered a few and sent out a few of his own.

'What's your name?' asked someone abruptly, jumping in front of him and clasping his hand. 'I've known you for so long but I don't know your real name!'

'Then there must be a reason for that,' he replied.

'You don't know?' shouted someone else full of surprise. 'Why, all his good friends know his name! He is the Mountaineer... because he knows the Mountain inside out. Three cheers for our good friend, the Mountaineer!'

'Yes! To the Mountaineer! Hip hip, hooray... Hip hip, hooray...'

He glanced around. Not everyone was cheering. A few were cryptically silent, shaking their heads and sighing softly. They caught his eyes and nodded at him, and he nodded back at them with a smile. Then he headed up the trail, towards the plateau, and they followed him in silence, leaving behind the rowdy fanfare. There, on top of the mountain peak, in the middle of a mountain-range, they stood together, looking out onto the vast rugged landscape sprawled all around them. There they stood, with feet planted firm in the ground, paying homage to the bonds of life in shared silence. And as they did so, from the depths of the mountain-range a roaring thunderclap arose, riding on the crisp afternoon wind and shaking their hearts. It ripped through the air, flanked by four fierce thunderbolts, one for each corner of the world, tearing the sky and pummelling through the carnival echoes until there were none to be heard, reclaiming the land from the vice of chatter.

There, in the heart of a rising land, on top of the world, stood a small group of friends paying silent homage to life as life paid a roaring homage back to them.

The Man smiled. He had finally gotten his answer. Those standing around him were his true friends. The Mountain had spoken.

He turned around and looked at his friends, thanking them silently for what they'd done and for who they were. Then, after a long and meaningful silence, he sat down on one knee and placed his palms on the ground, his eyes closed and his lips quivering. Little whispers flew out of his mouth and billowed over the rugged land.

His friends watched in silent accord. They knew he had the rare gift of communing with the Mountain, who, as legend had it, spoke to those who listened to her and listened to those who spoke to her. She knew his name and he knew hers. He and the Mountain were friends. Not just in need and in principle. They were friends in substance and essence. When one hurt, so did the other. When one fell, the other came to the rescue. When one needed, the other didn't have to hear a plea. They knew each other's name and they knew each other's nature and what they were all about. No dawdling, no doubts, no fears nor droughts.

His name? He told me his name and tale one day near the trail and plateau. He told me because I sat there and asked. I sat there to listen and learn.

He told me, and then he leaned forward and said, looking me straight in the eye: 'And what about you, my friend?'

I looked around. The whole nature was watching. Watching and listening...

Xavier Thorntrail

Tale of a Modern-Day Samaritan

"Look in a mirror and one thing's sure; who we see is not who we are"
—Richard Bach

The Great Collapse

I. Terribly Sorry

A man was lying on the pavement in a busy street. He was drooling heavily and his body was twitching worryingly. He groaned for help to the many people walking around but they all passed him by without paying any attention to him.

'Please help me,' he shouted to a hurried passer by, grabbing him by the ankle in a desperate attempt to gain some much-needed assistance.

'Terribly sorry,' replied the passer by aloofly. 'I... I am in a hurry. There is something I have to do first. I have to mail this letter here, see? It's very important. Let me mail it and I'll be right back to help you.'

Surely enough, he returned after a little while, but there was no sign of the helpless man. Only a few smudges of spit and snot on the grey pavement remained, right around where he had been lying. Other than that, no trail, no trace. As if he had been picked clean off the street. As if he'd just dematerialised...

Years later, the passer by was short-listed for a charity award. His name was featured among other public figures, all of them celebrities in their own right, all of them great contributors to society. Every member on the shortlist had been known to devote a significant amount of time and resource to help the less fortunate, and they were all perfect candidates for the esteemed Golden Heart, the greatest charity award in the country.

A day after the shortlist had been published a paid announcement was featured in every newspaper available. It wrote the following:

"In the sixties, a field study was conducted called 'The Good Samaritan Experiment.' This was an experiment in social psychology which investigated various factors and parameters behind an individual's willingness to help someone in clear and apparent distress. The experiment involved numerous setups, trying to illuminate the various different factors associated with altruistic behaviour under a wide range of conditions, spanning from favourable conditions to unfavourable ones.

"Specifically and in a nutshell, the designers of the experiment recruited seminary students for an ostensible study on religious education. Upon arrival, students were briefed on the supposed details of the study and were then asked to go to another building where they would carry out their assigned tasks. Some of them were told that they would have to talk about seminary jobs while others were told that they would have to give a talk about the parable of the Good Samaritan (a person who had stopped in the street to help a man in need, unlike the priest and the Levite who had just bypassed him on their way to other holy deeds and duties). Also, some of them were told that they should get to the other building at their own leisure whereas others were instructed to get there as fast as they could.

"Unbeknownst to the study participants, the way to the other building was rigged. Specifically, it passed through an alley where an actor would be waiting in a slouched position, moaning, groaning and pretending to be in distress, waiting for some kind of assistance from the passing by students. And there lay the real juice of the experiment: the response of the seminary students to a person in need of assistance.

"Sadly and shockingly, in a great number of cases the students simply bypassed the distressed person without offering any help. Some even literally jumped over the person, moving hurriedly to the building where they would give a talk on seminary jobs or on the principles of altruism by referring to the Good Samaritan parable!

"This is just one of countless experiments dealing with altruism that have been conducted over the years in many forms and variations.

"In another experiment, an even more shocking tendency was revealed. Notably, it was established that individuals sitting in a room that had begun to fill up with smoke would report the smoke – or resort to any kind of corrective action – much faster when alone than when in the presence of other people in that room. As far as the scenario where all other individuals in the room were confederates – who had been instructed to ignore the smoke – and act as if nothing out of the ordinary was happening – the subjects seemed to be decidedly affected by what those confederates were doing. As a result, the rate of response to the emergency dropped when in their presence.

"The aforementioned experiment was subsequently modified and made to record the response of individuals not to smoke but, instead, to what appeared to be a severe seizure that could be heard over an intercom device. Again, the rate of response to the emergency situation dropped dramatically when the individuals under scrutiny were in the presence of others. People seemed to just not take initiative when others were around. They would just react less sharply and with dilute conviction.

"In general, these experiments revealed an overall tendency for people to help an individual less when in the presence of other people. In other words, the more people around, the less initiative taken – and the less assistance offered.

"It is worth noting of course that most of these experiments and studies involved the setup of artificial cases and scenarios, which helped identify and quantify the various rates of response in different circumstances, but which are widely considered unrepresentative of real life situations. Naturally, there has been intense criticism against this type of investigation, branding it as a made up and spectacular array of strings that are essentially meaningless in the complicated fabric of the real world. Meaningless, useless and irrelevant.

"In response to these criticisms, a few years ago a team of renegade social scientists decided to conduct an independent study on altruism in the streets of three major cities (London, New York, Paris) and of three provincial cities (Swansea, Syracuse, Nantes). Their aim was to measure the response of a passer by to a person in need of assistance without setting up artificial situations or manipulating a number of scripted scenarios. The idea was to simply place an actor on the street and monitor and record the reactions from those passing by.

"In order to prevent the needless deployment of medical units, affiliates were placed in all medical emergency units and other key places during the duration of the study, their responsibility being to engage any calls made in request of help for the actor or actress on the streets, thus, severing the calls' flow to centres of response and reversing any instructions for paramedic deployment. To assist the actor, a privately owned ambulance on stand by would be dispatched to his location accordingly, removing him from the street in the most natural way. This setup not only reinforced the legitimacy of the situation but also helped bring the whole issue to a smooth close, especially in cases where passing-by police forces or other civic units had gotten involved.

"The results of the study were deeply disturbing. In fact, this study revealed a tragically decreased tendency to offer assistance. Rather than list and explain the whole array of results right now, though, here is a revealing snapshot of one part of the study instead. It is quite representative of the whole set of results and is very relevant to current affairs.

"In particular, here are three pictures of a passer by, retrieved from the archives of the study. These are pictures from a setup conducted in central London on February 29th, on a Thursday morning.

"In the first one, at 09:21 – as shown by the digital camera clock – this man has clearly stopped over our fallen actor and seems to be conversing with him. In the second picture, again at 09:21, he is seen leaving the area of distress without having offered any help. In the third picture he is seen returning to the area of distress fifteen minutes later, at 09:36, by which time our actor had already been removed by a team of affiliate medics. (Our actor had in fact been lying on that pavement for exactly twenty three minutes in that setup, from 09:07 to 09:30, during which time he received no help from any of the 495 persons who had been documented to have passed by him. Furthermore, it was later established that not even a single call had been made to the emergency medical units of the city regarding our man's plight that day.)

"Now, here is a close up of the passer by who returned fifteen minutes later. If you look closely, you will see that this face belongs to none other than a person who was nominated yesterday for a Golden Heart. Ironic, isn't it? On second thought, though, it may not be ironic at all. Just typical, very typical.

"Well, whatever the case, not all that glitters is gold. And not all golden hearts are valuable, especially fake Golden Hearts like yours. Terribly sorry, you lousy Samaritan. Terribly sorry but the charade is over. Your actions have finally caught up with you. They always do. From Little Brother, with compliments!"

And that's all the paid announcement wrote.

II. Many Bad Apples Spoil the Standards

One week later, the man in the picture received the Golden Heart. In fact, he was hailed as a hero across the whole nation, being the only person among 495 who had actually returned to help the twitching man in distress. A veritable Good Samaritan.

He was invited on every TV show imaginable, giving interviews, sharing his thoughts on issues of caring, helping, cynicism, and the modern society. The TV hosts treated him royally and the audiences loved him. He would glide through the questions like a silk kite, riding the currents with effortless ease and soaring higher and higher into public acclamation.

Once in a while he would encounter a provocative or even hostile question regarding the reason behind why he had gone to mail the letter before actually helping the twitching guy on the street, but he would shrug off the presuppositions of such questions with a simple and disarming argument: 'I really don't understand why we are talking about the letter when we could instead be focusing on the others who never even stopped for a second to look at the fallen guy, or on those who never returned to help at all. Let us not spin my contribution into a scandal. Goodness knows there's enough spin-doctoring in the world as it is. I am not the villain here. But neither are those who didn't stop to offer help. The real enemy here is the callousness of modern life. The enemy is the sordid state of affairs that is being augmented by the rampant pace of life that we are progressively getting into. In fact, let me share with you a couple of thoughts on how we can all help our fellow citizens...' And on he went, speaking of the noble values of life with explosive fervour and conviction.

Of course, when the hype went away after a while another paid announcement was featured in every newspaper available. It read as follows:

"In a relative world of multiple views and viewpoints, where everything is being perceived, analysed and understood through various and varying perspectives, one person's villain is another's hero, and one perspective's hypocrite is another's visionary leader.

"If, by objective standards, we are to judge a man's response to another man's plight by what that man himself has actually done to help the other, then we may say that walking away to mail a letter first and then returning to offer assistance to a convulsing man on the street (a whole fifteen minutes later) is quite unacceptable, if not criminally inconsiderate and negligent. But if we are to a judge that same man by comparing his actions to the overall reactions of all those who had also passed by that area, then we might find that our man is an actual hero by comparison. He is worthy of praise, an idol, an icon, the one to look up to and glorify. He is the Golden Hearted Man.

"Undeniable as it may be, this assessment of course says less about our relative hero and more about the sordid depths to which our benchmarks have sunk. It is a sad instance for us all indeed. For it can be nothing less than sad when we realise that the best apples in our bunch are not firm, shiny and tasty anymore, but are actually rotten and fermenting. Of course, by comparison, since they are not completely and utterly putrefying like the rest of the bunch, they are nothing less than the best of the whole lot. And the more the bunch rots, the lower the benchmarks sink, down to the bottom and straight into filth.

"Golden Hearted Man, you are less of a deadened soul than the remaining 494 in your bunch, but you are still a deadened soul, and your reaction was totally unacceptable. Yet, if you think otherwise, then we wish you from the bottom of our hearts that when in dire need of assistance, you receive no less and no more than the kind of help that you yourself offered – and so fervently advocate. May you receive what you offer, and let your own self be the judge of such assistance. We wish the same to those who support you and to all those who share your values and ideals. From Little Brother, with compliments."

III. The Irrepressible Power of Cause 'n' Effect

Two years later, a newspaper article read as follows:

"Investigations are still underway regarding the controversial case of Masante Smirtic's collapse.

"Smirtic, AKA the Grand Golden Heart, or simply 'the Grand Beat' (as the media referred to him), was a successful entrepreneur who had started from virtually nothing and worked his way through the system, eventually creating Grand Enterprises, a group of companies dealing with a wide variety of products and services. A sleuthing businessman and a 'self-made amateur politician' (as he liked to refer to himself), he was known and loved for his wide contributions to society through various charity setups, most importantly through workshops he had recently set up around the country.

"These admirable workshops had taken the cause of charity to the next level. By departing from the commonplace monetary donation and the occasional celebrity visit, they had set a new standard by establishing educative venues where people could analyse and explore the various aspects of caregiving through a series of systematic seminars.

"The Grand Hand, as this initiative is known, is in fact an institution that has been expanding for the past two years, now boasting 66 venues across the country. It is partially subsidized by the government – the rest being funded by Grand Enterprises – and provides its services at no charge at all, making it accessible to everyone, especially those who cannot afford much more beyond their immediate needs. Some call it 'Smirtic's greatest achievement,' but sceptics refer to it as the 'most elaborate and seductive PR strategy ever conceived.'

"The Grand Hand was first conceived by Masante Smirtic shortly after a controversial announcement by the mysterious group known as Little Brother. Specifically, in reaction to Smirtic's name having been short-listed for a Golden Heart, Little Brother had issued a damning statement regarding a past encounter of Smirtic with a person in distress in the street, who turned out to be an affiliate in a social psychological experiment. Little Brother claimed and corroborated that Smirtic had bypassed the man in distress in order to allegedly first mail a letter, returning to help him fifteen whole minutes later.

"In the backdrop of the reaction – or non-reaction, to be more precise – of hundreds of other individuals to the man in distress, Little Brother's exposure of Smirtic's behaviour backfired, shooting him straight into public approval. He had apparently been the only one among the 495 passers-by to actually display an interest in the distressed man, even if belatedly, and that made him a hero rather than a villain.

"Smirtic immediately seized the opportunity and embarked on a nationwide campaign, whereby he promoted the nobility and necessity of sacrificing some of one's time and resources to assist those in need.

"The weeklong campaign proved to be highly effective; it won him not only the Golden Heart, but also every person's approval and affection. His appearances on TV shows would shoot the ratings through the roof. His interviews would sell magazines and his name and face were everywhere, splashed across every bus and billboard in the country. He even arranged five lecture shows in stadiums, which were sold out in no time, creating a short-lived but frenetic black market. Tickets were reportedly being sold on the street and over the web for a whopping £10,000, leaving motivational speakers like Tony Robbins far behind and matching the likes of rock 'n' roll giants such as the Rolling Stones and U2.

"Shortly after that, Smirtic launched the Grand Hand in schools and community centres, urging people to get to know 'the lighter side of their selves,' as he called it. The initiative was a huge success, drawing attendance from every part of society, and the seminars and workshops were constantly overbooked. The media called it 'a Wave of Grand Handedness that was sweeping the nation clean of its self-involvement.'

"But critics branded the Grand Hand as just another moneymaking scheme that had been carefully crafted to fit what they called 'the blatantly spin-doctored attitude of Smirtic towards his fellow citizens.' There were reports that only the first classes were free and that as one progressed along the ladder, they would have to pay for the more advanced classes. If one could not afford to pay, then they would be employed by the Grand Hand and work their way through, though no one has verified these claims. Individuals involved with the Grand Hand seem to be very secretive about their personal ties and obligations with the institution. It has been claimed that people of poor economic status and educational background are specifically targeted, eventually being totally absorbed by Grand Enterprises, and that the Grand Hand is nothing more than a recruitment and training camp of Grand Enterprises – although that, too, remains to be verified. Clearly, the critics of Smirtic are not mincing their words, making them public at every chance they get.

"Smirtic has been repeatedly accused as a 'hypocrite who could charm a cobra into giving him eggs.' Many of his critics are raising the issue that Smirtic's return to the scene of distress on that fateful day was an accident that had been inadvertently brought to light by Little

Brother in an attempt to discredit him, an attempt which had backfired monumentally. According to the critics, Smirtic and his PR professionals seized the opportunity and subsequently spun and marketed his return to the scene into a modern-day legend.

"The critics also argued that the story of Smirtic rushing off to quickly mail an urgent letter was hogwash since a man of his stature would probably have taken care of any urgent mail through his Mayfair-located office headquarters instead of running in the street to mail it himself. Others simply dismissed any validity whatsoever in the urgency of that letter – or any letter in general, whether real or imaginary – arguing that no letter could supersede the act of dropping everything and bending towards a twitching man in need of assistance in order to hold his hand while making a phone call to emergency medical services.

"Some critics have in fact gone so far as asking for the CCTV tapes that contain Smirtic's trail for that day to be given out in order to crosscheck his claims, but the police have refused to publish that footage. They insist that any such move would impinge on a citizen's rights to privacy, and that such information is published only in cases where individual or public safety and security is in immediate danger. According to them, Smirtic's trail is a matter of controversy rather than safety and security, so they have decided to withhold that information from the public.

"Smirtic was no stranger to controversy, and he remained as such all the way to his untimely demise last week. Yet, even after his collapse, he still stirs controversy.

"Smirtic, who has been reportedly pounding through life with all pistons firing, collapsed in a trendy restaurant last Sunday night. His close friend, Archibald Gabriel, who was with him since early that evening, said that Smirtic was his usual energetic self. Nothing out of the ordinary had happened and everything seemed normal. Yet, abruptly and without a sound, he collapsed to the floor. 'It was most peculiar,' said a witness who wishes to remain anonymous. 'One moment he was talking and the next he just melted to the ground. As if he'd been switched off. Most bizarre.'

"Bizarre is perhaps the only way to describe the incident and the set of events that followed it. Notably, when Gabriel called the emergency services, he was put on hold for quite some time, and was then disconnected. According to our reports, he tried calling back but his phone appeared to be momentarily out of service, resulting in more confusion.

"Having parked his car two blocks away from where they were, the panicking Gabriel asked the bystanders for a lift without further ado. A man offered to help them and bid them over. Amazingly, he dropped his car keys in a street drain as they were approaching his car. A woman then stepped up and offered to give them a ride to the hospital but disaster struck once again; she crashed into the front of the car parked behind her as she was hastily pulling out of the sidewalk. In her panic, she went into second gear with the gas pedal on the metal, slamming into the car in front of her too, totalling her engine. Gabriel then pulled Smirtic out and carried him to the car of a calm and collected middle-aged man a few yards down the street. His car, though, would simply refuse to start.

"So they started waving at the passing traffic. Most cars were just whizzing by and only a few were slowing down, but none of them were stopping. Someone then reportedly started banging on them as they were passing him by, shouting that the Golden Hearted man was dying right there on the street. A black Mercedes Benz is said to have pulled over just then, offering them a lift to the nearest hospital.

"But the torturous twists of fate were not over. Remarkably, on their way to the hospital the Benz driver took a wrong turn and lost the way, wasting precious time trying to get back on track through a web of restricted turns and one-way labyrinths. It took twenty two minutes to reach the hospital.

"By the time he was rushed into the A&E, Smirtic was not breathing. He was pronounced dead on arrival. The official cause of death has not been disclosed.

"A great number of people are being questioned in relation to the baffling circumstances surrounding Smirtic's death. The police have issued a statement that no further comments will be made on their behalf until all involved persons are questioned and all clues have been thoroughly investigated. They have also urged the media to not fuel the whole situation with outrageous reports and unverified claims about the whole issue.

"Smirtic, aged 44, was divorced and reportedly in very bad terms with his ex-wife, who had retained custody of their three children after a fierce legal battle. She'd made allegations in the past that Smirtic had been abusive and neglectful, calling him 'a veritable egoist with a smooth tongue,' and referred to their divorce as the best thing that could have ever happened to her and her children.

"Strangely enough, though, she has now reportedly filed a manslaughter lawsuit against the state, blaming the system for her ex-husband's death and asking compensation in lieu to her children's trauma of having lost their biological father to 'an unfortunate but potentially avoidable set of events.'

"Many people are pointing their finger towards the controversial Little Brother organisation. Little Brother had notoriously wished Smirtic assistance similar to the kind he'd offered to the man in distress on the pavement on that fateful busy morning, assistance in harmony with the principles which Smirtic was so loudly advocating and defending ever since the controversial pictures had hit the press.

"Amidst the growing conspiracy theories that are stemming from the bizarre and highly improbable set of incidents and co-incidents that surround Smirtic's swan song, Little Brother issued a terse statement yesterday in relation to Smirtic's demise. They denounce all accusations categorically and point the finger back to Smirtic and his ethos, which, according to them, is exactly what precipitated the highly peculiar factors surrounding his tragic end. 'Everyone's past catches up with them sooner or later,' they stated laconically. 'This is just the way it works. It's the ultimate lesson that no one can avoid.'

"And in a way which seems too ominous for comfort, this reporter humbly admits that they seem to be right... dreadfully right."

Victor Gente Delespejo

∞ Niet and Snie Have The Same Goal... ∞

Sometime along the 23rd century, two strange figures are conversing in the warmth of their abode. A translation is necessary because they speak in strange tongues and mannerisms.

Niet: How's your food?
Snie: Edible. How's your drink?
Niet: Drinkable. How was your day?
Snie: Just like yesterday and any other before that. How was yours?
Niet: Just like tomorrow and, oh, you see what I mean.
Snie: No, I don't see.
Niet: Eat and shut up.
Snie: Then I shall explode or die from infections.
Niet: You know what I mean!
Snie: No, I don't know.
Niet: Just eat, will you?
Snie: I will drink too.
Niet: Oh, come on!
Snie: Maybe later. I'm busy now. Can't you see I'm eating and drinking?
Niet: ...

Let's follow this strange couple's conversations a little later in the day when they're not eating or drinking.

Niet: Gnikwah spoke to us yesterday.
Snie: And...?
Niet: He spoke of a great hero.
Snie; Who?
Niet: Onion the Great.
Snie: Did you cry?
Niet: Yes.
Snie: Then don't tell me. I don't want to cry.
Niet: I was joking, you fool. What great hero is called Onion the Great?!
Snie: Don't know. What?
Niet: *(whispers)* Some day, I swear... *(turns to Snie and speaks loud)* Anyway... And don't say "what way!"
Snie: Why not?

Niet: JUST LISTEN!

Snie: That's all I'm doing, am I not?

Niet: ... *(waits a while, then speaks)* This strange figure was known as the Great Yeller. He started fading away, becoming ash, dying. There was no hope. All was lost. He went round the world, looking for answers. One day, he found a black box. Could it be? Had he found the Black Box? The mythical Black Box? "Do not open," was written on the cover. Yes, this was it, the Black Box, the box which should never be opened! That's what the stories said anyway. The Great Yeller sat down and began to play back those stories in his mind, stories he had heard in his youth. All who had opened the Black Box had died. They had all died terrible deaths. So said the stories. But weren't they supposed to be legends, myths, old wives' tales? Well, apparently not. The Black Box was right there, right before his eyes. He picked it up with fear and admiration, with awe. One part was light, the other heavy...

Snie: Like us?

Niet: Kind of. Now...

Snie: Did someone carry the Great Yeller around in a box too?

Niet: What do you mean?

Snie: You said the Great Yeller was becoming ash. How did he move around? And who carried him if all was lost?

Niet: Why you dumb... you... It was special ash, all right? The kind that sticks together and doesn't disperse in the wind.

Snie: Doesn't what?

Niet: Doesn't disperse... doesn't scatter... you know?!

Snie: You could have said so sooner. What, are you stupid?

Niet: Well, I must be!

Snie: I know. But I forgive you.

Niet: Shut up!! Now... where was I? Um... oh yeah, the Great Yeller sat down and looked at the Black Box anxiously, wondering whether or not to open it. He was dying. Was there anything more to lose? No. So he grabbed it with his frail limbs and in one desperate attempt he tore it wide open...

Snie: ...

Niet: Don't you want to know what happened?

Snie: Aren't you going to tell me?

Niet: Yes, but aren't you eager to know?

Snie: Not if you're going to tell me. Mind you, if you hadn't stopped to ask me these stupid questions I would know what happened to the Great Yeller by now. So stop asking me if I want to hear the story and tell it to me!

Niet: Yes… perhaps you're right on this one.

Snie: You are very stupid, you know that?

Niet: Don't push it, will you? Ah, sh, sh, say nothing… no comment please… ok… The Great Yeller tore the Black Box wide open. A sheet of some sort fell out. There was something inscribed on it. It said: "You have just found eternal life. If you do not warn others against the Black Box, eternal life will be taken away from you. You will die. Have a good life." The Great Yeller was ecstatic. 'So that's why curiosity killed the cat,' thought the pale figure. 'Well, better mind my own business and tell others to do the same.'

Snie: …

Niet: Are you getting any of this?

Snie: Is the story over?

Niet: No.

Snie: Then I can't get it if it's not finished, can I?

Niet: Sometimes things just stand on their own too, you know, before they get integrated by the ending.

Snie: No, I do not know.

Niet: Alright, alright. Now listen. The Great Yeller rode around the world for a while, minding his own business. But as time went by, he noticed that his condition was not improving. It wasn't deteriorating either, but it was definitely not improving. He was caught in a form of stasis, still pale to the bone. One day, though, and just like that, he had an epiphany. He remembered all those who had spoken of the Black Box and its lethal dangers… They were all very old, degenerate, sick people, but somehow still alive. They'd been around for ages. He had thought it strange then. How were they managing to stay alive? But now he knew… for he was becoming one of them.

Snie: Good story. Fantastic!

Niet: I haven't finished!

Snie: Oh… ok.

Niet: Ahem… The Great Yeller decided to do the unimaginable. He decided to tell the truth about the Black Box and its secret…

Snie: But… but then eternal life would be taken away from him!

Niet: That's what he'd believed during all that time. But now he wasn't so sure anymore. So he decided to do what he'd always felt was the right thing to do. He decided to speak about the Black Box to others. And as soon as he did he felt the impact of his actions. The change was sudden and very dramatic.

Snie: What? What happened? He died, didn't he? He died in terrible pain.

Niet: No, on the contrary! He regained his colour and his life. He was resurrected.

Snie: What?

Niet: That's right! He was resurrected and well back on track. In fact, this new approach was so rejuvenating that he began spreading his vibrancy on others. The more he told people the truth about the Black Box, the better they became, and so did he. So on he went, rolling around the world, immersing everyone in a healing bright yellow light. And the world shone once more.

Snie: So why wasn't eternal life taken away from him?

Niet: Simple. Those who had found the Black Box had never dreamed of challenging the warning. They never found out how to stay alive in a dream and not a nightmare. But he, he did what *no one* who had found the Black Box had dared to do. He *told everyone*, loud and clear. And it didn't kill him.

Snie: Why? Why didn't it kill him? What did he tell everyone?

Niet: To stay away from the Black Box… because it can cause eternal pain, eternal 'suspended animation…' unless, of course, they open it and then warn others to stay away from it… You understand what I'm saying? He warned others away from it by acknowledging its existence rather than denying it. He warned everyone away from it by speaking out about it rather than keeping it a secret. And he lived a life of quality while offering the same to the rest.

Snie: What?

Niet: He paid it forward! He didn't keep the Black Box to himself. He paid it forward and told everyone about how they could gain eternal life by opening it and then cautioning others… telling them to keep warning everyone else forever and ever… warn against the Black Box and gain eternal life by spreading the word and fanning the will to look for it instead of creating a monster which others should avoid…

Snie: …

Niet: He gave life to everyone he met by inspiring them to go on their own personal quests! He gave them a reason to live!

Snie: Hooray! Hail to the Great Yeller. Where is he now?

Niet: He is dead.

Snie: What?!

Niet: He gained eternal life, not stasis! Gnikwah said that his spirit still lives among us though, watching us, guiding us, inspiring us.

Snie: Really?

Niet: Really, metaphorically, who knows? Maybe both. If we don't try, we won't know what eternal life is like.

Snie: The Black Box.

Niet: Come on, let's go look for it.

Niet and Snie got out of their warm abode and stepped into the great wide open. To the east, the ruins of the devastated metropolis still lay waste. They had been left there to remind everyone of the Big Inferno. There were dozens of dilapidated great cities like that one, and thousands of smaller ones, all over the world. That was the rumour anyway.

It was also said that to the west of every necropolis, a giant new metropolis had been erected, just like the one looming in the far distance… Giant fortress, with walls three miles high and a shiny dome to shield it from the radiation and the scorching winds. It was known as 'Ecosystem 9.' It was impenetrable.

Niet and Snie had never gone near it. They didn't venture out often in any case; it was forbidden. If caught by the patrols, it meant unequivocal and instant death. Or worse. They could be captured and taken to 'The Bubble,' as the metropolis was charmingly referred to. Those caught had never been seen again. No one knew what happened inside those walls.

They turned their backs on the ominous fortress and scampered off in the opposite direction. Into the barren wasteland. Towards the necropolis.

Snie: Where are we going? I can smell trouble.

Niet: We're looking for the Black Box, not for rocks in a quarry. It's going to be tough.

Snie: No, *you're* looking for the Black Box. I can't see, remember? I am sniffing for it.

Niet: I know you can't see you nitwit. So sniff away.

Snie: I am! And I smell foul odours in the wind. Are we… are we going towards the Dead City?

Niet: Yes, we…

Snie: What? Are you mad? We are searching for the Black Box, not black death.

Niet: Relax, relax. We are going towards the Dead City only until we reach Skeleton
    Canyon. After that, we turn south.

Snie: South? Why… To the Mirror Plains, yes!

Niet: That's right. Where no one dares to go. Not even the Black Patrols.

Snie: Where it is so hot that the sky melts to the ground.

Niet: Where we will be invisible!

Snie: Yey!

Niet: Now, the only trouble is getting there.

Snie: Don't worry! Just keep your eyes open and steer me through. I'll do the rest.
    You're my eyes, I'm your legs.

Niet: Black Box, here we come!

Snie: If only the Great Yeller could see us now.

Niet: Who knows? Maybe he's right here with us.

And off they went, the cripple Niet riding the blind Snie, into the
barren wasteland.

∞ ∞ ∞

Tennis

Quiet Please... Play!

Tennis. I've been thinking about it a lot lately. I guess it has something to do with my sudden move to London. As you probably already know, I came in at the beginning of June, anxious and apprehensive. What you don't know, though, is that I was assigned to Wimbledon. And then there was tennis!

Tennis used to be one of my favourite sports, you know. I used to follow it, and played a little too. But as I grew older I grew busy, and I slowly fell away from it. It became a memory – a memory that I knew I had but could not quite recollect – and then just an idea in my mind, an idea that was always on vacation. It was gone for good.

Then I got assigned to London and ended up in Wimbledon! Bang, there went the idea, bursting back into memory with the threads of my past firmly in its hands. Tennis was back in my life, and it was here to stay.

Everything seems just more alive now. The roots are working, the blood is pumping and I am waking up early enough to see the sun rise. Tennis has reinvigorated me in ways I never thought possible. I guess you were right... Life is exercise. I remember now... I remember!

Victor Gente Delespejo

Advantage Lector

I am glad you are rediscovering and reinventing yourself. You gotta do what you gotta do, and if it's tennis that gets your heart pumping, then that's what you must do. And let me be honest with you… tennis is one hell of a sport. It's chess with balls. And it's tough, tough as nails.

You know, somebody once told me that tennis is like life. And she was right. Tennis is a lot like life. Hard to master, let alone maintain at top form, it's one hell of a competition. A truly remarkable experience. But aren't they all?

Now, let me ask you a question regarding the local tennis scene – nothing complicated, just a simple question. Um… Is it always game, set and championship overseas?

If it is, then, well – how can I put it mildly? – …beware, lest you become too comfortable there. It's dangerous business, getting comfortable in places where victory is sparse, so don't set your expectations just yet. Just keep questioning your goals and recalibrating your efforts, and do so without indulgence, lest you want to be defined forever by the motions of a once achieving but now just musing inventor, an inventor who just loves to bask in the reflected glory of past inventions while trailing behind all those who may not have invented those exact things but who are, nevertheless, doing a damn good job of excelling in them! Not a nice place to get comfortable in, I assure you. But bear in mind that such is the fate of all pioneers; given the time they can fade to the rear – especially if they begin to define themselves by their past rather than by their present and future. Pioneering is risky business and requires hard work, creating a very demanding legacy, and so do success, triumph and excellence. So beware – and work hard, very hard – for the forefront can never be taken for granted.

In other words, 'Caveat Explorer,' 'Caveat Inventor,' 'Caveat Discoverer.' Caveat.
Xavier Thorntrail

Henmania

Actually, now that I think of it, and with your warning fresh in mind, there's a thing or two I've noted about British tennis – contemporary British tennis, that is. Well, fairly contemporary anyway. So let's see. Ahem…

June 2004. Two tennis players are going at it like gladiators in the arena. One is British, the other isn't. The match is turning out to be a gruelling bout and the only thing missing is the blood and gore. It's what you'd expect from a truly dramatic and jaw-breaking tennis duel, the kind that has everyone talking about it for years to come.

What you wouldn't expect, though, is a crowd that is flirting with hysteria and behaves more like a football crowd rather than a tennis crowd i.e. it is hyper-partisan, cheers only for its side, and is not far from actually jeering the opponent. You'd expect this to happen at some random Tennis 'n' Barbie Fest, sure, where people enjoy a nice day out by watching the local heroes bash tennis balls while munching on a piece of meat, but anywhere else? No, not really. Especially not here!

Well, think again. The venue – Wimbledon. The perpetrators – the Henmaniacs!

It is very sad to see the historically greatest tennis championship of them all reduced to an event that is permeated through and through by a desire for a Briton to win – a desire turned to hysteria, that is. The line has been crossed. Wimbledon is treading on dangerous ground, and the tradition, the prestige, and the regal status of the king of tournaments will not be worth a penny when such hysterical behaviour is taking place, and worse, when it is actually encouraged to take place and even take over.

While the administration of Wimbledon cannot – and should not – stop the rowdiness that craves a British victory so totally utterly desperately, it could certainly stop feeding it and feeding off it. Henmania, the magnetic entertainment concept that has Britons rooting for their man, has turned Henman's supporters into sheer maniacs and has all other tennis fans pulling their hair out, for Christ's sake! It's not a pretty sight to watch – hair pulling and Henmania – if you are not a Hen-Maniac, and it better go away, lest the king of championships is turned into just another common tournament by none others than the Britons themselves! Is a mere victory, however coveted, worth a century's history and prestige?

Wimbledon must choose. It can either soar above the rest of the tennis events through well-earned and deserved merit, or it can be the tournament in which any opponent's double fault is applauded loudly and obnoxiously, and where the TV commentators of all people incite the thousands of Hen-Maniacs on Henman Hill to shout in support of Tiger Timmy during a match's rest periods! I mean, what is this, the village fair? Or do Britons want Wimbledon to become the tennis equivalent of those few but notorious football grounds where visitors are beaten not through the home side's talent but through sheer intimidation by a violently ravenous for victory crowd?

These are heavy terms, 'notorious, intimidation, violently ravenous...' But let's not forget that violence is not just a physical act; violence entails any form of excessive behaviour that violates an established code of conduct. So, when the Hen-Maniacs begin to behave in rowdy and unsportsmanlike ways, one could safely say that they are becoming increasingly violent – by tennis standards that is. Hardly a scene for hooligans to get excited about, it nevertheless creates a venue that is not only becoming violent in its own unique manner, but which is also well on its way to the point of no return; Wimbledon may be turning into the Roland Garros – or any French tournament – where rowdiness seems to be an asset, not a liability, wouldn't you know!

Hen-Maniacs may be doing nothing more than having the time of their life, but the rest of the tennis world – players and their supporters alike – are being rubbed the wrong way by Henmania, which seems capable of turning tennis, one of the few sports that have not been tainted by excessive partiality, into just another sport of civilised violence. What a shame this would be. Wimbledon has always been the beacon to tennis culture by flying its standards high; it is the last bastion. Must it be tainted so, all in the name of a player that never wins anything? If only Henman won something once in a while, Henmania would be a little more palatable, and a rowdy Wimbledon would at least have something to show for its misdemeanour!

Of course, as a final note, one can see that this sort of standpoint stems from having taken offence at a specific form of fan behaviour in the hallowed grounds of Wimbledon. It is in fact nothing less than the result of an uptightness quite similar to that which has enveloped British tennis for so many years, asphyxiating British victory. For let's face it folks, if you want your man to win, you have to support him all the way, and screw the obsessive-compulsive etiquette. It's time to choose: the Champions of British Wimbledon? Or a British Wimbledon Champion? Prim and proper, or fucking winners? Oh shut up you silly tart! Go take offence in the vestiary, among the other hanging coats, and let Great Britain become great again. And if that means getting down and dirty and quite improper, then so be it! So be it!

Victor Gente Delespejo

Henmania? You Cannot Be Serious!

A few years later, Henmania has in fact faded in the distance and is nothing but a memory, a piece of wishful thinking, a misplaced band of hope in a willing but essentially incompetent tennis player. It is gone for good, never to be resurrected by a carefully publicized comeback streak or a stuttering miracle run. We have been spared the pain and agony of another hyperinflated attempt by Tiger Tim to go for Wimbledon's crown, or any Grand Slam really.

To be perfectly honest, Henman didn't fail for lack of intention. He wanted that title, and boy did he want it badly! If ever there was a player more in need of a Grand Slam title, it was him. But watching Henman go for gold was like watching sperm cells dashing forth to fertilise an egg only to smash their heads against a condom's walls. Noble but futile. Sure, a small chance always existed that the bloody raincoat would just break, but it seems that he never went for it hard enough to cut through the clutter and float home with flying colours. He was never horny enough for the title. More needy than horny, his attempts projected desperation rather than resolution. And, thus, he failed, time and time and time again. What a sad icon for a great nation.

Enter Murray. A talented, feisty, always in-your-face competitor with a wide array of shots and a fierce determination to beat the best players in the world. Enter Murray, the spoiled brat, who throws tantrums at the drop of a hat and misbehaves in ways totally unacceptable. Enter Murray, the improper tennis player, the incorrect sportsman, the misfit, the lemon, the grape from the sour vine. He grouches, he swears, he slams his rackets around and he is just totally reprehensible and immature, even when he appears calm and focused. A total opposite to Tim Henman in every sense of the word. This fucker's a winner.

Murray has the sparkle in the eyes and the talent in the body, but he also has the cojones to carry himself to the next level. He is ready for distinction, not needy. He is fired up and he shows it. His impulse is obvious and it makes its mark loudly. It is a force to be reckoned with and it stems from personal drive, still uncontaminated by the pressure placed by a whole nation parching in one of the driest spells in its sports history.

Perhaps this is the key behind Murray's effectiveness; not the spunk to carry himself to the next level, but the mental authority to play tennis first for himself and then for a whole nation. Maybe this boy has the guts to withstand the crushing pressure of a United Kingdom – and its 60 million citizens – because he has decided to first train himself, getting fit and strong and able, before attempting to actually lift the weight of Britain's world on his young gladiatorial shoulders. Now, that does not take only great cojones. It also takes great brains, and a little rebellious streak.

Still, breaking the rigidity of British culture – and all the condoms it wraps around its aspiring cells – requires something more than just the rebellious streak of Murray. It requires the sharp blade of an American and the downright pragmatic approach that stems from his fresh culture, a culture where tradition is something that is being created now through the achievement of great feats; a culture that looks ahead, and not over its shoulder; a culture that is defined by "what you *can* do" and not by "what you *mustn't* do."

Brad Gilbert was asked to come on board the Murray ship for this exact reason, and it seems that he has a strong hand, fit for the helm and ready to lead. A good captain, Gilbert knows not only how to manage and handle a ship, but he can also read the currents, the weather and the night sky. His sights are set on the greatest prize of all, excellence, and he knows that the only way forwards and onwards is the one that makes you excel, taking you there, wherever it is that you want to go. And to find this way one must prepare diligently. Such is the way of a discerning mind and such are the ways of a warrior, a winner, a champion. Intention, drive and talent are not enough. They are all too common among individuals and can only be made to count, to truly count, when the right and fitting preparation is made. Fitting preparation is what gets the thruster engines going, sending the shuttle out of Earth's pull and into its chosen course. And Gilbert seems to be doing his homework. But, most importantly, he seems to be getting through to Murray, convincing him to do his homework too. For, at the end of the day, it is Murray who must get on the ship and board the shuttle for this greatest of journeys. It is he who must aim high. And only he can burn the fuel that will send him out of the world of the plain and ordinary and into the company of stars.

Back in the plains of gravity-riddled earth, Tim Henman was

allegedly asked by a notoriously volatile fellow named John McEnroe if the sessions with his sports psychologist were going well. Henman allegedly replied (although it is not certain) that he actually didn't employ the services of a sports psychologist, to which McEnroe allegedly replied, 'You must be fucking joking!'

Henman's reply may have probably been, 'I don't need a psychologist. There is nothing wrong with me. I am perfectly fine,' to which McEnroe probably replied, 'You're as nuts as they come and a goddamn fool! No one in their right mind would expect to excel in professional tennis and go for a Grand Slam title without utilising the benefit of a professional mental coach.'

Henman probably said, 'If I am to win, then let it be through my own true worth,' to which McEnroe probably responded, 'Snap out of it, Winnie the Pooh! If that's how victory is earned, then you'd be speaking German now, and your title would be Herr Henman. In this world, my dear proper fellow, you use every tool in the shed and every weapon in your artillery to come out on top. And if you need to employ the help of a professional sports psychologist who has the tools and weapons to get you through to number one, then that's what you should do.'

Henman probably coughed a little and then may have said, 'Can you imagine the headlines, John?'

- "Tim Henman has finally lost it!"
- "Henman has an identity crisis… Calls in the head doctors!"
- "How Tiger Timmy lost his stripes and teeth!"
- "Henman… Couching Tiger, Ridden Wagon!"

And McEnroe most probably said, 'You cannot be serious! Get a backbone, man! Get a backbone or quit. Goddamn prissy boy! I used to eat sissies like you for breakfast, on and off court. If you're gonna be a prima donna, then at least have some style. Do you see what I'm saying?'

Henman may have replied, 'I'm sorry, I just can't forget what they said on TV about me yesterday,' to which McEnroe probably said, 'Answer my question, you goody-goody-two-shoes!'

Henman may have gotten upset by the remark, spilling some of his tea on McEnroe's lap intentionally, all the while pretending that it was an accident, to which McEnroe probably responded by getting a racket and smashing it on Henman's head.

'That's how you deal with an incorrigible opponent,' he probably said while pouring himself a fresh cup of tea above the sprawled-out Henman. 'Follow your instincts, do what they least expect you to do, and screw what everyone else thinks. If you're good enough, they'll come to love you, respect you and embrace you no matter what. Get it? Now, if you'll excuse me, I have to get going. I'm late for an appointment with a few other flickering flames. There's some things I wanna tell them before it's too late.'

...

Henmania? Sure, if you want to lay flat on your back and look at the stars every day, wondering what it must be like up there. But if you want to fly among them, and eventually become one of them, you better embrace another course, a course that can shake gravity off and break through the barriers of rigid traditional legacy. The moment is not yesterday. The moment is now. Time to play with the best of them. Good morning, and good luck! And I'm very fucking serious!

Xavier Thorntrail

Superman Juggling Kryptonite

"When looking for faults use a mirror, not a telescope"
–Unknown

Loss of Faith: Our Kryptonite

Christopher Reeve was an inspiration to society because he fought against a handicap that had crippled his body, holding him captive in immobility for the rest of his life. He was also admired for championing the cause of medical research and was one of the few persons that could free this subject from the political electric chair it had been strapped into. Such was his impact that he was mentioned in the 2nd US presidential debate on Oct 6th, 2003, on the issue of stem cell research.

Three days later he suffered a heart attack. On the fourth day he passed away.

Some may focus on the irony of it all, others on the tragedy of the timing. Whatever the case, the occurrence will probably be registered as just another unfortunate coincidence. It is reminiscent of the case of 'Prisoner F—' in a Nazi death camp who had a dream in February 1945 that he would be released on March 30th of that year. Yet, when he woke up on March 31st, he was still at death camp, still a prisoner, so he died a prisoner, apparently from typhus, on that very same day.

Like we said, an unfortunate coincidence.

Viktor Frankl notes this co-incident in his book "Man's Search for Meaning," where he also notes that in the week between Christmas, 1944, and New Year, 1945, the death rate rose to unprecedented levels. While the deaths were attributed to the usual suspects (malnutrition, exhaustion, disease), Frankl adds an inconspicuous factor to the fatal formula: the majority of the prisoners had cherished the hope that they would be home again by Christmas that year. When these hopes disintegrated into disillusionment, so did their will to live. And so, in the wake of those unfulfilled dreams, they gave up and died en masse.

Frankl's assertion is not farfetched by any means. Over the years, numerous studies have provided solid support for the dynamic between meaning and quality of life, between faith and survival, between the loss of faith and the decrease in immune resistance.

Something in that presidential debate may have drained Reeve's faith. It may have been Bush's policies on the issue, or the tactical manner with which Kerry mentioned Reeve and approached the whole matter. It may have been the relative meaninglessness of such debates and the disillusionment that usually follows them. It may have even been the perception of the thick haze that keeps the essence of a cause out of sight and out of mind while political discussions revolve around invisible points. Helplessness they might indeed induce.

Yet, "He who has a why to live for can bear with almost any how." This quote by Nietzsche threads the tapestry of Frankl's book and is one of the most basic truisms regarding human existence. Let it now weave a vigorous deliberation regarding Reeve's decease.

He who has a why to live for can bear with almost any how, yet, on Oct 10th, 2003, Christopher Reeve ceased to bear with 'any how' and died from a heart attack.

The question is: why?

Xavier Thorntrail

When Kryptonite Is Revealed

The US 2006 Vote proved to be a turning point in US history. It marked the end of an era and a shift from one end of the spectrum to the other. Faith in the republican policies and agenda proved too eroded to hold on to the majority control of the Senate. So out went the conservatives and in came the liberals. A bold statement for the coming presidential elections, this shift marks a great change that is probably already well under way.

Yet, upon closer look one may argue that the change will not be so great after all, for a shift from a republican to a democrat majority is not such a big of a deal – not if the essence of the matter is taken into account. Sure, policies will change and so will administrational principles. There will be a massive change on a theoretical and practical level, and the US will slowly swing from right to left. But so what? What difference will that make? Will the corruption in government be reduced greatly? Will injustice and prejudice be eradicated? Will the cynicism that pervades every facet of society be replaced by some sort of idealism that shall bind the loose parts of a diluted way of life?

Hardly. The underlying problems will remain. The roots of the problem will be untouched. And so nothing will be really solved. Not in any substantial way. New coats of glossy and impressive paint will be passed over the cracked up walls and grounds, and life will go on as usual until the cracks resurface. How typical! And then we seriously argue that real and substantial change has taken place and that we are moving forwards when the only thing that has in fact happened is that we have taken a leap towards the left as a reaction to the leap taken towards the right some years ago, which was a reaction to the leap towards the left… right, left, right, left. Not forwards or onwards, but sideways. And we have the nerve to talk about real and effective change!

Choosing between the political left and right nowadays is like having to choose between the Church and the Monarchy in the Dark Ages. Two different parts of the same eroded coin. Denominations of a hyperinflated and useless currency. Not only in the US, mind you – it's the same in the UK, France, Germany, Italy… Wherever you go and whoever you ask, they either say that left and right are not so different anymore, or they don't realise the current fundamental similarities between the two sibling paradigms, and then they wonder why the inequities they had voted against seem to be hanging around, being continuously recycled into novel, yet, familiar forms. The dysfunction is present either way, and so is the impression across the globe – as it is common – that citizens are being taken for a ride down the loops of ridicule by a great bunch of worthless politicians who have turned politics from the 'responsibility of making policies' to a 'soap-opera of politicking.'

The political left and right of the world are nothing more than different aspects of the same trunk. Once a little shoot, this trunk grew bigger and propelled society forwards and upwards by being approached from either side, depending on the circumstances. And society grew with it. But now this trunk has grown old, foul, decrepit. It no longer reaches for the sky. Whichever way we look at it, whichever side we approach it from, it is evidently withering away, killing everything that depends on it. It is just a soul-eroding relic, a monument atop a great pyramid whose maintenance requires the painstaking efforts of the whole society. Every individual's life is dedicated to keeping the monument bright and shining for all to see, and every function of society revolves around that idol until dedication becomes actual sacrifice – not the good kind of sacrifice in which individuals give something up in order to gain something else, but the bad kind in which people are thrown to the mill and made to turn it round and round and round without the possibility of parole. As far as real progress is concerned, it has been forgotten. Welcome to the coordinates of a highly decadent society, where the representations of progress become more important that progress itself.

Isn't it about time for a change in capital? Not left, not right, not centre and in between, but a new line that will not be based on political divisions of the 18th century. The world has changed a lot in the past two hundred years. From a ship of wood and steel it has become a ship of space metals and high-tech reactors. There's no use in trying to patch it up with a bucketful of tar and a few spits and bangs. Time for new tools and ideas. How about a political stance that shall speak the truths that everyone knows but is afraid to speak out in public? How about a new currency that shall replace the old and worthless one? How about real progress for a change? Is it time?

It certainly seems so, for as time passes, individuals around the world are losing faith in the whole system. When left, right or centre begin to share more similarities than differences between them, our infrastructure begins to erode. The cracks that lie underneath the coats of glossy paint resurface faster and faster each time, telling tales of compromised foundations. Democracy, liberty, modern economy and progress in general begin to suffer greatly, and so do those of us who ostensibly uphold them.

It is time to look in the mirror and face the reflections. No more shrinking away from the challenge or shying away from responsibility. We have a legacy to uphold and a way of life to improve. It is our turn to take the torch and run our piece of the track. Let us do so gracefully and with unrelenting determination. Or are we to remain in history as the generation that not only dropped the torch, but who also walked off the track and sat down to have a snack and a drink in order to soothe its overstretched body and mind?

...

Victor Gente Delespejo

When Kryptonite Is Revealed 2

…And one more thing – what about those other parts of the world where democracy doesn't exist in the first instance? These places are for real and they are starting to grow in power and influence. While the absence of democratic practice from their affairs may be inhibitory to their overall development, it nevertheless fortifies their growth and conditioning with a stalwart unity. Such unwavering courses of undemocratic growth naturally give rise to agenda that take advantage of the weak points of the democratic world – with which they are competing. And these agenda use democracy against democracy itself in order to promote their own self-interests, whatever they may be. They are attacking the 'inalienable right to exist in a given set and system' – a system that has chosen to function in the safety of a free society – while their actions are harassing and enervating the whole dynamic of the globe. In essence, their snouts are slowly locking on to the vascular system of the free world.

Dare we allow our way of life to continue bleeding much longer? Dare we keep juggling pieces of Kryptonite around as if nothing is happening? Dare we pretend that we are not in great need of an overhaul?

Finding a new ideological currency that will bind our disintegrating society suddenly seems less of a theoretical argument and more of a practical necessity. It is an imperative, a demanding and unwavering imperative, and is the only tool that will fix the cracks efficiently; the only solution to our predicament; the only weapon that will defend us from the demands of the emerging undemocratic powers that are rising aggressively in the horizon. Without this currency we are broke and defenceless. And because we cannot afford to remain exposed very long, we, too, have begun to seek protection in the unwavering course provided by undemocratic choices, just as others have done. A poor option in itself, becoming tough and militant at least provides us with a decent fighting chance.

Nevertheless, militancy still remains a very poor option, especially when the choice to seek out the immense power that comes out of truth and enlightenment is readily available to us. All we have to do is remember what our ancestors did when they realised that Theocracy and Despotism were no longer acceptable. All we have to do is create another option. A working, fitting and functional option.

But in order to do so we must first acknowledge what the problems are and where they lie. First the questions, then the answers. That's the way it's always worked, and that's the way it always will.

Xavier Thorntrail

The Momentum of Rising India Meets the Pale and Ailing Superman

Here's an interesting figure I just came across. 86% of young Indians are religious i.e. they share some sort of spiritual ideology ranging from Hinduism, Christianity, Islamism, Sikhism, Jainism, Judaism, Buddhism and Zoroastrianism. Quite a syncretic assortment.

Assuming that they don't turn against each other when they grow up, these youthful motley believers will be working under the umbrella of an emerging super-economy called India, and will be pitched to compete against a shrinking population of increasingly cynical and self-doubting Westerners whose only ideological bedrock seems to be a loose definition of freedom to do whatever one feels like as long as there are enough resources to keep us busy.

So where do you think the balance will tilt when the two populations meet? Inspired growing population or disenchanted shrinking population? Throbbing erection or flaccid retrenchment? Take your prick. I mean pick. Pick. As in grab the ice pick and cut me some ice cubes on the double – if the bloody pick doesn't fold on impact that is. I'm sorry, I can't seem to stop. I can't control myself. I'm picking on the prick aspects of the situation. But maybe that's good. Good. Perhaps I'm on water that moves… that makes waves… that stirs itself up and makes a commotion instead of spreading itself flat as a glass pane waiting to be shattered. So take your pick son. Take your pick and smash the glass in one swift motion. The future awaits you. In there. Behind the shattered gloss. Behind the shattered mirror. You goddamn prick. You prissy twitchy super-modern flaccid and complacent prick.

I'm sorry. Strike that through. Strike it through completely. But keep in mind that this is how a vast majority of the non-Western world (which is a majority in itself) regards the West. Unsubstantiated or uncalled for as it may be or not, the representation is there and we have to deal with its widespread presence. And keep in mind that where there's smoke there's fire. There may actually be some validity in such attitudes, like it or not.

It's not the kind of thing one wishes to hear about oneself, surely. When the acerbic viewpoints of others appear to be well founded they sting all over, marking the time for recollection. But herein lies the good news, for the only way to neutralise and overcome any such representations is to actually face them. Only thus can they eventually be transfigured. Only when faced.

Yes, I truly fear we are on the wrong path my friend. I fear that our way of life is facing a great crisis, whether it is in the explosive scenarios of the warmongers or just the implosive scenarios of the peace bearers. Either way, we don't seem to be able to rise to the occasion if you know what I mean. Impotence flows many ways, many unfulfilling ways. The only way to lift the burdens of our affluent, yet, ultimately unfulfilling way of life seems to pass through an incisive recollection and transfiguration that will reconnect the mojo of the perennial principles to our current way of dealing with things.

Let me ask a question.

The hollowness that people have in our part of the world... how do you define it? That sense of incoherence and dissonance where one's life is great on paper but, nevertheless, feels slightly wrong or dubious or off course? Or, conversely, when it feels not totally right, or slightly unjust, or subtly unjustified? How do you account for the general sense of helplessness whereby the way ahead seems AAA OK but not exactly as one had imagined it and not quite right, as if something substantial is missing from the recipe, something that is necessary for holding the dish together and making it taste good too.

For how long will people suspend their inner core beliefs in order to match the development of a system that is assuming a life of its own, leading down a path where people either have to be torn between the ideal and the pragmatic or they have to somehow lose their soul in order to bring the two together to be in harmony within the world? How long can we as a whole accept the compromises we make in order to fit into this system as a natural part of life while denying that some of these compromises are in fact part of the problem rather than the solution, protracting certain profound inequities inherent in our system instead of suppressing them?

When the system's basic vibrations are so far apart from perennial values such as justice, love and respect, the average compromise may indeed succeed in giving a person that edge which is so necessary in our naturally competitive system. The not-so-average compromise, though, goes much further. It rips the internal world apart, prying open a huge rift inside – between what one truly believes in and what one must adjust to for practical reasons – creating a hollowness so pervasive and overwhelming that it drives people mad, sending them spinning to illicit drugs, legal antidepressants, workaholism, disillusionment, greed, cynicism and learned helplessness.

I, for one, admit that this hollowness is haunting me; a sense of general helplessness that can be ameliorated by family, sex, companionship, a job, money to spend, holidays to make, shows to see and things to do... holes in the grounds for an ostrich rather than lasting solutions, for even the life of families and partners and friends and activities slowly succumbs to the pervading helplessness rising when individual enters system. Instead of being the main drive forward, these activities turn into damage control and patch up the constantly battered hull. For such is life without shared purpose – a passage through reef barriers and jagged rocks in the midst of a storm... a constant battering and repair... a life in the Colosseum, continuously spent battling troops, gladiators, wild beasts and machines of war... a ceaseless and merciless fight to the death in the grandest stadium of them all, in the system arena.

The only way to escape the deadly vice of the arena and enter the city as free men and women is to face the Colosseum itself and not the gladiators it spawns and spews against each other; unite as one under common goal and fight our way through whatever comes out the portals until we reach the stadium's outer gates. Then we smash them open and enter the city of Rome, liberated and imbued with a binding purpose, ready to join the rest of the population and become part of the city. Let everyone know that they face free men and women here, not slaves.

A vibrant spirit is the only approach known to work well against induced helplessness, inspiring individuals to not only survive the system arena but to also surpass every limitation conceivable while binding everything as hard as diamond. And as the idea shines, its principles illuminate the darker parts of the land, spreading change and innovation everywhere, promoting and setting the foundations for a better and more functional world. For a little while anyway. For with the passage of time the ideals get tarnished and the whole city turns into an arena. And as Rome turns into a gargantuan Colosseum, so does the whole world. For a little while anyway. For with the passage of time the chaos and purposelessness are dissipated by a set of new and growing ideals, magnets and cores that bind people together again into new adamant form, inspiring great wonders once more.

Where in the process are we now? In a city that is creating new and great wonders, or in the Colosseum? Well, let's just go back and look at Rome, that beacon of beacons which set the foundations for the modern world we now live in, to sharpen our senses.

Rome thrived for centuries, not only by force of the sword but also through the impact of her groundbreaking ideas. Rome the Republic spread her ways across the world, where they entrenched themselves deep. She brought light and progress to the world, laying down the firm and sound foundations of Roman Law, Arts, and Sciences, setting a grand precedent for the centuries to come. But Rome the Empire was not so sturdy. She began to shake under the tremors of her grandiosity and the blows of her proliferating enemies. And when she perished, during the Age of Bread and Games, in the Era of Entertainment, Rome did not pass away as Rome the Republic, nor as Rome the Empire. She collapsed as Rome the Whore, a cynical, needy, greedy, and soulless entity, too self-involved and jaded to survive let alone innovate and lead. With her spirit raped and deadened and her idealism eroded away she was just another victim of the arena, trying to make a living by offering entertainment until it killed her.

In her dying moments she remembered what she had long forgotten – that which had driven her to greatness in her youth, which had inspired those around her to excel – and she sighed with delight. She saw it very clearly and sensed it with all her dying heart and soul for a very lucid moment. Then she perished, with her eyes open, just like Athens, Sparta and Macedonia.

She was greater than those states, though, and her implosion was astounding. Never had the world seen such a collapse, nor would it see one again, not until the fall of Constantinople one thousand years later, the fall of a city known as The City. She, too, fell because her spirit and ideals had been eroded and tarnished by the passage of time, the great corruptor of matter and men.

Five hundred years on, at the turn of a millennium, roughly where the Roman and the Byzantine societies had begun to shake in their foundations, we are looking back wondering what went wrong then, trying to understand what is going wrong now, struggling to shed light on why our society seems to be disillusioned, sickly, in need of medication and very adept to creating enemies out of thin air. Have we perhaps reached that turning point where we are losing our spirit too? Is it perhaps time to reinvent ourselves and reconnect with the cornerstone principles of our way of life in order to reinforce our lives? Or are we to take the risk and go down the road that has been travelled to ruin and proven fatal without exception?

It seems that we have reached our moment of choice and that whatever we do or don't do will determine our course. Action and inaction are now synonymous; they simply represent different choices. And whatever we do, however loudly we act or however deeply we burrow our heads in the sand, choice cannot be escaped, nor passed on; it can only be affected. And the question is: if we have to make a choice no matter what, shouldn't we make the responsible choice? This, of course, leads to another question – what constitutes the responsible choice? And the conundrum begins, bearing a barrage of options with it.

Yet, the answer need not pass through the Bermuda Triangle of complication. We have reached the point where all we need to do is augment our elaborate knowledge with the straightforward power of inspiration. It is once again time to return to basics, to reconnect with our driving force, which we have forgotten, and to envision the future through eyes that are not simply aware of the past but very mindful of it too, determined to analyse and comprehend previous mistakes in order to actually prevent them from repeating themselves at will.

The way out of this labyrinth is simple. We have to go back to the ideal, back to the source, back to where our soul once grew and where it can grow once more. There we will stop wilting and start flourishing. There we will grow. And with a bit of luck, we may even inspire others to do the same.

***

Why are people in the West so afraid to embrace the need for new ideals? If Hitler and Stalin have indeed managed to taint the notion of ideology so lastingly, then they didn't lose. They won. Those murderers won and we are living out the aftermath of their horrible dreams. For there is only one thing worse than a bad ideology... and that is the fear of one in the first place. Our allergy to ideology as an ideology worth having will be our undoing. Enter limbo. Orderly chaos. Like ants in a colony. Free will gone. Everything is up to the whims of a massive invisible hand and to those who control it – those few and obscure figures residing in parapets of influence who pull the strings – and we lose ourselves in the midst of a cold machine. Having money or resources makes no difference. No substantial difference at all. They can distract us away from the problem and make things better for us, but they make no difference on the whole. We are still parts of the machine. Not part of it. Parts of it. Individual parts.

Isn't it ironic that material resources seem to be the chink in the armour of the material-driven system of individualism? And isn't it even more ironic how a haywire sense of individualism creates a system so pervasive that everything is not only an individual part of it but also succumbs to its collective machinations?

Parts of a machine we remain, individual constituent parts, and the only way to transcend this position and become truly free individuals is to climb the ladder and cross over into the realm of self-serving economic and political superiority. Our problems don't stop there though; they persist, the only difference being that we are now an active part of the problem instead of plain victims i.e. a lot more in control and a little more soulless – like those politicians you see on TV and immediately know that they are either speaking lies through their teeth or just spinning the truth for a number of obscure reasons with a sort of absolved look on their faces, as if they have acquitted themselves from the accountability inherent in distorting the truth, convinced that their selfish and single-minded actions are in the best interests of everyone. Politicians on the payroll, speaking not out of their ass but through their force-fed wallets, they are everywhere and growing cheaper by the dozen.

Between you and me, some of the vilest people I have ever met are individuals of such clout; empty, opportunistic beings of arbitrary values that stand for nothing other than making their interests bigger; greedy and mindless expansionists who equate happiness and achievement with the exponential rise in money and power... people of many houses but few friends; of huge house parties but few substantial relationships; of big personal fortunes but small personal wealth; of diverse portfolios but monolithic values; of great needs but of little to offer despite their vast possessions; living bodies with a deadened soul, roaming the world in search for that peace of mind that no mansion or investment or takeover can provide them (as they will eventually find out, the hard way, in the midst of a life lived in the company of many people, yet, lived in total and consuming isolation).

Few are those who rise above the floating shit. Few and far between. And they shine brightly, for something else fuels their being, such as values beyond the "more, more, more..." that eats away at the Takers. Values with substance that are geared to giving back not just for the sake of show or PR, but out of a heartfelt wish to do so. These rare individuals are Givers, individuals who believe in the ideology of solidarity, respect, sacrifice and other such perennial values that not only sound good in theory but which also keep the world working properly, effectively and efficiently.

Yet, in this increasingly cynical world we forget about the practical and pragmatic aspect of these values and reject them as utopian hogwash fit only for fairytales and New Age Flake-isms, as we also forget that pragmatists are in fact more easily corrupted than ideologues. After all, it takes a long time for a strong ideology to be twisted. But how long does it take to corrupt the likes of Kenneth Lay, Donald Rumsfeld or Jacques Chirac? How long does it take to corrupt these economically-driven, ideology-free, practically-oriented individuals?

As far as ideologues are concerned, though, they aren't all saints either, nor are they immune to corruption altogether. Some of them fall as quickly and easily as the practically expedient Chiracs of the world do. The George Dubya Bushes, for example. Eager to save the world, the Dubyas of the world get sucked into the vortex of their affirmations and distort their ideology rapidly, implementing it in ways that defeats the purpose while supporting the arbitrary. Dubya Bush himself is, of course, a special case of a puppy dog who has been assigned the power of ideology and who is now abusing highly precious ideals just so he can further the personal gains of his owners.

If not for anything else, ideology must be embraced in order to protect it. If not, then it will be seized by the likes of people like Bush and Chavez who will have no qualms about twisting it from the onset, and we will have to face the limitations of their interpretations rather than our own. And I purport that it is much better to face the corruption of our own ideology rather than that of someone else's. Take issues in our own hands, see? Carpe fucking Diem. It's my life, isn't it? Well, I don't want to live it solely in terms of Bush's or Chavez's or Bin Laden's applications. It is time to fight for what I believe in, and to seek others who feel the same.

At the end of the day – and the beginning of another – I am looking for ideas from people with insight, ideas to release into a system that we consensually regard as immutable only because such a behemoth of an infrastructure is considered impossible to change. But change is impossible only after one thinks that it's impossible; suspend confidence and you suspend all possibility. After all, one cannot achieve that which one does not believe in – or cannot even imagine for that matter. But begin to entertain crazy thoughts and the odds go up. Entertain imagination and probabilities increase. Entertain folly... and the impossible becomes possible.

We have a chance to do something good. For the first time in decades we have something substantial to work with. This is the chance that comes along once every couple of hundred years. This is it, the chance not every generation has, the chance to make a difference. Time to go to work and shape a better world. Time to set the wheels in motion, kickstart the engine, get the wagon back on track. Time to go to work.

I am not vying for an activist approach. Not necessarily. But I am asking for contribution, for ideas, for a stand against what feels wrong while upholding what feels right. I ask for your deep and unspoken opinions, those kept hidden under silence because they would provoke some tension if they were voiced, stirring the waters more than we have become accustomed to dealing with in this twitchy touchy era of theoretical but not fully observed free speech. For that is what we have come to: fear of voicing our beliefs; fear of standing up; fear. Just fear.

When opinions are swallowed for fear of disturbing the waters it is a bad sign. When positions are not made public due to fear of social stigma or just peer and sheer pressure, then we are neck deep in trouble. When our cries are trapped in bubbles, then we are surely drowning. Perhaps it is time to speak the mind once more. Speak the word. Speak the thought. Time to live again. Jeez, how hard can that be?! Just say out loud what you really, truly think, what you actually truly believe in!

Given our increasing need for a healthy society and a more fulfilling life, the loss of faith in ourselves and in our way of life's ultimate meaning seems to be the kryptonite to our existence and the last thing we want to hear. But the best criticism is the one conducted on one's own complacency, and the health of society can be restored only when a vision is re-established. Not before.

What kind of vision it would be is up for serious and exhaustive discussion, though, and another matter altogether, for in order to be able to even tackle the answer, let alone grab it by the horns, one has to first bring it out with the right sort of questions. First the questions. Then the answers. That's the way it's always worked. It's a quite reasonable setup. Don't you think so?

Indians certainly do. They are asking the right questions under the shelter of an inspired society that is gradually coming together as it rises from the depths of ignominy into the global horizon. Scanning the area in the distance, far into the West, India sees a watery soup shining across her horizon. She smiles at the sight and then kneels to pray. Silence. Silence... Then, after a short while, she opens her mouth and a great chant echoes all around, reverberating around the globe and drowning out everything else... everything except the resonant chant coming out of the northeast, from the direction of China.

Ideology anyone?

Xavier Thorntrail

Global Issues

"*Our environment, the world in which we live and work,*
is a mirror of our attitudes and expectations"
–Earl Nightingale

X marks the spot but Y marks the territory

Dear Readers of Once Upon a Time,

During the French revolution an envoy went to the mayors of two neighbouring villages and asked them to resist despotism and join the movement that was fighting for freedom. He explained to them how things would change for the better and that they would all benefit from these changes greatly.

After a long discussion, the two men were convinced by his arguments. Excited, they went back to their people eager to report to them the new developments and convince them to take up the revolutionary cause.

The first man, X, was faced with many critical questions. By focusing only on the practical short term issues, though, and by addressing his people's needs and fears, he eventually convinced them to support the movement.

The second man, Y, was also faced with many critical questions, which he chose to explore further. So he decided to go back to the envoy and discuss the issue in depth with him in order to understand the essence and the value of this coming change.

They had a lengthy and comprehensive meeting in which his queries were addressed and expanded upon. Satisfied and informed, he returned to his people and clarified the key issues. After an incisive discussion – and now actually knowing why – they all agreed that they would support the revolutionary movement.

A few years later the Revolution was getting out of control. It was evidently turning oppressive and the Reign of Terror had started spreading throughout the country. No place was safe and the two neighbouring villages were wondering how long it would be before the Reign of Terror would reach them.

Surely enough, an envoy of the Revolution was eventually dispatched to the two villages to meet with X and Y and ask for their support in defending the new and ultra-radical factions behind the revolutionary movement at any cost. According to them, the whole of France was under the threat of Royalists, Federalists and counterrevolutionary forces that needed to be crushed immediately and without mercy. Anyone suspected of supporting these insurgents would be considered a traitor and executed without hesitation.

X was persuaded that it would be in his immediate benefit to support the new radical approach and its proponents. He returned to his village where he promoted the new envoy's positions. Eventually, he succeeded in getting his constituency's support.

Y had his doubts. After discussing it with his people, they decided that the new envoy's positions were in conflict with the basic and fundamental values of freedom, and so they vowed to resist the Reign of Terror and to continue fighting for liberty.

The Reign of Terror was ended shortly after and the Democratic French Republic was restored.

Some years later, Napoleon rose to power and started tightening his grip around the country. He sent an envoy to the two villages to assess the situation there.

After a short discussion, X decided to back up the demands of Napoleon's envoy and went to inform his village of the new changes ahead. Y, on the other hand, had his reservations but kept his disagreement private. He told the envoy that he would relay the matter to his people promptly and left with his heart beating in the middle of his throat.

Surely enough, after a long meeting the new positions were rejected because they were judged to be going against basic freedom values, and the Y village resisted Napoleon with all its might.

Shortly after, Napoleon's Empire was dissolved and the democratic French Republic was restored. For a little while.

When Hitler invaded France a century later, one of the villages resisted the invasion and occupation, fighting for their freedom and independence. The other village looked at their immediate interests and collaborated with the Nazi regime.

Who do you think resisted and who collaborated?

In essence, it all boils down to this: unless subjected to informed analysis and critical judgement, resistance and collaboration are nothing more than a pawn's move. The Y-Factor knows it, and that is why it is always stronger than the X-Factor. The X-Factor knows it in turn, and this is why the X village always envies the Y village.

This is also why, deep down in their souls and whatever the circumstances, the Y village is always free.

Victor Gente Delespejo,
A disgruntled Western Citizen,
A worried Citizen of the Globe.

The Human Ice Age

Dear CNN,

It is just becoming worse, turning from serious to worrying, to comic, to threatening, to revolting, to revolt-inducing, to potentially tragic. I am talking about the growing mentality which accepts that the US need to blatantly dictate the course of the whole world – including friendly nations that have dissenting opinions – with an iron fist.

Does the assertion go too far too fast, employing quick and radical judgement while inviting the same exact judgement upon itself? Not necessarily, at least not if you compare general mentalities within the US – and the outlook of others regarding the US, an evaluation which is pragmatically driven and founded on practical criteria, for it is based upon the interpretations of the majority of the rest of the world i.e. 200 odd countries and 6.5 billion people. I think these figures should count for something, right? We do live in an age of representation after all.

Tell you what! Why don't we clear the air from the misty stereotypes and clarify the argument, shall we?

Dear CNN, this caustic feedback stems from and relates to the wording of the Quickvote that you held on your website sometime in November 2003. To be specific, you posed the following question: "Should countries that opposed the war in Iraq be allowed to compete for reconstruction contracts?" The option was to answer either "YES" or "NO."

And the answer is, "What kind of a presupposition is operating within such a Quickvote question?" What kind of nationalistic mood are you setting through it? I hate to use the term 'imperialist' because it's been abused too much, but there's no other term to describe the environment that is being created. Then again, perhaps there is. 'Supremacist.' Or 'covertly supremacist.' Or 'tacitly unilateral.' But let's not get carried away with the name calling here.

What is more relevant (and eloquent) is that CNN is part of this "whatever you want to call it" atmosphere. I understand why Fox News creates such tense circumstances. Fox News is a blatantly biased news station that thrives on creating a polarised nationalist mood and on setting the standards along a strictly American yardstick, a very conservative, God-obsessed, Bible-stricken, self-righteous, pompous, and vengeful yardstick. Something straight out of the Old Testament. But CNN?! Where does CNN fit in with all this?

You see, dear CNN, if the decision on Iraq's reconstruction were taken by a world body of authority (a global one), I'd say that the term "allowed" is pertinent. But when the US decides to act unilaterally, then the term "allowed" begins to assume ominous undertones. Especially in the mouths of Bill O'Reilly and his type.

Truth be told, this unilateralism is considered ill-advised and reprehensible by a great variety of bodies and organisations, including your own. You do not speak for it. You even speak against it. Yet you still come up with Quickvote questions such as these.

It is hardly surprising then why the presupposition solidifies – the presupposition that the US is the master and commander of all that grows and shrinks. And it is equally unsurprising why the impression that the US wants to be the master and commander of all that grows and shrinks is solidifying with it.

Eventually, such questions and comments, such presuppositions, spread slowly but steadily through the media, seeping into the minds of the American public and creating a mentality which accepts that the US is indeed the master and commander of all that grows and shrinks. And after a while, this mentality shifts a little and becomes one that expects and demands that the US commandeer and domineer over everyone and everything under the sun and moon – at least in the minds of many American citizens. Quite a worrying attitude to spread around, wouldn't you say? And let us not mention the naturally apprehensive interpretations and reactions of the rest of the world, those 200 odd countries and the odd 6.5 billion people, who are already experiencing the ripple effects of these mentalities, feeling rather threatened, angered or disillusioned. Let us not even mention the complications of such apprehensions.

Ok, let us be realistic and pragmatic. The US, same as other great powers, sets the course of the world on all levels and in more ways than one. That is what superpowers do. They have the muscle to flex, so they flex it. Who can blame them? Can you blame the strongest person in the arena for overpowering everyone else?

The problem is that the world is not just an arena. There are other qualities to it, which do not benefit from constant and unilateral muscle flexing. The world is also a school, a workplace, a sports retreat, a summer camp, and the jock is not always the star in these places, especially when he seems to be strung out on some sort of amphetamines and kinda walks around all nervy and jittery, believing he is carrying out the work of God and looking for a fight all the time because he has a short fuse and gets easily offended by almost everything. This is, of course, why he seems to have no real and lasting friends. Nobody really likes him, not anymore. And why should they? He bullies them all the time, at every chance he gets, even when they are on the same team, doing some sport together, or when they are sharing dinner in the dining hall. Or is this just the work of the current US administration, whose attitude has given the US a bad global rep?

In fact, to be more specific, the US has only just recently begun to bully its way around the world, including at the dinner table, in unacceptable and intolerable ways (not that there is an acceptable and tolerable way of bullying, but this is geopolitics so let's allow some room for pragmatism and practicality). The US, or should we say, the current White House, is now openly dictating the course of countries such as France and Germany (still allies through NATO), and Russia and China (potential nemeses) by shoving them around and not showing the amount of respect or restraint necessary. The lack of inspired strategy is apparent. Yet, it did not stop the voters from keeping this administration into power.

Well, this is not valour in the face of adversity. This is not determination in the face of danger. It is plain stupid naiveté. It is speaking loudly and carrying a small stick, soon to be known as the W contribution to society. The W Legacy.

The worst part of it all is that this way of thinking is no longer confined to the diplomatic echelons. It is being cultivated on the popular level of the average American citizen. It is being sown everywhere. Not just by Fox News, but by everyone, including CNN.

It is hardly surprising then that I've lately been running into Americans who bear true animosity to Europeans. Their feelings are genuine and not aimed at the Germans and the French only. The current mentality is that "It's the French now who are not totally with us, and it could be any European country later on." A divide is being fed, a chasm is growing, and its effects are seen in the everyday life of individuals. And it is polls like yours that feed its growth, especially when they are worded as yours was, oozing with a subtle W undertone; so subtle, in fact, that it almost sounds natural. But it is not. And the reactions of the overwhelming majority of people around the globe – of global citizens – testify to their arbitrariness and to the anxiety that they cause.

Even Europe has been affected, citizens of allied countries, countries that have been allies and friends with the US for the past fifty years at least. Europeans are having a massive change of heart about the good nature of the US. But it's hardly surprising. When someone begins to look at you differently, you begin to feel different towards them too.

This is not a good development. It does not fare well with global stability and is definitely worth further consideration. I am sure it is clearly apparent to most of us that any kind of rift with Europe will be damaging to the US – and to the world in general – over the long run. Even a mere batch of cold relations with Europe will cause global pneumonia. And a global pneumonia will not affect just certain parts of the planet; it will affect all of it. This will, of course, hit every household, every home and every individual. It is reasonable to assume and predict that most people will be affected negatively, and that the distribution of this adversity will be distributed across the whole globe. Everyone stands to lose from this.

The loss of ideologically sound vision by the most robust and most representative member of the West is indeed a major problem. And it is growing. The US is now far from what the US was in the 30's and 40's, both objectively and subjectively. It's not the gentle giant that hunted down the monster of Nazism, coming to the rescue of those under attack. Not anymore. Something more sinister has associated itself with it over the years.

If it truly wishes to regain its gentle giant status and begin to influence the world in benign ways – without the stigma of double standards damning its actions anymore – it should redevelop a political dynamic that is more in tune with the perennial values of life and less with the obsession on policing, governing, scolding and assimilating, lest the US becomes the new aging Rome, taking the whole West down with it.

And if the US thinks that radical Islam is the new Nazi

Germany, or the devil himself, then it should make sure that others see what it sees before expecting full support; it's the only way to enter any confrontation, the only way to win, to survive. One must have support. One must have the support necessary to go to hell and back to stop the devil in his tracks, any devil, any evil, any threat, uncouth or civil.

In Robert Bolt's play 'A Man for All Seasons', though, Sir Thomas More, the 16th-century Chancellor of England, raises a timeless caution about going to hell and back. He warns against the dangers of cutting down all the bushes and trees the devil hides behind when you are on his track and hunting him down. He warns against it adamantly, for he knows what will happen after you have cut down the last bush and tree – the devil will turn around and begin to turn the screw on you! And what will you do then? Where will you seek refuge then, o hunter now hunted? Where will the whole West seek refuge when the devils it is now hunting turn around and start to really crank the pressure up in a stripped down and shelterless environment? Or has this already begun?

***

The liabilities in seeing enemies and devils everywhere are an imperative that the US must realise, and so must bodies of influence and power like CNN. It is not just the globally marginal countries that are feeling threatened by the US, seeing evil (or counter-evil) in its shocking and awesome foreign policy. Not anymore. Now the West, too, is feeling threatened by the constant US-devil-hunting, on political and cultural and societal and individual levels. Everyday people, workers, managers, mothers, teenagers are getting frustrated and angry. The political US should know better than to go on disenchanting their like and disturbing functional homogeneity, thereby making enemies out of friends. God knows it has its hands full already.

Of course, enemies have their utility. Throughout its 200-year history, the US have been a master in identifying, isolating or creating Barbarians against which to unite and fight, thus promoting and preserving their own unity, their stability, their sense of righteousness. And they have been doing so while ostensibly acting in the better interests of the whole world. While that was part of the case in many instances (i.e. while acting in their own best interests they also did indeed help others), the US actions are now under the lens. People outside the US have begun to doubt the benevolent and constructive aspects of these kinds of US interventions more and more, especially the most recent ones, especially the ones that involve Iraq. Meanwhile, others are realising that the US have gotten carried away with this 'all-American' policy so necessary for US internal unity, national pride and righteous fulfilment. In fact, these individuals are beginning to react. And when I say individuals, I am not referring to Cubans, Palestinians, Indonesians and Salvadorians; I am talking about French citizens, Spanish, Dutch, British… And while the governments of some of these countries are supportive of US policies, their populations are disillusioned, threatened, and on their way to taking action, if not now, then later. The way is being paved for dangerous tension.

Is what is written here scaremongering? If it is, it is a scaremongering far more valid than the scaremongering primarily bred by the witch-hunters and their search for the evildoers, and most importantly, by the measures taken to conduct these hunts. Nobody denies that Al-Qaeda and their offshoots are a terrible threat to our way of life and to society in general. Nobody can deny that there is a "devil" out there that has to be fought, a devil that has always been around in one form or another. Nobody can reject that society's duty is to fight any devil and protect what is considered good or just. But there's a limit to what one can, and must, do, or to be more precise, there's a point beyond which the ends cease to justify the means.

Take a look at the Holy Inquisition. It decided to fend off the devil with witch-hunts, mock trials, exorcisms, torture and other such methods and techniques, and it failed miserably. Not only did it fail, but it also damaged the idea of Christianity irrevocably and permanently. The Kernel of Christendom was burned along with the witches in the Holy Pyres, and the average person still wonders what on earth the Post-Middle-Age Church and its policies in the Early Modern Period had to do with Jesus Christ and his teachings.

Pre-emptive strikes, self-righteous indignations, pseudo-morality, Big Brother eyes peering through your living room and mine… Are these the principles and tools of a society that defends and preserves peace, order, safety and democracy? Or are they the doctrines and the weapons of a new sort of Holy Inquisition that is trembling in the wake of reconstitution, having realised that its dogmatic past practices have sculpted this coming reconstitution into form?

In true Old-Testament fashion, this new sort of Holy Inquisition is fighting fire with fire and is seeking eye for an eye, oblivious to the fact that it is thus injecting the horrific sculpture it has helped create with a life force that vibrates with disillusionment, fear, passion, hatred and the instinct for survival, a process which can only lead to a conflict of gladiatorial nature; till the end. To the death!

Using the biblical phraseology currently so popular in the US, this new sort of Holy Inquisition – which, in this case, could be aptly renamed to 'The Somewhat Oily Inquisition' – is digging for Armageddon. And if the name sounds too dramatic, well… with disillusionment rising among friends, passion and hatred among enemies, fear among the rest and a technology of epidemic and annihilating proportions, what name other than Armageddon would you give to this looming state of affairs?

The Somewhat Oily Inquisition does not, of course, represent the whole of the US. It is the platform for a small extremist minority that is taking advantage of seminal noble principles inherent in American culture and its citizens, a platform from which they are manipulating every tense situation.

Yet, small as this minority may be, it is not minor at all anymore. It has gradually grown in influence and power and is dictating the US course despite the resistance it faces from within, which is quite lacklustre, yet, strenuous. Cronies meet Libs and the tug-of-war is on. In fact, if one stops and takes a good look, it is evident that the US as a whole is being torn apart in a ruthless internal tug-of-war. While trying to take the eyes of the enemy out with its right hand, the US is damaging its own eyes with its left hand. In essence, and in a unified bi-partisan effort, the injured US has been left blinded by its 'eye for an eye' policy – a national policy that is fast becoming a national mentality. And it is widely known that there is nothing more unpredictable and dangerous than a blinded giant.

We, the disillusioned, want to help this great giant recover and heal, for both its sake and ours. But we can only do so much. If there is something this monumental representative of the West – and of the 21st century, the first global century – must "allow," it's a change; a change from within and a change with the times, lest it become a dinosaur. After all, for true change to take place, minds must grow. And for minds to grow, effort is required, from within and from the outside, from top to bottom and back again. Certain decisions have to be made, action has to be taken, and measures have to be introduced. If not… does the term 'extinction' ring a bell? It goes hand in hand with 'failure to adapt' to a rapidly changing environment.

Unlike the proverbial dinosaur and despite its blinding pain, though, the US is not a pea-brained reptilian giant. It is an analytical being that is comprised of highly cognitively advanced cells and which possesses the capability to identify an impending Ice Age. It can even predict one long before it arrives. It cannot stop one in its tracks, true, but it can do other things, impressive things. It has the technological and cognitive ability to undergo a total transfiguration and survive an Ice Age, for it is an entity made up of human cells and not cells proper. It is a society. Thus, not only can it willingly mutate its body faster than a biological organism. It can also:

- Recognise its interdependence with the rest of its habitat's residents and devise ways through which to achieve an optimising transformation that will further help it survive.
- Comprehend why it must give up its agenda of total world domination and not flex its military muscle at the drop of a hat.
- Comprehend why it must stop generating supremacist nationalism through biased polls and subtly uniform – even if ever so generally standardised – journalism.
- Comprehend why it must stop spreading fear among its own population through racial manipulation, crime-related spins and health scares.
- Comprehend why it must stop intimidating friends.
- Eventually understand that it is accountable for actions it condemns, such as genocide (the Native American population) and mass destruction (Hiroshima and Nagasaki), and must take responsibility – not apologize, take responsibility – for its past errors, however inevitable or justified they actually were – or seemed to be at the time – in order to avoid the mindless occurrence of similar actions in the future, thereby reassuring the world of its present and future good intentions.
- Exchange pride for dignity to gain true and lasting power.

In order to do so, its cohesion must not be predicated upon, or be dependent on, the existence of barbarians. Its prosperity and welfare must not be based solely on material wealth and short-term gratification. It must create and add to its economy a value-capital that will be exchanged not around double standards, but instead around an ideological pragmatism that serves and enhances ideals of long-term utility, collaborative and symbiotic purpose, and true global worth.

This is the kind of capital that will enrich the US economy and the economy of this globalized world. In fact, everyone must make the adjustments where applicable, every group, every society and every individual, in order to help create together a truthfully substantial and essential New World. A new New World. Why?

Because the survival of each and every one of us depends on it.

If that is not good enough reason, then we will soon prove that it is size that matters in life and not cognitive capacity. In fact, the smaller and more primitive the better. The cockroaches, the bacteria, the viruses will be crawling and rolling along in full festivity, and humans will be nothing but an uncertain memory in the tiny brains and nuclei of ancient insects and micro-organisms. And if there is intelligent life elsewhere in the universe, we will at best be objects of investigation, fossils that will adorn extraterrestrial museums and living rooms. And we will have a great thing in common with the dinosaurs – we will have been both too big to survive. At best. Now, at worst... Well, it wouldn't really matter anymore, would it?

But fear not, for even in posterity humans will take the cake. It won't take long for a life form capable of intergalactic travel to realise that whereas the dinosaurs were eradicated by a natural disaster, the humans eradicated themselves. And, thus, we shall forever be the kings of our domain: Lords of the Earth in life; Lords of stupidity in death. Lords of the Earth for millennia; Lords of stupidity for eternity.

Sincerely yours,

Victor Gente Delespejo,
A disgruntled Western Citizen,
A worried Citizen of the Globe.

After the Surge and Before the Meltdown

Dear Everyone,

If one takes a moment to look around and observe what is happening, it becomes immediately clear that we are not threatened by falling temperatures. On the contrary, the temperatures are rising all over the world at an alarming pace. Thus, it is not an Ice Age that we should worry about. No, ladies and gentlemen, forget the Ice Age and start making way for the lovely threat of the sizzling Fire Age.

Scorching temperatures and melting ice caps are the charming companions of this coming Fire Age, and they bring with them the hard-rockin' "Extreme Weather Fluctuations," soon to perform in a venue near you. Watch out for their smash hits "Flash Floods," "Heat Waves," "Dried up Rainforest Makes a Good Patch of Farmland," and their unforgettable tune "Super Storms Pounding on My House." It'll be a great show, worth every penny you spend on it, but don't go overboard; keep your cool and save some money for your caring political party, which can always use your donation. Please donate generously and remember that your political party is here to look out for your best interests, so make a big donation and help us build a better and safer place where the threat of global warming will be dealt with swiftly and resolutely, just as the threat of terrorism has. Please don't forget to also screw the Kyoto Protocol up the ass in order to help our slumping economy recover, which will eventually stand to benefit greatly from a cataclysm, should one occur, for we aim to be the top supplier of relief technologies and equipment to the whole drowning world. In fact, this cataclysm will be a blessing in disguise, for – as God has confided to me – it will spawn an unprecedented level of research and innovation, placing humanity in a whole new tier.

Now, where's the sucker who said that Bushonomics don't have a long term vision? Has he shut his mouth yet, or does he wanna hear our plan again? No? That's what I thought!

So, any more questions? Ah, yeah, go ahead. What was the question? 'How will we live in an environment that is turning increasingly hostile?' Well, there's only one way to deal with this! The more hostile the environment gets, the more we bomb the crap out of it! What?

What do ya mean that this is not what you meant? What? So what's the question? 'How will we survive in a climate whose equilibrium is being disturbed?' Well, how the hell should I know? I just know that we will! That's all! God insassured me of it. Yes, he insassured me of it, and he insured me too! What's the matter with you? Can't you understand English? Next question. What? Did I ask God how we shall survive? Ma'am, I can tell you now that I, I do not have the audacity in me to ask our Lord and Maker how He aims to carry out His plans. I'm sure He knows best how to run things down here. After all, He's the Big Boss. And I certainly cannot take it in my liberty and start snooping around in His affairs. Nor can I begin to question His plans and wishes. I know better than that and so should you. In fact, I cannot believe that you are asking me this question. Shame on you, ma'am! Shame on you. May God have mercy on your soul. Now please, get on your knees and pray for our troops down in Iraq, which are getting ready to surge into victory. And that goes for all of you. Get on your knees and pray. If you do we shall win. God has spoken.

...

Oh boy! I mean, this is what we are predominantly dealing with here, dear Citizens of the Globe. This is what the leader of the strongest Western country of our time is saying between the lines – and sometimes out loud, too, although not in those words (his exact choice of words cannot be reproduced for fear of damaging the English language irrepairvocablishly, God bless his soul).

What is even more extraordinary, though, and quite worrisome, is the fact that W clones are beginning to sprout all over the globe, emulating this type of logic and applying it in their own special ways.

What do you say to this type of ill logic, whatever culture it comes from? What indeed?

Sincerely yours,

Victor Gente Delespejo,
A disgruntled Western Citizen,
A worried Citizen of the Globe.

Out of the Frying Pan and into the Fire

Dear Everyone,

The George Dubya Bush administration is responsible for many crimes against humanity, too many and complicated to list. So let's just put things in a nutshell.

The Dubya Bush administration has started an unnecessary war in the name of making the world safe from a loathsome dictator only to exacerbate the situation in the Middle East, creating a civil conflict within Iraq, allowing numerous terrorist cells to spawn from the chaos, and turning global opinion against the US – and against the West in general – at a time where it deserved all the support in the world. What a waste. What a monumentally stupid waste!

Yet, the biggest crime of the Dubya administration is not the illegal invasion of a sovereign state over ultimately unsubstantiated claims about the presence of WMD's, or Saddam's threat to global security, or his links to Al-Qaeda, etc etc; it is not the inflammation of an area already drenched in nitroglycerin – nor the killing of people like you and me, whether Iraqi nationals or American soldiers – nor is it the torture that has taken place in Abu Ghraib prison or in front of the cameras of a vicious butcher squad that chose to make headlines by sawing people's heads off. No, the crime is far worse than that, far nastier, far deeper.

The crime de la crème of the Dubya administration is none other than the rape and murder of idealism itself, in the name of which this whole goddamn mess was created. It was in the name of ideology that Iraq was invaded, and it is against that specific ideology that the criticism for the invasion of Iraq is pounding. The justified opposition to Dubya's stance is finally making headway and is gaining ground on him, but, unfortunately, it cannot contain itself and is delivering blows far beyond Dubya's ideals alone. It is in fact pounding against idealism itself, rejecting it in every form other than a loosely appreciated and barely shared concept of laissez-faire economics and practical politics. Not a promising development, to be sure.

Idealism is down and struggling. It will take a great deal of time and effort to resurrect its worth in our hearts and minds, appreciating its value once again.

While we struggle to regain it, we are an idealism-fearing and sceptical bunch embroiled in a sinister conflict that seems to be spreading. And there is nothing more dangerous than being in a sinister conflict without the benefit of a good ideology. Actually, there is, and it is none other than being in the shadow of a certain initiative-turned-conflict that has not only been started by you, but also been clearly proven and widely acknowledged to have been conducted under the pretences of a flashy but hollow set of ideals.

How terminal it all becomes when noble ideals are used as ashes in the eyes of the gullible so that the greedy can gain a few more millions for themselves.Once a group of legitimate businesspeople and politicians, these individuals possessed vast amounts of wealth and power, which they had earned through hard, legitimate work, and, truth be told, they deserved every smidgeon of it. But then some of them got greedy and decided to bend the rules to their advantage; they bent them, they broke them and rewrote them, trammelling the benefits of the global economy with their tactics and connections while disregarding the principles of justice and fair play altogether. Now these tainted individuals are nothing but a bunch of thugs in suits, who have used their power irresponsibly and with utter disregard to the workings of the now interconnected global dynamic, reaping the fruits of their cunning to quench their obsession for more wealth and power. Lords in ivory towers, building fortifications around the lands they are squelching dry, they are investing in the headquarters by ravaging the rest of the territory. Not very inspired or farsighted, is it?

Well, the good news is that in the day of globalisation, more things have gone global than just the economy; awareness has grown global too, and so has public perception. No action of that calibre goes unnoticed anymore, and, seen for the thugs that they are, these people are now wanted across the globe for the crimes they have committed – and gotten away with. Everyone knows who they are and how they have made it; the truth is out there, working its way through every individual's mind, sifting through the facts and turning the cogs of judgement; gradually and deliberately, a few billion bull's-eyes have begun to hone in on them. Justice will catch up with them sooner or later, and the wealth they have extracted by causing global tensions and bloody conflicts will be worthless to them. Nothing – not even all the money and influence in the world – can keep them safe anymore. Ask Louis XVI and his corrupt bunch. They know.

You see, when you invoke the name of God and the principles of liberty and democracy in order to lay your claims on oil or to conduct a socio-politico-economic experiment, then you are clearly in the situation where the shit has hit the helicopter rotor – hardly anything to complain about, for if one throws shit in the air, then one shouldn't complain when he gets shit stains on his clothes.

But there is a problem in all of this. When you throw shit around in the global village, where I, too, live, and when you are doing so from the neighbourhood where I live in, then not only do I get stained myself, but I also get targeted by those you so blatantly shat upon.

Now, this is not something I should have to put up with, surely. I had a voice the last time I checked, and I think it's about time I used it, for it seems that instead of being dragged by force in the crossfire of the greatest shitstorm to ever hit the planet, I am actually being cooed into it, like a moth to a flame. And that's no good! It doesn't speak well of my character and integrity. No, I will shout my opinions and fight for what I believe in rather than acquiesce. Acquiescence… The new plague.

But that's not all. There is another problem brewing up, volatile and corrosive. Its name is Cynicism. And while the Cynics gain ground, chiselling away at any form of ideology in the name of reason and sanity, little do they know that their tactics are stripping our society of its backbone. Soon the only thing left of it will be a saggy bag of skin sprawled all over the floor and going nowhere. Our self-defence from abused idealism and rampant zealots will turn fast to an equally monolithic paradigm that brands any sort of idealism evil or manipulative, purging the modern world clean of religious fundamentalism… and we have just made a 180 degree turn, boomeranging from zealous conservatism to zealous liberalism.

Clearly, the way forward is not the fear of idealism. Nor is the castigation of idealists. Just because a certain Dubya and his gang have abused certain noble ideals to further their personal wealth and schemes does not render all idealism obsolete or counterproductive. In fact, such a nullifying approach would only be expected of the Dubyas of the world and their narrow-minded gangs whom we are criticizing so harshly. Dare we follow in their footsteps, even if our path lies in the safe coordinates of a distant mirror image? Or is it about time to come together under something truly noble for which we will live together, and if need be, fight and even die together defending it? The proposition may sound ridiculous, but perhaps this says more about the times we live in rather than the proposition itself, times where fighting for what one believes in is considered ridiculous. And perhaps it is time to pause for a minute and actually ask ourselves if there is truly nothing that unsettles us enough to make us stand up and fight for it. Who knows? We may surprise ourselves, however placid we may be. After all, when diseased, people must do certain things in order to get better, no matter their disposition. They often surprise themselves with all the things they have to go through to heal themselves – things they once thought impossible – and they do what they have to do to get better, whether they be calm, placid or downright docile characters. If they don't, then it's goodbye cruel world. And while life on earth goes on even after the death of certain individuals, it is nothing more than a life born out of the prevalence of a disease. Quite a cancerous prospect, I assure you, and with a never-ending supply of disease in the pipeline of existence, we may begin to realise that the only thing that can run out is our demand to fight for our health.

Perhaps it is about time we stand and fight against the cancers to our way of life, whatever they may be, before they begin to claim ourselves or our loved ones. Perhaps it is about time to become free men and women again, men and women of dignity and self respect; humans in pursuit of higher principles and not animals chasing carrots and bananas and glittering gold coins. This is the time when few must stand against many, allowing the Cynics and the Takers to take no more. No more! It's time to reach out and reclaim our lives from them. Not an easy task, for sure, but it will be worth it, if not for our sake, then for our children. After all, they are the future. Our children are the reason why we do things; they are the core that keeps the adult satellites trundling, the force that gives us purpose, the reason why we care. They are the future of our existence… Or has this become nothing more than just another empty slogan that we have learned to squawk loudly to ourselves on our way to work and back?

Respectfully yours,

Xavier Thorntrail,
A disgruntled Global Citizen,
A worried Citizen of the West.

Jimmy Carter's 'Meet, Greet and Offer Teat' Approach

Dear Everyone,

While we are on the subject of sinister global conflict, let's just mention one little thing. Once the foot lands into the quicksand, sinking out of sight and taking the rest of you with it, you don't just sit around and start analyzing the geological developments that led to the creation of such a waylaid and treacherous phenomenon, nor do you wonder whether it was manmade or natural, or which idiot prompted you to take the path that led you there – not unless you have a genuine deathwish. If you don't, and your mind is working properly, then you will probably fight tooth and nail to get out of the trap and reach for safe and solid ground before attempting anything else. You will fight to get out of the trap before you start asking questions or pointing the finger.

Let's put it another way. Once you realise that your babies – whom you have reared so lovingly and tenderly – have grown teeth, you stop breastfeeding them. You move on to the next level. If you don't, then your tender little teat will be bitten off. And this is the best case scenario. For there is also the possibility that you have not reared your children well at all, in which case they not only grow teeth but also develop an appetite for malice. Abused children are like that, unpredictable in their tantrums and quite vicious at times, especially if they've been hanging out with the wrong crowd, playing with dangerous toys and listening to older kids who manipulate their desperate want for something real to believe in, something good to belong to, something great to aspire to. That's how it happens – switch goes the devious argument, crack goes the impressionable mind, and the teeth turn to fangs.

Let's make it even simpler. When you are facing an already unfolded threat, you don't simply refold it into a flat square and stash it away. Once opened and unfolded, these threats are like plastic wrap – however ingeniously you fold them up, they always snap, crackle and pop back into bent and disorderly form.

The only way to deal with them is to dispose of them once and for all in a neat and tidy manner. That does not mean nuking them or bombing the shit out of them, of course, nor does it mean rearranging your whole way of life around their existence. The neat and effective way forward is to come out on top of the situation one way or another – winning the war, the peace, the impressions, or whatever it is that needs to be won for stability to return – and then committing to a fresh and substantial cause. God knows we have a few of those out there just waiting to be fought. Health, family, legacy... Ideas that are more than just words on a paper.

Causes like these have something in common. They are all poised to defend life against oppressors, aggressors, corruptors, manipulators, and all forms of Cynics and Takers. And they are unstoppable. But they can cut both ways. So we must beware of feeding the fires of inequity, lest they turn into a well-founded cause that shall rise against us. And if such a fire has already been started, kindled and fed, then we must withstand it long enough to win so that when all is said and done we can then exercise justice ourselves rather than have those who have defeated us do it for us. For they will not be friendly. Victors never are. Not as far as the defeated ones are concerned.

Which is why we better save the questions for later. Let's tuck away that teat for a while and make sure we first win the fight. Then we can start worrying about feeding our new offspring under the auspices of a united house. And by we, I mean all of us. See?

Xavier Thorntrail,
A disgruntled Global Citizen,
A worried Citizen of the West.

All Politics is Local

Dear Citizens of the Globe,

One may be wondering what the reasons behind the US 2006 Vote were. And while a few of us may say that voters have demonstrated a preference for Democrat policies, most of us know that the shift of power in the US Congress is a result of dissatisfaction with the current administration and the GOP direction. And while most of us may say that the political adage regarding the dominant significance of local politics didn't hold up this time, a few know that this is not the case. All politics is and remains local. The only thing that has changed is the area of the local neighbourhood. In the era of globalization one must surely acknowledge that Iraq, Iran and any other place on the planet are parts of our back yard... and they can determine electoral results, now more than ever.

Victor Gente Delespejo
A disgruntled Western Citizen,
A worried Citizen of the Globe.

Let Current and Resistor Beware

Dear Citizens of the 21ˢᵗ Century,

Iraq is under attack by external forces.

Regardless of the interventional objectives or the objectivist causes behind such an operation, there is a local resistance that fights against the intruders. Naturally. A much-expected local resistance. Where would any nation end up without its resistant forces? What kind of a nation would it be without them?

Yet, resistance is sharp on both sides. Its blade can cut likewise whether used wisely and deliberately or unwisely and compulsively. Its vivifying fire can burn the waves but can also singe coil, wire and casing. Ergo caveat resistor. The device's proper and efficient function depends on studied calibration that can administer the buzzing currents within its complex structural elements properly. Too little resistance and everything goes up in smoke. Too much, though, and the device never even turns on.

The answer lies in optimal solutions that fit the predicament. Overachievement is as useless as underachievement. The response must perform a class glove act and fit perfectly, for only fit and fitting responses nourish survival. Everything else usually falls flat and withers away. Yes, nature must be cruel to be just.

Iraq is under attack by internal forces. Never mind what woke up the cockerels. Did the crack of dawn tap their eyelids open? Did a gentle breeze rustle their feathers up? Did the children from neighbouring farms throw pebbles at them again?

Who cares? The cockerels are up. It's time to wake up with them.

Even though these questions are interesting in and of themselves, they are inconsequential on one basic level: 'When dawn arrives, the cockerels respond.'

Why? Well, they just do.

The question is not why do they respond? The question is how do they respond? How 'well,' how 'bad,' how 'fittingly?'

Only now do the reasons for their wakeup become relevant, only after having realised that a cockerel reacts to the effects of the approaching day, regardless of the determining details that embellish it.

Cockerels. Defenders of Newtonian principles and supreme graduates of classical physics. Praise them… and they shall bow! Or they shall scoff back with arrogance. Or turn their tails on us. But whatever the case, praise them… and they shall react. Intrude upon their night and they shall resonantly let you know they saw you coming as clear as day and an hour ahead.

But remember that Classical Physics can only go so far. Beyond a certain level it withers away. Quantum Physics takes its place. The rules change. And so do the cockerels and everything else around them.

Iraq is under attack by violent forces. A great transition is about to envelop it. Will the sun rise and shine in its sky… or will the night cast its cold and dreary blanket over the splitting desert land? After all, the sun also falls. And the cockerels also sleep.

Victor Gente Delespejo,
A disgruntled Western Citizen,
A worried Citizen of the Globe.

What do you mean "It takes two to Tango and to Box?"

Dear Citizens of the 21st Century,

Since it takes two parties to tango and two sides to create a pervading conflict across the global arena, and since the US has been taking the heat for almost everything that has gone wrong in the past sixty years or so, let's just remind ourselves of a few key things. We won't analyse them. We'll just mention them so that they become salient.

The US has been accused of a number of illicit and immoral acts such as covert intelligence operations, meddling with the internal affairs of other states, funding civil conflicts, organising coups, supporting certain despots, invading sovereign nations etc etc, and justifiably so, for it has certainly done these things. Yet, it has perpetrated all these questionable actions in reaction to a certain set of global affairs. It didn't just wake up one day and say, 'I am bored. I have discovered the light bulb and the atom bomb. What else is there to discover? What else is there to do? Um... Wait!" Bling (an idea lights up on top of the US head). "I shall bomb the shit out of a couple of places, invade a few others and force everyone to eat McDonald's at gunpoint to make my economy grow.' It didn't do that. Or did it?

There is evidence to suggest that it actually did, despite the common misconceptions that have been spun to confuse people. The truth cannot remain hidden for long and the evil plans of the US are finally coming to surface. It is now widely known, for example, that McDonalds are not just a 1950's phenomenon that just sprung out of nowhere. Its roots run deep in time, farther back than any imagination would consider, and its utility is supremely sinister. McDonalds precedes the atom bomb and was devised to be used in tandem with it in the most Machiavellian plan of all time.

Namely, McDonalds was in fact invented in the early 1800's as part of a clandestine US plan to take over the world, but was kept under wraps for more than a century until the proper means to induce widespread fear would be developed. This was by no means an easy task, and it took quite some time to make possible, but who dares and perseveres wins.

It has now been firmly established that the US fuelled the

ascension of the German Empire and the First Reich, secretly causing WWI, which would then lead to the Treaty of Versailles and the subsequent rise of a very bitter Hitler and his Nazi Regime and, of course, the Axis Powers. To be precise – and this may come as a surprise to most people – Hitler's real parents were American agents on a mission to give birth to a dictator who would plunge Europe and the rest of the world into chaos, providing the appropriate conditions for US global intervention and hegemony. WWII was nothing more than the platform wherefrom the atom bomb would be launched, paving the way for the widespread tension that could support the McDonalds franchise invasions.

There are many who of course reject such claims as utter nonsense. They know that what really happened was that the McDonalds are just a business product invented by the British in the late 1600's, which didn't kick off till centuries later.

But even among these true believers, there's only very few who know that McDonalds was actually the brainchild of the British East India Company and that it was to be initially launched in the Indian subcontinent – only to be frustrated by research predicting a severe resistance to the culinary imposition from the West. Hence, McDonalds was retracted and eventually launched with great success on the other side of the globe, in America – a continent which had initially been confused with none other than India itself! Aha! Devilish coincidence? Or devilish imperial conspiracy?

While you rack your mind on that thoroughly profound question, let's look at the other side of the issue. It is made up of what are widely considered to be unsubstantiated claims and outrageous arguments, so brace yourselves for what have proven to be seriously stretched arguments. Or have they?

Let's see.

The beginning of the 20th century saw the rise of Communism which swiftly turned from a noble cause to a monstrous regime. With Stalin at the helm, that regime came to the rescue of Europe from the Nazis in a joint Allied effort. And as the swastika came crumbling down, the hammer and sickle came rolling in from the borders of Russia, spreading into Eastern Europe and central Asia and reaching into the remote corners of the Far East.

So the US found itself in an immense tug-of-war, pulling against a USSR that was standing across the mud hole on very different ground. There they were, the US and the USSR, two superpowers of superpolar proportions, each standing for a wholly disparate and opposite ideology, representing different interests and fighting for a piece of the pie in the biggest zero-sum game ever played.

If one forgets for a minute who started what and all that adolescent whining, it becomes clear that there was a severe brawl going on, plain and simple, albeit covert and undercurrent. We refer to it as the Cold War. And during that brawl certain outrageous things were done by both sides in an effort for one to gain the advantage over the other. So when the US went to Korea, it did so in response to an invasion being carried out by the Soviet-backed North Korean army. And when it went to Vietnam, it did so in response to Soviet interference in Vietnam's regional affairs. Now, while the Vietnam War is a whole chapter in itself, and admittedly one of the greatest blunders of the 20th century, both morally and practically, let's not forget that there was a USSR on the other side of the spectrum and that the US didn't just wake up and say, 'With the Japanese firmly in my grasp, it's now time to force-feed the mainland Orientals with McDonalds, so let me just set a foot in South Korea and then step across to Vietnam from where I can deploy numerous squadrons of choppers that have been modified to shoot burgers straight into every Asian orifice in sight.'

Those who point the finger at the US all the time have probably forgotten the existence of the USSR and think that the world was always operating under the dynamics of a single superpower with an itchy military-industrial complex. Either that or they are probably people who for some reason were actual supporters of the Communist cause, calling the US an imperialist nation... like the camel in the desert race who started making fun of his rival's hump, calling her names – like "hunchback" and "Quasimodo" – and laughing his head off while he scampered alongside her with a giant lump on his back, thinking that he himself was some sort of swan-like creature straight out of a beauty pageant, poor soul.

The race was on and so was the brawl. The two main competitors were at each other's throats, fighting for the domination of the world or just plain fighting each other's domination away. And after a long and global struggle, one of them fell.

A great judgement followed, whereby responsibility and blame were assigned all around. Most blame fell to the loser, the USSR, and life went on normally. Then, as the world began to feel the after-effects of the Cold War, and with only one superpower in the spotlight, the blame began to shift and the fingers started pointing at the US – especially when the new thorns in everyone's side came with the names of Bin Laden and his Mujahideen-turned-Taliban (guerrillas initially armed and funded by the US to resist Soviet incursions in Afghanistan) and Saddam Hussein (a dictator funded and armed by the US in order to counter the Islamic regime of Iran). One, of course, has to go further back in time and bear in mind that the Iranian Islamic regime had come to power in response to the authoritarian rule of the Shah, who had been placed in power through a CIA-backed coup, which had been conducted to oust the nationalist Prime Minister Dr Mohammad Mossadegh, who had nationalised the Anglo-Iranian Oil Company, which had been under British influence following the Allied invasion of Iran in 1941, an invasion geared to prevent Iran from joining forces with the Nazis and the Axis Powers during WWII… An endless minefield of loops and knots, one leading to the other, pointing fingers back and forth, spinning the issues around until there is no clear answer.

In the tracks of history, one can get lost amidst the haze of perspectives. But there are loopholes. One can always collapse things down to simple issues and make comparisons. For example, in the backdrop of the early 20th century, in the turmoil of WWI and WWII, and during the global brawl that followed, cold as it may have been, there is one way to establish relative blame: look back and let the results speak for themselves.

So, let's mirror some of the more characteristic examples of either side against each other and see what they have to say for themselves.

- Nixon and Stalin.
- The systematic bombing of Vietnam and Cambodia to establish democracy and corporate rule in the area and the systematic starvation of the whole of the Ukraine to get its wheat and sell it in the world market to sustain a failing communist economy.
- US influence over Western Europe and USSR influence

over Eastern Europe.

- US incursions in Latin America and USSR annexations of a number of countries in Europe and Asia.
- Any US-aligned right-wing regime (like Pinochet's Chile, 1973-1990) and any Soviet-aligned communist regime (like Romania's Ceauşescu, 1965-1989).
- McCarthy's witch hunts and Stalin's witch hunts.
- Guantanamo and its media-drenched existence and Soviet concentration camps somewhere in the obscure depths of Siberia.
- The growing economic system of capitalism – unjust and rampant as it may be – and the shrivelled up communist economic system which totally paralysed twenty odd nations from the head down, leaving them to atrophy.
- The millions killed outside the US during wars or interventions in the name of democracy (or US interests) and the 20 million Soviet citizens alone killed during Stalin's command by their own government in the name of the Communist cause (or Stalin's paranoia) so as to sustain the union of the Soviet Federation.
- The overall contribution of the US to world affairs such as development, research, technology, science, art, knowledge, entertainment, growth etc compared to the overall contribution of the USSR to such world affairs.

The differences are unambiguous and unequivocal, and those individuals who still aspire to the Communist way of dealing with reality while blaming the US for all the evils in the world, in spite of the plain facts, are doing nothing more than choosing the results and after-effects of the failed paradigm over its surviving alternative. A monstrous choice whereby all logic is bent in the vice of a noble ideology gone terribly wrong – a failed but sadly not abandoned ideology, despite its monumental collapse – it is still alive and obvious, like a minatory shadow, lingering around and constantly trying to blame others for the disasters it has so undeniably aided to spawn.

So when they begin to accuse the US of crimes against humanity, they forget that no incident is a runaway bead and that all actions pass through strings which cannot but have to be compared with each other

– no matter how deep in the cracks they may have fallen.

At the end of the day, in a harsh and unjust world, individuals have to often choose between two sets of beads. They must choose the better of the two. For that is what constitutes justice in the complex world we live in. At any given time, during and throughout the long process of progression, it's always about which of the available choices is better.

The question is: McDonalds or Siberian vodka? McDonalds or Middle Eastern Halal and Haraam? McDonalds... or Bin Laden, Ahmadinejad, Kim Jong-Il, and Hugo Chavez?

I have to be honest with you... If the US falls, I cringe to imagine how its antagonists would run the world.

Xavier Thorntrail,
A disgruntled Global Citizen,
A worried Citizen of the West.

An Ugly Swan Is a King among Ducks

Dear Misguided Perfectionists,

At the end of the day, in a harsh and unjust world, individuals must indeed choose between two given sets of beads. They must choose the better of the two. And if the beads are extremely unattractive, they must simply opt for the lesser of two evils. For this is what it boils down to: choosing a side, speaking your mind, improving on the situation, and moving on. Harsh but true. And unavoidable. That's how it is. However unattractive the available options may be, individuals have to often choose between two given sets of beads. In a harsh and unjust world. At the end of the day. At the beginning of the night.

Victor Gente Delespejo,
A disgruntled Western Citizen,
A worried Citizen of the Globe.

What do you mean "Our Hands and Minds Are Tied?" And If They Truly Are, Do You Enjoy Being Tied Up?

Dear Citizens of the World,

When comparing the fouls committed by the two superpowers of the 20th century, pitching Nixon against Stalin, or US interventions against Soviet interventions, one could regard both sides of the spectrum as the manifestation of something good that stands for certain values and defends one's own side from looming threats. On the other hand, one could regard them as the manifestation of something aggressive, expansive and evil, that takes death and destruction wherever it goes, and, thus, reject them both. But even in such a case, where any form of intervention is considered an unnecessary act of brutality and an abomination to a modern and informed way of life, one must still choose a side – if not one of either two, then definitely a third, a side that will stand up to the brutal alternatives and counterbalance their effect, eventually neutralising them and shoving them out of the picture. If war and conflict and political expediency are deemed primitive and unacceptable, then only a third side that does not abide by such rules can counteract their effects. And one shall have to commit to that side in order to promote such ideals and establish them over the prevailing ones.

But the question is: How will such a side succeed if it does not fight for its ideals? More importantly, how does it survive when the other sides get annoyed and the game gets rough and dirty?

Herein lies the defining problem of pacifism. How do pacifists survive when the warmongers attack them?

A haunting question for anyone who aspires to a better way of life and a world without war and conflict, it also shows that the system has to always be tackled from within if change is to be brought about successfully, whatever the change may be. Being too far ahead is just plain dysfunctional. Things must work within the confines of the existing Norm and its practical consensus. And if change is due, even overdue, then it must work from outside those confines but still within close proximity to the current and established way of doing things.

When the Gods of Olympus were discarded they were substituted by one God in Heaven instead of the whole notion of religion being erased; when the one God in Heaven was challenged during the French Revolution, He was replaced by the Supreme Being of Reason – temporarily, of course, for He returned very soon; when the surviving one God in Heaven was challenged again a little later, He was challenged by a systemic order called Science. And when Ghandi waged his campaign of non-cooperation with the British, he resisted through non-violent means. But he resisted. Averse to violence as he was, he still resisted in his own non-violent way. He chose a side and was not afraid to stand by it. He had a purpose, a goal, an ideal.

Those who reject the notion of picking a side, rejecting all ideology as an outdated tool of societal bonding that can potentially turn evil, are forgetting that it does not suffice for one to evolve beyond certain parameters for a change to occur successfully, or for the new rules to even begin to apply, let alone work. The whole environment must evolve as well. If it hasn't done so yet, then the newly evolved rules do not apply in general. And the only way for the transmuted ones to establish those new rules firmly, and live by them, is to abscond from that environment and set up home somewhere else, somewhere where everything may be rewritten on a blank slate that will face no interference from outdated ways of operating anymore.

But that is easier said than done. People cannot just pick up and leave, nor can they set up a country that is completely isolated from current parameters so that they can make a totally fresh start – not nowadays anyway. Perhaps it was possible in the 18th century, but not anymore. Times have indeed changed and the world has become geographically finite. That is why Communism failed, and that is why the neo-con experiment on a totally free and unregulated market economy in Iraq also failed. The involved practitioners did not take into account the already operating Norms of a finite world that would interfere with their experimental paradigm. Trying to rewrite the framework in a totally new algorithm without any consideration for the supporting ground and the surrounding environment – and their general modes of operation – was an act doomed to fail. So they failed in their cause, as do all utopians who get carried away, reminding us that the secret to a revolutionary change is dreaming far enough to get out of the box, but not too far and beyond all reach, lest the utopia become a dystopia.

Those who believe in a world free of ideological wars are currently blaming the ideologues for the stalled development of society; if only people would get over their presumptions and follow a pragmatic path consistent with scientific truths and economic principles, all based on a loose and free-flowing idea of constructive values, the world would be a better place… or so the anti-ideologists think, for they believe that they have evolved beyond the need to implement one's belief system over each other and can, therefore, coexist peacefully in a multilateral world of no conflict at all. And they may be right, totally and undeniably right. But there's a problem inherent in that belief, a deeply fundamental problem. We could state it but let's not. Let's instead bring it out in the open through a metaphor.

…There was much turmoil in the jungle. Species were attacking and eating other species in order to survive and flourish, and life was getting increasingly tough. The food chain was a brutal dynamic that required total conviction and ceaseless concentration, giving no room for error to anyone, without exception. Even the kings of the jungle were vulnerable – miniscule parasites waited in their millions for a small gash to open… Like we said, there was no room for error at all. Without exception.

At some point in time a certain species of the jungle got tired of the brutality and began to envision a dynamic whereby all species could not only survive but also flourish without battling and eating each other. It was a wonderful notion. The more this species thought it out, the more it seemed like a plausible idea. When it told the other species its idea, though, they all sniggered and sent it away.

Dejected and angry, the visionary species went home and continued thinking out its new vision. It laboured over it for many days, dissecting and analysing it from many different angles. It played it over in its mind and began to develop it into form. Gradually, the concept began making sense, solid sense. And the more it coalesced the further it developed, reshaping and moulding the mind of its developer.

The change was evident and began attracting a great number of species eager for an amendment in the jungle rules. They got together and worked hard on the idea day in day out. Slowly, their work started paying off and, with time, they all began to evolve to a point where they could actually put these new insights to work and sustain them; they could find nourishment through a number of means that did not involve the killing of others, making it theoretically possible to coexist peacefully with anyone and everyone.

Gradually, new and groundbreaking values began to be developed and observed. Things had definitely changed for the better. There was a growing feeling of achievement and confidence floating around, promising huge success, and the visionary species was very content with itself, for it was evident that it had found the new path in evolution's landscape. It was now ready to lead all life down that path, all the way to fresh and exciting grounds. The time had come go back to the species that had laughed at its idea and convince them to follow its vision. It would be easier this time round. All it had to do was show them the undeniable effects of its innovative – and now tested – approach, and they would believe.

This is exactly what it did, in the middle of a stormy night.

When dawn broke the next day, there was an unusual lull in the jungle. The storm had subsided and the clouds had vanished. Nothing was moving about. There was silence all around. Total silence and peace.

Suddenly, the sound of carnage emerged from somewhere. Mighty roars and screams of pain tore through the great jungle in a series of terrifying waves. They continued for quite a while, tearing through the lull, bearing havoc and curdling the blood of every living creature in the vicinity. Eventually, they subsided. A wave of total silence made its way through, lasting a few minutes, followed by a huge explosive belch.

After a while, the jungle was once again oozing with danger and brimming with battle. The sky was a crystal rainwashed blue and the brown earth was slowly turning crimson. Species were once again fighting each other for food, territory and light, as they always did. As for the visionary species and its followers, they were nowhere to be found…

Clearly, development and progress do not depend solely on intellectual or theoretical advancement. They require a diligent and exhaustive framework that will meld the old and the new, successfully and efficiently. And if there is resistance, then it requires that its evolved members fight for what they believe in – lest they become breakfast

– even if their beliefs support the actual need to eliminate fighting altogether. Sad but true.

Like we said, fate is at its least charming when it is ironic. But that's fate. That's life.

So, it becomes more than evident that for anything to stand a chance and survive in the world, let alone flourish, it needs to believe in itself and to fight for its ways whether they be rough or refined. Fighting is a given, not a variable. The actual variable in this formula is where to stand.

***

All this raises some interesting questions. I cannot help but ask, for example, where is that side which not only reflects one's core beliefs, but which also represents the way forward in a manner that is relatively constructive and beneficial towards society in general? Where do I oblige myself and what do I have to do for my ways to survive and be effective?

And if I think that the available options are no good anymore, what do I do? Do I stick with the lesser of two evils, or do I build a new platform from where I can represent what I consider fair? Or do I just give up and reject everything, defending my new vision of a 'world without conflict' by absconding from all dynamics of ideology, expecting the magical hand of modern economy to prove me right?

A swift look around makes it eloquently clear that a number of these things have happened. Some people have stuck to their guns and are supporting their side, warts and all. Others have left the scene disillusioned and are waiting for some kind of magical correction of the system that will rid the world of manipulative ideology while they just live their lives in peace, minding their own business without contributing anything new to the world. And others have chosen to envision new paradigms and to take responsibility in life by fighting for them tooth and nail, thereby also filling up the space which could have been taken by an ideology gone berserk.

At the end of the day this is what it's all about. If one really deems ideology the scourge of world affairs, then this is all the more reason to project a strong ideology to support those claims, for that will at least prevent the spreading of other aggressive ideologies operating at any given time.

Those who regard the game of the jungle primitive and in need of an overhaul, though, don't think so. They disagree vehemently and have instead chosen to recede to the wasteland of disorganised beliefs and individual self-promotion, essentially taking themselves out of the picture and far away from any real impact on world affairs. Like sheep with advanced cognition, they have chosen to remain sheep and just graze the fields individually (while they ironically consider themselves the most awake and advanced of the lot) under the moral canopy of nothing more than plain wishful thinking. And while grazing in the fields may be their inalienable right to do so, it may be time to consider that it is also their ticket out of this world. After all, this kind of attitude, permissive as it may be, can do very little for itself, or for anyone else for that matter. In fact, it does nothing more than defeat the purpose of checking aggressive ideology in the first place, for it falls apart like soapstone in a stream. It seems that we have gotten so carried away by all this progress lately that we've actually forgotten that freedom and acquiescence are two very different processes, two highly separate concepts altogether.

...

At the end of the night, in a harsh and unjust world, individuals often have to choose between two sets of beads. They must choose the better of the two. And if the beads are extremely unattractive, they must simply opt for the lesser of two evils.

But if the available options are totally unacceptable, then they must craft a third set, a new and valuable set that they like. For this is what it boils down to: building a new side when none of the available can be chosen, speaking your mind, improving on the situation and moving on. Harsh but true. And unavoidable. That's how it is, at the end of the night, where another day awaits, where another circle begins.

Xavier Thorntrail,
A disgruntled Global Citizen,
A worried Citizen of the West.

Here Comes the Ball 'n' Bash AKA What do you mean "This is a Rock 'n' Roll Party Shaking to the Beats of a Wholly Partisan Corruption?"

Dear Victims of the latest global tensions i.e. dear All,

Here is an ode to the current Rock 'n' Brawl fest:

'Spun around like a roulette ball, I am back where I started. But something has changed. I am dizzy. Numbers 9 and 11. Next time you spin, I rack the cash against solid security. Phoenix rising in the desert. The neo-conomicsperiment. God bless my great indignation, the one that overwhelms me when I gamble and lose my wages and esteem. In the name of all, ah… all, ah… gee, had it, now I lost it. All coulda, all shoulda, all woulda, but in the name of all, eh, well, eh, gee, had it again… um, we are, all, ah… merciful, ah, beautiful, ah… seventy verge in… waiting for room E. Stall in the name of the Union. Off, gone is a ton. Chai? Nay. Ham? Er, no, that's sick, all, ah, sick I say. Just join the dance… We're all having great fun here. Who started it? Well, who cares? Just grab a partner, toss 'im round, grab another, toss 'er to the side, we're having so much fun here… Step to the left, step to the right, centre spin, bump your heads against each other, yeah, and here we go again! Yeah! Dick Tator, meet Dee Spot. Lord Absolute, meet Lady Monarch, she's the heiress to a fortune, to a country filled with options. Most Bishops, meet Most Popes. Mr Mull Ah, meet Mr Hate Red and the strapping and alarming 'Dyna Mites and Homemade Bonbons,' who've exploded on the scene, they're all over, have you seen them? Oh, by the way, Sir Self Righteous, I would like you to meet Mr Self Righteous and Dr Self Righteous and Professor Self Righteous. Yes, thank God for your titles, otherwise it'd get confusing. How would we discern one Righteous from another? Yes, thank God for your titles. What, there is a God you say, but His name's different? What? There isn't one? We couldn't know it? Well, dance away, talking never saved the day! The rest of you, you know who you are, you get the drift, so meet and greet, wine and dine, grab your partner from behind, slide your members, don't be shy, throw him on the jagged wall, throw her on the liquor stall, rock 'n' roll, waltz and shout, belly dance and shake that ah, the Cossacks came, time to kick to overdrive. Oh ma word, it's so absurd that we are having so much fun. We're here to dance, so dance away, and here we go again till late. It's on the world, they're buying, blessed be their names!'

'In the name of peace and quiet, will you turn that racket off? Some people are trying to live around here. It's hard enough as it is without your crazy hollering. Why don't you organise an educational trip in space, in the deep seas, in the rainforest? Why don't you quit brawling about and do something truly constructive for a change?'

'Well, we would, but we'd all have to pitch in. All of you, too! Less enjoyment, less trinkets, more hard work and responsibility, more devotion to a target, an ideal, a common goal...'

'Eeh, no, that's fine... Just turn it down a notch. Come on darling, leave those idiots alone, they got a point. Where were we everyone? Oh yes, grab a partner, toss 'im round...'

'In the name of all that's sane, will you keep it down a notch up there? We're trying to dance down here you know.'

'Oh, shut your mouths down there!'

'Everyone, please stop shouting and keep calm!'

'You stop shouting and keep calm!'

'Why you little ingrates...'

Crack, slash, boom... Grab a partner, toss 'im round...

Xavier Thorntrail,
A disgruntled Global Citizen,
A worried Citizen of the West.

And Here Comes the Theatre AKA What do you mean "The Whole World's A Stage And We Are Mere Factors In A Brutally Bad Play?"

And the title of the play, dear audience, is:

"The Politics of Conflict: A Group Discussion." That's the title, my dear Cofactors. Here goes.

'...

- Cool, I have an idea.

- So do I!

- Me too!

- I like your approach but I'm afraid I disagree on a couple of points.

- But those points are the cornerstone of it all!

- No, they're not!

- Yes, they are!

- No, they're *not!*

- *Yes, they are!*

- Oh, jeez. These two idiots are going to spoil it for the rest of us.

- Hmm, maybe you're right. Well, I better take over the proceedings. Someone has to take a stand, or no solution will ever be found. All words and no play never saved the day you know.

- My milkshake, it's better than yours. Damn right, it's better than yours.

Crack.

- You broke my milkshake, o sorrow of sorrows!

Slash.

- You tore my straw, you piece of shit!!

Boom.

- You sir [sic], are a degenerate person and a threat to the cause. You are undermining every chance of success we have. But I respect your point of view. So I will bear it in mind. Let's just try and get along, shall we?

- Wh-what's his angle? What the hell is he on about?!

- He has a point. Put aside our differences and try to get along. All of us. That's all he asked for. That's all he did.

- He's an appeaser and a coward in the face of danger and challenge, backing out and giving more than an inch, giving mile after mile, that's what he did!
- Maybe so, but he still has a point.
- Maybe so, but he's still a coward and a traitor.
- And you're a thick-headed idiot… and a traitor!
- Who's the traitor? You're the traitor. And stupid too!
- Where's Waldo? Where is he? Point your fingers if you see him.
- Right, the Tower of Babel was never completed. So one language for all. Assimilation. It's the only way. You're either with us or against us.
- All, ah, we here all, ah, agree with the concept. With one small, ah, detail. We want our tongue to be the one you all coulda speak. Without exception, without mercy from us all, ah, the merciful. Thank you for the great ideal, ah, though.
- I see. You are clearly against us.
- You are damn right we are against you, and we shall, ah, take over your dominion and enforce our system of beliefs everywhere with brute force.
- You are the Axis of Evil.
- You are the Axis of Evil, ah.
- Will somebody stop these two from dragging us into another fundamentalist ordeal?
- Alright everyone! Let's all have a nice bottle of vodka and relax. It passed through 15 different countries before it could be made into such a fine product. They could have been more… never mind now. It is called 'Mujahideen Heads,' and it is based on the death of those who had been funded to oppose our expansion.
- You started it, goddamn it!
- And you used the devil to beat the devil! The greatest damage our stalling union ever did to your spangled union was to drag it into our dirty game.
- Let's have some warm ale, shall we?
- No! Let's have some wine. It is good for the heart, is it not, mon ami?
- It most certainly is not, I say!
- Rice for one dollar anyone? Plenty of rice for one dollar each. One dollar!
- Silence! We are the Chosen Ones, we shall rule over the earth. God said so. Who said that not having a country for 2,000 years is that bad? Look what it did for us. All countries are our countries now. We are the over-citizens. God was right.
- We think that all, ah, all, ah, all of us are right too. Our God says so.

- Pipe down, will ya? Now, come on everybody. Let's have a Bud, the king of beers. Here you are. There's plenty for everyone!
- Don't forget us. We have brought cashmere to keep you warm. In case it gets really really cold.
- I beg your pardon but that cashmere sweater is mine to offer for sharing.
- No it is not!
- I am sorry but it is!
- It is not!
- It is!
- Don't worry about that my dears. I have brought a deployable steam bath. It is called 'The West-bound Crescenstar,' AKA the 'X-Tarmeniator.' We can warm ourselves in there all together… atchutchu!
- Did someone say traitor?
- Traitors? Down with the traitors!
- Did someone say king a while ago?
- The Kings are alive. Long live the Kings!
- Shhh! Quiet. You want the whole world to know?
- Blow? Yes, I got some pure 'blow' delivered this morning.
- Yeah. Now you're talking! So let's get down to business. Sniff – sniff – aaaah…! Yeah! YEAH!!! WHO'S WITH ME? WHO'S WITH ME?
- Enough! Perhaps we can develop a common language through informed cooperation. That's the best way of smoothing out the edges of inescapable conflict in opinions… the best way of bringing out the positive aspects of pluralism. Our subject is still conflict I believe, isn't it? Integration then! That is the solution.
- But some will be left behind, won't they?
- Well, what do you expect? That we all magically agree on the perfect solution? Some have to adjust to the rest. It's the downside to informed discussion, well-examined enquiry and fruitful cooperation. At least we shall reach an agreement through a majority vote and mutual consent, not through scimitars and swords. Thus, we shall also come to a better and more efficient solution regarding how to deal with our differences and with conflict.
- Hey you, what's your bank account number? I would like to wire you a donation.
- Hey you, if you turn a blind eye on this, I do the same for you.
- Hey you, if you don't vote for me, I shall embargo your behind. No more soup for you!
       …'

Welcome to the futile coordinates of nihilism, where it makes no difference where you go or what changes you try and make. Many have given up on purpose here. Others have gone mad or committed suicide. The spiral is vicious and merciless and can send you spinning to the depths of senselessness (or sense).

The reason of illogic or the unreason of logic? That is the question – one of them, anyway.

And the dance continues. Back in the loop, and here we go again till late, grabbing partners, tossing round, smashing them on jagged walls and tossing them on liquor stalls. That's how it is, and that's how it will stay until we evolve beyond the state that has to compulsively pass from all the stages of dog eat dog.

Until then, the spiral keeps recycling. From the green grass comes manure. A perspective held by pessimists. The optimists don't agree with it. They see the upside instead. Out of manure comes the green grass. What do they do about it though? Nothing. They just go about their business, waiting for it to grow while the pessimists tell them that it won't.

Then there's the other kind of optimists and pessimists. These ones make a choice. They take a stand on one side and go for gold. "If the bash never ends, if nothing makes a difference anyway, and if it's all up to the perspective one holds, then might as well do my own thing." And so they do.

Some become great leaders. Some become monsters. But they all go for gold, leaving their rivals behind. The question is, though – at what price?

And the questions rise, dear all. Does great leadership depend on how many people have been helped on that highest of pedestals? Or do the methods employed make a difference? Do the ends justify the means? Must they? Let us return to "The Politics of Conflict: A Group Discussion," and find out.

...

- Hey you, to hell, ah, with you all, ah. In our tongue the answer is, 'Death to the infidel, ah'. Blow…? No my friends! Blow UP!
- Is that so? Well, I hereby propositionise the usation of nucular weapons against heathens… I meant against terrorism. For the sake of democracy and liberty. Meanwhile, the absolute monarchy in Saudi Arabia is to remain intact. For

the sake of practicalicity. Did I say that right? Darn! I am smart you know. I just have a form of dyslexiasis. DARN!!! So… who's with me?

- I most certainly am, old boy.
- Warmongers! You think that you can stop the turmoil by blasting the others to bits?
- Oh shut up, you hippy liberals! You think that you can stop the turmoil by graciously retreating, retracting, and pretending to be Good Samaritans?
- It's a double whammy everyone; both fists have connected with each other's face, and they are both down, warmongers and liberals alike.
- All, ah, all, ah, all of us are getting what we wanted. You are fighting amongst yourselves and your democracy is being eroded in order to fight us effectively. Our people, ah, don't all agree with us and our tactics – at least it appears so – but we try to convince them all, ah, to support us. You are helping very much. And leave Saudi Arabia as is. An absolute monarchy. Continue supporting it. Keep licking its behind. Help us all, ah.
- Is that so? Why don't the Saudis wage their own revolution if things are so bad on their stinking-rich peninsula? Why do we have to wage it for them?
- Wait. More wine anyone, mes amis?
- Rice? One billion plus and rising fast. Very fast. Cha-ching!
- We are the Chosen Ones, we shall rule over the earth. God said so.
- That's right fellas. With only one difference. *Me* shall rule over the earth. Now will someone turn the heat up? It's getting cold in here. Boy, I miss the ranch. It's so comfortabled down there. Come on damn it, turn the heat up!
- …I said that this cashmere sweater is mine.
- …I beg your pardon. This cashmere is mine.
- Mine!
- Mine!
- Mine…
- Mine…
- Hmmm, now that everyone is preoccupied, perhaps we have time for one more genocide. Let's finish off the Kurds before we enter the Eunion.
- Relax everyone. Nazdarovia. There is nothing like a good drink to warm someone up, except another good drink of course. So… More vodka anyone? My God! Catastrov! I have lost my precious 'Mujahideen Heads!' My volatile fuel is missing!! Where is it?

- Well, ah… What do we have here? We all are not supposed to drink, but we make an exception for you. Time to let the volatile fuel do its job. Time for blow up. To your health, to your hell, ah.

- No, to hell with *you*. You want to blow something up? Blow yourselves up in the middle of nowhere, not in the middle of a crowded room, you fucking freaks! That's why the whole world is against you! That's why you've already lost the fight!

- He's right. But let me add something. To hell with all those who blow people up, wherever they come from. And to hell with those who don't fight back to defend themselves and their team, too.

  …'

Warning. The last statement has brought us dreadfully close to a catch.

Now let's take a break and listen to a message from our sponsor.

'…Hello everyone and welcome to the Watch. We are happy to inform you that the terrible play 'The Politics of Conflict: A Group Discussion' is taking everyone by storm. It's a cracking blockbuster. But wouldn't you know it, there are other things we have to unfortunately report on apart from this play. We are under contract, you see. So here goes:

'A cat was rescued off a very tall tree in Oregon while a bus fell off a cliff in the Himalayas. 126 dead in Baghdad from insurgent bomb raids while we forget that the news shows over there can say whatever they want about the matter, such as "The devilish West has struck again, planting bombs through its operatives and aided by traitors. It is about time we slay this devil. Those who blow themselves up in the middle of a busy Western street or on a full passenger aircraft will be greeted by seventy virgins in heaven…"

'We also forget that these are the words that recruit one suicide bomber after another, or why this morbid recruitment is spreading with even more morbid success. We just live our merry lives grazing the grass under the culturally-sensitive canopy of everyone's right to do whatever they want without challenging them one bit. And when we do challenge them, we do so through double standards that are rotten to the core. Which brings us to the editorial.

'Tit for tat. A nuclear explosion for a nuclear explosion. If 9/11 was bad, think giant mushrooms on TV, loads of them. "Oh, come on," you might say. "Who'd be stupid enough to detonate nuclear bombs?" Well, it doesn't matter who'd detonate them. That's important only before they go off. Once they do, though, priorities change. For the vast majority anyway.

'Reckon it's gone about as far as it could possibly go without chiselling large percentage chunks off the territory with each blow? The cartographers and demographers can stay where they are. We can't afford their industries and sectors to boom. Not all business is good business. They may be decent professions in themselves, sure, but we can do without their proliferation quantity-wise, if you know what I mean. Quality-wise, let it rip.

'Now, if you are still unclear about the issue of unwanted booms, see your local undertaker and ask how business is doing. "Never been better; people are dropping like flies," is exactly what you don't want to hear – unless you own a chemical factory or the only real estate left in the area, which will make you a very wealthy person. Dead but wealthy.

'Suffice to say that a point of no return looms on the misty horizon. After a certain level the methods employed and the number of people helped onto the highest pedestal doesn't matter anymore coz there won't be a stadium left. There won't be an audience. Whoever the number ones are, they will be celebrating a Pyrrhic victory, standing on a singed pedestal and waving their radioactive medal to a swarm of fear-ridden mutants.

'Perhaps we cannot altogether avoid mutating to a new state after all. Still, if we are to change so drastically, let our mutations not come through a radioactive conflagration. It would not be advisable. Our stylists would not approve.

'On second thoughts, though, we shouldn't really worry. A thermonuclear hydrogen bomb is clean of radiation. Those who will survive the detonations will not have to worry about claws growing out of their foreheads. Now isn't that a comforting notion?

'And with that little brainteaser we have come to the end of this hour's version of the Watch. Stay tuned for the next and final part of "The Politics of Conflict: A Group Discussion," which critics have called

the best terrible play to hit the globe since "Sodom and Gomorrah."
Enjoy yourselves.'

'...
- Want a sip of my milkshake?
- Yeah, but *my* milkshake... it's better than yours. Damn right, it's better than yours.
Crack.
- You broke my milkshake, damn it!
Slash.
- And you tore my straw, you piece of shit!!
Slap.
- Did you just fuckin' bitch-slap me?!
- Yep!
- Did this guy just fuckin' bitch-slap me?!!
Grab your partners, toss 'em round...'

Victor Gente Delespejo,
A disgruntled Western Citizen,
A worried Citizen of the Globe.

∞

∞ ...So After A While, With A Great Big Smile... ∞

Somewhere out in the middle of nowhere, two strange figures are trudging through the barren wasteland. They seem to be communicating with someone or something through strange tongues and mannerisms.

Niet: O' mighty Great Yeller. Please reveal yourself to us. Come to us and show us that you are by our side. We can feel your presence, but it wouldn't hurt to see you with our own eyes too.

Snie: Why would it hurt to see him?

Niet: I said it wouldn't hurt to see him.

Snie: Ok... Why wouldn't it hurt to see him?

Niet: It would just be very helpful to see him, that's all.

Snie: He's by our side, isn't he?

Niet: Always. Can't you feel his warm and guiding presence?

Snie: I do.

Niet: Then stop asking stupid questions and keep walking.

...

Snie: Um... Niet?

Niet: Yes Snie?

Snie: If the Great Yeller is by our side, then why wouldn't it hurt to see him?

Niet: I said that it would just be very helpful.

Snie: But if he is right here, why would it be very helpful?

Niet: Because it would reinforce our beliefs.

Snie: But... is he here for real or do you just believe that he is here?

Niet: I don't believe that he's here. I know that he's here.

Snie: Then why do you need to see him?

Niet: Because... because it would relight my fire, ok?!

Snie: Fire? Are we on fire? Are we...

Niet: No, you idiot, we're not on fire! It's an expression for... ouf, sometimes I just wonder how I manage. (*waits for a minute, takes a deep breath, then speaks*). Seeing the Great Yeller would reinforce our convictions... our determination. We would be recharged.

Snie: But if you know he's right here beside us, why would you need to see him to be recharged?

Niet: Because! Once in a while, it's good to gaze at what you already know. It's like the occasional pat on the back. It keeps you going. Like you and me. You are blind, so you have me to tell you what is going on and where to go, giving you that pat on the back when you need it. Now shut up already, and keep walking.

Snie: Why?

Niet: What do you mean why?!

Snie: I mean why should I keep walking?

Niet: Because you are wasting our time with your pointless questions. The Black Box is somewhere out there in the wilderness, and we are not going to find it if you keep stopping all the time to ask silly questions!

Snie: Why not?

Niet: What do you mean why not, damn it?!

Snie: I mean why will we not find it if I keep stopping? Will it move away?

Niet: No, you nitwit. It won't move away. But at the pace we're going we'll be lucky if we find it while we're young!

Snie: But we are not young.

Niet: YOU KNOW WHAT I MEAN, DAMN IT!!

Snie: No, I don't. We are old.

Niet: (whispers to himself while clasping his face with his hand) Oh dear goodness… please give me strength… strength to deal with this moron… (drops his hand and lifts his head again, speaking out loud) Yes, we are old, and this is why we don't have much time to waste. We must keep searching for the Black Box without stopping here, pausing there, and marauding everywhere apart from where we need to go just so that you can ask some stupid questions. I swear, if only I could walk, I'd show you how things should be done.

Snie: Good thing you have me to carry you.

Niet: Yeah, but without me you wouldn't see where you're going. Remember that!

Snie: I know. That's why I am very grateful for our arrangement. Without each other we would be lost. I thank the stars that we are together. I thank them every single hour. Don't you?

Niet: Yes… yes… you know that I do! Now stop wasting time, and keep moving. Go on.

…

Snie: Um, Niet?

Niet: Yes Snie?

Snie: If we have to see what we already know in order to keep us going, then what happens to the blind ones like me?

Niet: I told you not to worry. I am your eyes. I will tell you what I see.

Snie: But I won't see it with my own eyes.

Niet. It doesn't matter. I will describe it to you in full detail.

Snie: Yes, but… didn't you say that the point is to see it for ourselves?

Niet: Yes, and so I will describe it to you when I see it for myself. I will see it with my own eyes and I will tell you what it looks like with my own mouth so that you will be able to hear it with your own ears.

Snie: So it's ok to hear something we already know instead of just seeing it?

Niet: Yes, it's ok to hear it too!

Snie: Good, because I have been hearing Great Yeller's voice in my head for quite a while now. He's been telling me that we are way off course. We've been going around in circles for a while now.

Niet: What?! Oh shut up, will ya?

Snie: I'm telling you exactly what he said. He insists that we are off course, and that the Mirror Plains are over there.

Niet: Over there where?

Snie: Over there, towards the buzz.

Niet: What buzz? I don't hear any buzz.

Snie: Well, I do! Thank our lucky stars for my good hearing.

Niet: What are you doing? Stop! Where are you taking us?

Snie: To the Mirror Plains. To the Great Yeller. To the Black Box.

Niet: Are you mad? This is the wrong way! Turn around. Turn around I tell you…

Snie: Here we come, Great Yeller… Here we come. I can hear you clearly now…

Niet: Stop, you fool. Stop this minute. I'm warning you! I said stop…

And on they went, the heeding Snie carrying the hard-of-hearing Niet, into the barren wasteland.

∞ ∞ ∞

The Chemistry Within
(A collection of short stories)

"I give you the secret of secrets –
Mirrors are gates through which death comes and goes"
–Orphée (1950)

Nitroglycerin

'One Black Label. No ice… Nope, no soda… Yep, straight up.'

Bartenders pretend not to be surprised when you ask for a neat shot of the Scottish Highlands nectar, especially when you are young. They just put on a casual face to hide behind, merely affirming your uncompromising choice, but they fail, and their surprise shows.

'No ice?!'

Some omit the question mark altogether.

'No ice!'

But they add it elsewhere.

'Water? Soda?'

It's as if they're on a mission to dilute your intake. Why?

Who the hell knows? Maybe to protect you from the one inch punch of Malt Lee. Maybe coz they're surprised that you're doing what they'd never even dream of. Maybe coz they're cranky. But the truth is simpler than that; they just think you are showing off. So they try to shove one right back atcha.

'Scotch, straight up? At my bar? Here's some ice. Who do you think you are, asking for neat scotch here?'

'Well, I'll tell you who I am. My name is Bravestomach. My creed is "Purity" and I take no prisoners at night. Keep walking. And hold the ice cubes. They ain't fit for everything. Now, if you'll excuse me, I have somewhere to go to.'

He took his measure of liquid dynamite and began to saunter back to our table in true Bravestomach fashion. He made a couple of pit stops on the way to rev up his acquaintances, people he hadn't seen for a long time. Yeah, it was that kind of party, full of images from a distant past, and most of them were better off lying were they'd been, in oblivion, emaciating skeletons, forgotten, rotten, discarded, thrown away. They'd been tucked neatly out of sight and mind for such a precious time. Why open those bloody closet doors now? Leave them be. Just throw the rotten storage away, for good.

But you can't do that in real life. Wherever you go, whatever you do, the past will always catch up with you just like that, in an instant and when you least expect it.

'Hi.'

Zang. And you can't say 'Bye.' Doesn't make a difference even if you do. It can curb the damage but the connection has been made. Hi – Zang. Like touching a live wire!

Still, the past holds more than skeletons in its closet, pleasant things, welcome things, missed, longed and cherished; flowers on the stretch of memory banks, growing by the stream of consciousness and nurtured by the ceaseless flow of recollection. At least one hopes so. Woe if there are no flowers; desolate riversides bear nothing but barren legacies and empty lives.

What did he say once? To forget is to sink in the middle of nowhere. To not be able to recognize what is front of you, though, is to die in the ocean waters only ten strokes away from land.

And yet, countless people choose to drown in the waves, off the coasts of remembrance. It's plain and blatant suicide. Must be in the genes, hardwired in there somewhere, activated by certain stressors. Must be a utility for it, surely. After all, there is utility in every futility, however miniscule it may be.

'Well, well, Mrs Abe Issy, how the hell are you?'

Skeleton or flower? Not sure yet.

'Haven't seen you in a long time.'

The distilled bomb-juice swirled in the glass. A wave slid up the tubular wall and bounced off with a trickling splash back in the circular pool. The lack of icebergs was resoundingly evident. No tinkle, no rustle. Just a muffled 'blop.'

It confused her. She could see that he was holding a short heavy glass, the proverbial whisky glass. She knew it was full, for he had just come from the bar. But she couldn't make out what was in it. His palm was covering the rim like a tipi and his arm was hanging loose waist high, swirling the mute glass around. So what was in it? Where were the ice crystals? Where was that joyous clong?

'What are you up to these days?'

The hand stayed down and the conversation was not flowing. It was moving with skids and skips but certainly not flowing, just fragments of conversation being shot around so as to cover as much of the field in as little time as possible; a battery of one-liner questions and answers bouncing off each other but not necessarily responding to one another.

Not a pleasant way to pass time. Like a pinball trapped in a pinball machine, he wanted out.

'How long has it been anyway?'

Suddenly, the arm began to ascend. As it rose, the hand started shifting position and the palm began falling to the right, uncovering the bucket underneath. Thumb and middle finger were now gripping the glass on either side as if an invisible axis joined them. The wonder of a hand's mechanics were in full operation and display. As the palm fell, the indexes rose and the glass emerged into sight, the force of gravity keeping it hanging straight during the whole motion. The rotation was smooth and seamless, like that of bucket seats in a Ferris wheel.

Then the whole dynamic changed and the grip suddenly tightened. No more collateral adjusting. The glass was under complete control. The unthinkable had commenced.

The hand began to move and turn towards the body. The glass began to tilt. It met the mouth. The nitroglycerin started flowing in, through the pharynx and down the oesophagus, uncompromising and pure. It burned everything it touched, leaving a trail of fumes in its wake that rose to the nose signalling potential toxicity underway. Toxicity or intoxication? Same difference. The chemical interaction was irreversible. The liquid bomb was surfing down the glossed tract, through acid-reflux land and pipedream ruminations, straight into the simmering stomach. And there it exploded.

'Goodbye Mrs Abe Issy. Do not worry if the hinges are not oiled. The closet doors may begin to squeak but the attic door is firmly shut. And only I have the key to that one. So go crazy if you like. The attic room is all yours. Now if you'll excuse me, I have a table to go to. Goodbye, and good luck. God knows you'll need it. Terrible monsters breed in the dark corners of the room you just crept into. And they don't like each other. They don't like anyone. Not even their own dejected selves. As for newcomers, well… they loathe them. So good luck again. And goodbye. Or should I say good riddance?'

He walked to our table and sat eagerly in the sofa with glass in hand, sighing with loud relief. It was about time. Seemed like ages since he'd gone for that drink. His eyes were gleaming with anticipation. He looked around and settled in… stretched his legs… took a modest breath. Then he realised that his glass was completely empty! He scowled and turned his head towards the bar where the bartender was busy shuffling some ice in a mojito. Behind him, in the huge glass mosaic on the wall, stood an amber jewel bathed in light, a black label hugged around its stem… a few steps and a whole world away… on the other side of the room.

He looked around. The way there was strewn with skeletons and apparitions, haunted, overrun. But his vessels were pumping pure neat dynamite, waiting for action, itching for reaction, thirsty for more friction. He extended his neck and looked around, recoiling and loading up. Nothing would catch him by surprise this time. Nobody could get to him. He was prepared for anything and throbbing like a time bomb. He got up and began sauntering towards the bar…

It was his 8th consecutive trip there. How many more he had left in him nobody knew. Not even him. It was all in the past's hands now, floating in the restless waters that separated our table from the bar.

Victor Gente Delespejo

Freak Lightning

'Whaaat I've doooone...'

He barely moved his eyelids as the ringtone kept singing. He barely moved at all. Just sat there. Silent. Motionless. Apathetic. As if nothing was happening.

'I'll face myseeelf...'

No response. No reaction. No sound except for the ringtone – and the furious storm, of course, raging on the other side of the window.

He turned his ear towards it. Fat drops of water were pounding on the window ledge, beating it in. He smirked. He knew that if it rained long enough, there would come a time when there would be nothing left of that ledge. Just an outline of where it had once stood. But with time, it, too, would fade away.

'I'll face myseeelf...'

Nothing. No response. No movement.

Then silence – as if the ringtone had been severed with a scalpel; the umbilical connection to the outside was no more and he was on his own now. For a little while anyway.

'ZANG...'

A flash of lightning tore the night, casting shadows in the dark room. He turned towards the window and smiled, waiting for the thunderclap.

'CRRRACK-SHHhhh...'

He continued looking outside for a while with a grin on his face. Then he turned away from the window and looked towards the phone on his desk. Funny how when the ringtone had stopped, the whole world had stopped with it. The storm had been erased, even if for a brief moment. The rain had stopped, the wind had died down, and a lull swept over the land. Silence settled in, like a silk sheet falling from the sky in the still of the night, under the light of the moon.

'ZANG...'

The lightning tore through the silk sheet and set it on fire. It burned instantly, in a silver-white blinding flash, shedding light upon the land. The lull was consumed, vanishing as fast as it had appeared, and the storm barged in stronger than before. The rain began to pound on the window ledge mercilessly. Clouds swept into the sky and collided with each other furiously. Thunderclaps latched onto the howling winds and rode them all the way to the horizon and beyond. The still of the night was gone.

'CRRRRRACK-SHHHHH…'

This one hadn't taken long to arrive. A couple of seconds only. ZANG… one one thousand… two one th-CRRRRRACK-SHHHHH… The storm was drawing nearer, fast. Almost on top of him now.

'I'll face myseeelf…'

Still no response. The ringtone was falling flat with every repetition. Flat on its undulating head.

He sighed, and his eyeballs twitched. They rebounded around in their sockets for a moment or two, firing off some fleeting thoughts, and then fell still once again. His breathing returned to its normal slow pace. His lips came together and settled into a slight smile. His face froze. His whole body solidified again.

'To cross out what *I've*… beee… coooome…'

He just sat there, in his chair, staring into thin air. The leather cushions had started sucking the sweat out of his skin, but he didn't notice. He just sat there, amidst the lightning flashes that kept lighting up the room, smiling back at them. He just sat there, frozen stiff, with one solitary expression on his face. The flashes kept coming, in stroboscopic frenzy, as if God was taking pictures of him, but he remained still, unmoved, unperturbed, like a marble statue posing in a night club… Posing… Waiting… Frozen stiff…

'Erase myself…'

'ZANG… CRACKSHHHHHH…'

The singing stopped again. But there was no silence this time. The storm was right on top of him now. There was no delay between thunder and lightning anymore. The clouds were spewing out thunderbolts, zapping and cracking all around him, one after another, relentlessly. The rain kept pounding on that window ledge, harder, faster, foreboding disaster. There was no disregarding the storm anymore.

'Erase myself…'

No response. None at all. Absolutely none.

'Erase myself...'

He'd let it ring. Just let it ring. On and on and on, until it would stop singing. Until there was no more sing in it. On and on and on.

'And let *go* of whaaaaat...... IIIII've...... dooooooone...'

His brow began to drop. His eyelids were tensing up. Wrinkles. A frown. A heavy, sinister frown. Then a glare began to appear out of the depths of his eyes, glistening and sharp. Something was brewing up inside, something devastating...

A gust of wind hit the window. The frame shook violently. Clusters of raindrops crashed into the glass pane, bursting like paintballs. His eyeballs dashed towards it.

He saw it coming. A thunderbolt shot through the night sky and straight through the wall, blowing up the front part of the house. The walls started falling apart in a short-circuit bonanza of sparks, setting the floor and furniture on fire. Another thunderbolt followed, striking the rear of the house, blowing it apart too. Then the raging wind started drilling its way through the crumbling walls, tearing them apart, razing the whole house to the ground, inch by inch and brick by brick, followed by the rain, which pounded its way through the ruins, striking him all over in a long merciless barrage. But he did not move. He just sat there, in the middle of the storm, glaring right through it. Raindrops were pounding his bulged eyes, but he wouldn't blink. He just sat there and glared into the wind and rain. He glared into the storm with searing eyes as the house came crumbling down around him and the singing went on and on and on.

Just then, in the midst of chaos, the singing stopped. A waft of tranquillity blew through and a soothing lull swept through the land like a silk sheet falling from the sky. And for a moment, everything was calm. For a moment.

Suddenly, a voice emerged through the chaos, drowning everything out.

'I'm sorry... The person you called is not available. Please leave a message after the tone...'

His muscles tensed up and his face contorted; his upper lip rose and his teeth were revealed, while a raging yell began rising from his lungs; his eyes started spewing sparks with a menacing buzz...

'CRACKSHHHH...'

And just like that, he spontaneously combusted in a deafening explosion, leaving behind no traces of his existence.

***

The woman who'd been calling him heard about the explosion the next day on the news. Frustrated and shocked, she called a bunch of people to ask if they knew what had happened. None of them answered her calls though. They didn't even return them. Strange!

So she went to find them.

They all had the same story. Seven missed calls from the same man over the past three days. None of them had returned his calls for various reasons. Some of them had even heard them every single time but had nevertheless chosen not to answer them. They had just let their phones ring all the way to voicemail, intending to call him back some time later in the day, or in the week, or sometime.

The question she asked was 'Why?' As far as she was concerned, she had been working hard all week and was unable to pick up personal calls during work hours. And by the time she was off, she didn't have the energy to talk to anyone anyway. So she hadn't been able to return his calls, not until late last night. But what about the rest? Why hadn't they called him back? Did they all have a reason like hers?

Well, they did! Each had a reason of their own, a valid reason. Or was it something else? Something equally reasonable but less truthful? Perhaps a valid excuse... an excuse... just like hers!

***

Forensics eventually concluded that there had been nobody in the house when it got struck by what they referred to as 'freak lightning.' The police issued a broadcast thereafter and notified their members to be on the lookout for the missing man.

A few days and not a single clue later, he was officially declared 'missing.' The search intensified.

A few months later, with all hope vaporised, he was deemed dead.

Soon after, he was mourned.

***

Three and a half months after his disappearance, his few acquaintances came together to bid him final farewell during a pretty mundane ceremony under a stormy grey sky.

When the service was over, as they were saying goodbye to each other and getting ready to leave, their phones began to ring, one by one. They took them out and answered without looking at the screen. But as soon as someone pressed the button to receive the call, it would be dropped.

They all looked at each other perplexed. Then they started calling back the numbers which had called them. One by one, they put their phones to their ears and waited for an answer.

'Ring ring...... Ring ring...... Ring ring...... Ring ring...... I'm sorry... The person you called is not available...'

And one by one they burst into flames – and out they went – in a series of blinding flashes, vanishing without a trace. A couple of seconds later, there was nothing left around the empty casket, nothing whatsoever, except for a bunch of black, silver and pink phones scattered on the lawn, blinking dimly, vanishing in the midst of a tombstone geometry...

'...Please leave a message after the tone...'

Victor Gente Delespejo

The Snarling Beast

We were exhausted. Marching around in snow and ice for one whole day can do that to you. And not just any whole day – a whole early summer arctic day...

We had been up since three in the morning, chasing after shots for the documentary. It had been terribly windy throughout the day, gusts slashing across the plains relentlessly, whipping the land with sleet and making it impossible to get decent views of the landscape. We had tried but it was pointless; with our ability to work impaired, our self-defences naturally went down and we eventually felt the full sting of the bone-biting cold. It had been a truly exhausting day in every sense of the word.

When we finally came back to camp, it was just after midnight and almost dark. You see, we had run into trouble with one of our snow sledges. It had broken down in the middle of nowhere, and all five of us worked on it relentlessly. We were not leaving it there, and we were definitely not leaving anyone behind to work on it while we got back to camp to get more tools. The problem was simple enough – some trouble with the fuel pump – but it gave us hell before it finally got its act back together again.

Smashed with fatigue and a long day's frustration, we cooked something up in a flash and guzzled it up like wolves. Then we hit the sack. Running late on a deadline and in desperate need of those shots, we needed to catch some much-needed rest, for tomorrow was not going to be any easier. The weather seemed to have it in for us. The gusty winds were not subsiding – in fact, they were getting worse – and our chances of shooting good film were slim and thinning.

As soon as I closed my eyes I started drifting away. I thought I heard someone ask: 'Did anyone wash the dishes?' Then nothing. Just the sweet embrace of a deeply-needed summer night's rest in the warmth of a heavy-duty sleeping bag. Outside the wind rasped, stirring up the snow and blowing it across the endless plains. Inside our little hut, though, there was absolute peace and comfort, warm and accommodating, and a slow-burning stove. It felt like being with family. I began drifting into a cosy dream…

I don't know how long I'd slept or how deep I'd been, but when the door banged I felt I had been ripped away from something soothing and thrown headfirst into something terrible. I scoured around, hearing the others jumping out of their sleep and reaching for their Mag-lites too, their legs rasping noisily inside their sleeping bags. Then came another bang, much louder than before, followed by a growl… a coarse, menacing growl.

I flashed my Mag-lite towards the door and saw it shaking under the pounding of something beastly outside. With my stomach crunching up in knots, I fell to the ground and shone the beam at the bottom of the door frame. Two pairs of paws were standing behind it… white paws… their white hairs frozen into small short pleats, covered in ice crystals, refracting the light into the dark night outside. I blinked. At the end of each paw, long claws were pushing out, tearing through the icy ground.

'Get the gun… Get the fucking gun!'

Somebody rustled through our things, looking for our single-barrelled shotgun.

'The slugs… where are the goddamn slugs?'

Tin cans and utensils were flying all over the place along with maps and camera equipment and what have you as we scraped frantically around the small room.

'Get the goddamn gun… hurry up!'

'I'm trying to find the slugs. Where the fuck d'you put'em?'

'There, in the bag… on your right… somewhere there!'

The bangs on the door were getting louder and the growls more menacing.

'Hurry up goddamn it!'

'Got' em! Oh shit… these are film rolls! Fucking film rolls!'

'Cut the crap and find the slugs, goddamn it! Look, there they are, behind the stove… there, behind the….'

Suddenly the door broke open and a claw entered the room, followed by a frothing snout. Its jaws unhinged, breathing out steam and unleashing a bloodcurdling roar that flooded the room. Then a beastly body began to make its way through the entrance, barging into the hut slowly, etching its way through a crackling doorframe. It was huge…

186

huge and uncompromising. A mighty polar bear.

'Oh shit shit shit shit shit… fuck… oh fuck…'

Somebody threw a heavy can of food at her. It hit her on the left shoulder and made her back up half a step. But then she went berserk, letting out a howling roar of pain and fury.

'Stop throwing things at her, you'll make her furious. Stay perfectly still.'

'And what? Wait for her to just leave?!'

'Yeah… yeah… just lay perfectly still…'

'No! She's already inside you moron. She's here and she's hungry. She ain't leaving unless we throw her out. Attack her!'

'What?!'

'Attack her or die. Come on, attack her! ATTACK HER! Show her who's boss.'

'Are you nuts? Lie down…'

'Come on… make her fear us… throw those cans at her like we mean it and snap at her… like we mean business… stare her down… threaten her, attack her… GO ON… GET OUT… YAAA… YAAA…'

Another can of food spun through the air and struck her in the leg. She growled and stood up on her back feet, towering over our heads, roaring like an earthquake.

'Now goddamn it… it's now or never… throw everything you got and scream like madmen… scream goddamn it, SCREAAAM… YAAAA… YAAAA…'

We suddenly began snatching whatever we could get our hands on and started throwing stuff at her… cans, forks, papers, knives, cameras… screaming and yelling like mad wild dogs.

'COME ON… STAND YOUR GROUND… STARE HER DOWN… DRIVE HER OUT… YAAAAA… YAAAAA…'

We could certainly feel the effects of this primal mentality. A transformation was taking place. We began making harsh noises that made no sense. With every growl she made we growled five times back. Our minds stopped thinking in rational terms and another kind of intelligence began emerging from the depths of our ancient brain circuits… an animal intelligence… an urge to fight our foe on equal terms… a surge for survival.

She began hesitating. Her growls were not so confident anymore. Not so menacing as before. Her steps were shorter and lighter. We saw the change in her and reacted to it without any thought. It was time to just fight back and reclaim our space.

We assaulted her immediately, like a ferocious beast… five different sets of eyes glaring back at her from five different directions… five heads lashing out at her mercilessly… five sets of teeth jumping at her from everywhere, sometimes in unison, other times in relentless waves, one after another… after another… after another… and then back in unison, like a surging tidal wave… like a ton of raging bricks.

We were frothing at the mouth, yelling and snarling like mad, jabbing our way into her, edging our way onwards. She began to back away.

'THIS BEAST CAME HERE TO HARM OUR FAMILIES… TO KILL US, AND LEAVE THEM BEHIND TO SUFFER OUR LOSS. ARE WE GOING TO LET HER DO THAT? COME ON, WHAT ARE WE WAITING FOR? ATTACK HER! ATTACK HER!!!'

And in one furious surge, we assaulted her with everything we had, throwing a barrage of food cans at her and trying to scratch her eyes out with our claws, furious at what she'd tried to do. She turned around and took a couple of steps back, then growled once more. But this was a different kind of growl. She was now defending herself, carving out her retreat. We pushed on, banging on the walls with our hands, stomping on the floor, making a racket with our tools. She backed down, out of our hut and into the great wide frozen, and then slowly disappeared into the gusty thick night. We stood in front of the door for quite a while, yelling towards her direction, chasing her away, into the desolate distance. Our yells were now turning into cheers, comprehensible cheers. Grammar and meaning were beginning to flow back into our communication. The animals within us began to evanesce and our human capacities slowly settled upon us once again. We started laughing and fooling around, making fun of each other and of how we had all just shape-shifted into a pack of wild beasts. We even laughed about the fact that no one bothered to go for the slugs once we had driven the bear back out the door. We laughed, but we didn't wonder why. We knew now. As long as we snarled together like one ferocious beast defending its family, nothing could threaten us. Not even a hungry polar bear.

Xavier Thorntrail

Ipsum Prophecius

Mr and Mrs Dankeman were working around their house when they heard a cry. They turned around and saw a fellow emerge out of the woods and approach their farm at a calm and steady pace. He was wearing peculiar spectacles and was carrying a big leather pouch on his back. He looked strange, but that didn't bother them. They hadn't seen a stranger in months and were all too keen to hear what he had to say.

They welcomed him warmly and offered him a huge mug of beer that had been crisped in the afternoon chill of a late-autumn forest. He thanked them and smiled widely, following them into a cosy living room. They sat on two thin wooden stools, offering him the blanket-clad chair on their right, and began to ask him questions. They were eager to know what was happening in the world. He told them all that he knew and they listened with delight. Then they began to ask him about himself. They were curious to know more about him and about what had driven him to heart of the Dark Woods. So he began to tell them his story.

He was a young scientist, investigating the physical universe. His predecessors had discovered many years ago that the Earth was round and that it revolved around the sun. Over time, their discoveries had been corroborated and established, yet, very many people were still unaware of these facts. So he'd decided to travel around the countryside to educate people and accustom them to the emerging knowledge.

He'd been walking in the woods for many days now – unsure of which door to knock on – and was quite exhausted. The first visit had to be just right; it would set the tone for the rest of his expedition, so it was well worth the effort and wait. He had already passed through two forest communities, but none of the houses he'd seen had called out to him in any sort of way, so he'd moved on without a word, searching for that perfect starting point. He knew it was out there somewhere. He could feel it.

His heart raced every time he saw a house. Perhaps this was it, the one! But time and time again he was disappointed. So on he went, deeper into the woods. Days passed. He began to reconsider his whole approach. Perhaps he should just knock on the first door he'd come across and introduce himself. Just then, the Dankeman farm appeared through the trees, so he made his way to it without second thought.

They were the first people he was visiting during his expedition, and, full of enthusiasm, he confided in them that he felt honoured, deeply honoured that he would now be sharing his insights with them. He wiggled in his chair for a moment, getting comfortable, and then he began to talk about his predecessors and their groundbreaking discoveries with great enthusiasm. He talked and he talked and he talked...

'But *we* are the centre of the world,' retorted Mrs Dankeman with surprise, when he was done. 'God created us in His image and put us here to repent our sins so that we can enter His Kingdom as worthy subjects. How can *we* be revolving around the sun?'

'The story is a bit more complicated than that,' replied the scientist earnestly. 'If God indeed exists, then he is working through a set of rules that we are just beginning to discover.' He paused for a moment, scanning the two perplexed faces across him. He took a deep sigh, and began to talk in a more accommodating manner. 'The universe, this wonderful, wondrous place we live in, is made up of different energies that some of my colleagues believe can be harnessed. We have in fact discovered a few of them. Here, let me show you so you can see and judge with your own eyes.'

He took out a gadget from his pouch and placed it on the table with care. The couple clasped each other's hand as they watched the man join some wires. They looked in each other's eyes with apprehension, then leaned forward towards the trinket, hands still clamped together. Sweat started forming on their brows. They'd never seen such a contraption before. It was of weird shape, and the prancing shadows in the dim candlelit chamber were making it look alive.

The scientist worked on his trinket for quite a while, deeply absorbed in his task. His aura began to agitate the couple.

'What was his name?' whispered Mrs Dankeman in her husband's ear.

'Fool Filler,' he replied.

'What kind of a name is that anyway?' she retorted. 'Fool Filler? Strange name for a person, my love.'

'I know.'

The scientist muddled about for a few more seconds and then lifted his head.

'Lean back,' he told them gently, 'and do not be alarmed. You are about to witness the wonders of science.'

He grabbed the trinket by its crooked lever and gave it a few fast turns. An array of sparks exploded out of the gadget with mighty cracks and shot through the pale darkness.

'Oh mein Gott,' shouted the couple as they sprung up from their chairs.

'Yes!' cried the scientist exalted, raising his hands in revelation. 'Electricity! We have electricity!'

Mr Dankeman ran towards the kitchen. His wife opened the window.

'WITCH! WE HAVE A WITCH IN THE HOUSE... HELP...'

'No, no, listen to me,' stammered the scientist, 'this is not witchcraft, this is science...'

'WIIIITCH... HEEEELP...'

Mr Dankeman scuffled around the kitchen noisily while his wife kept screaming. Within moments he barged back into the room holding a sharp cleaver. The scientist instinctively lifted his dynamo by the lever and raised it high to face the puffing farmer. He thought his seconds were numbered. Any moment now the farmer would dash at him and cut him to pieces.

But the farmer had frozen midway. His gaze was once again fixed on the gadget. He was glaring at it through bold but terrified eyes, trying to resist his overwhelming impulse to drop everything and run away. The scientist, equally stunned, was transfixed on the giant blade and breathing heavily, wishing he could just disappear out of harm's way and back into safety. Deep in the heart of Middle Europe, life was now balancing on the tightrope of a standoff between a cleaver and a lever. Not for long though. Balance doesn't last forever.

The scientist made the first move. He instinctively rotated the dynamo a couple of times while shuffling his feet on the spot. Sparks flew in the air and the farmer jumped back in fear, his eyes wide open and bulging out of their sockets. The scientist seemed to be gaining an advantage.

But the farmer recoiled. He swiped away the sweat from his forehead with his free hand, wiped his thick moustache, and then took a deep breath and a few little steps forward again, a few very hesitant little steps with cleaver held high.

The horrified scientist saw the farmer's indecision and took his chance. He started swinging the dynamo around like a chain mace, and slung forth towards the farmer while screaming incoherently to scare him off. The sparks started bombarding the room, slicing the darkness into shreds and shooting terror into the farmer and his wife. Mr Dankeman dropped the cleaver cold and jumped out the window headfirst, screaming hysterically. Mrs Dankeman shrieked at the top of her voice for a couple of short seconds and then dived out behind him.

'WITCH... HELP... HE ATTACKED US WITH A BURNING BOX... HE CAST A SPELL ON US... HEEELP... heeelp... heeelp...'

The scientist gathered his stuff in panic as the voices were quickly fading away towards the direction in which he'd seen an abandoned hut on his way there. Perhaps it wasn't abandoned after all! He opened the door and darted away in the opposite direction.

As he sprinted away, an inscribed leaflet flew out of his half-open pouch. It swirled around a bit in the twilight breeze and then landed softly on the ground. The calligraphy upon it read as follows:

"This is the beginning of what I hope to be a lengthy and detailed journal, describing my adventures in the wilderness of ignorance, recording the developments as they arise, providing a coherent and longitudinal narrative for others to study and refer to. My name is Ipsum Prophecius, but I will refer to myself exactly as I will introduce myself to the inhabitants I meet henceforth: FULFILLER. I shall, thus, fulfil their wishes and reveal to them the real workings of the world. I hope they will expect of me exactly what I expect from them: the truth. I imagine..."

That's all the paper wrote. And as the scientist disappeared into the woods, the sun bled into the horizon and began to evaporate into the twilight sky.

Victor Gente Delespejo

Have a Nice Day

'Thank you for calling Global Communications Corporation. We would like to convey a warm welcome to you and let you know that your business is our pleasure and that your pleasure is our business. It is of the outmost importance to remind our valued and esteemed beneficiaries like yourself that communicating liberates your soul. It is our duty to help you break the barriers of isolation, and it is the least we can do for your wellbeing. Please note that all calls will be recorded, monitored, processed and analysed for security purposes and for your own safety. A safe world is a better world, and we take pride in contributing our share to this better world, a world where everyone is always connected.

'Please stay on the line for the easy-to-follow automated menu.'

He lowered his telephone receiver for a second and turned his eyes toward the TV, where muted documentary images of cold and dreary mountains were passing through the plasma screen. He glowered at them for a few moments, his eye slits narrowing and his heartbeat picking up slightly, and then began to turn away from them, reaching for the remote control next to him, but the closed-captioned subtitles snatched his attention up and pulled him in, deep inside the world they were so dramatically describing.

'...Isolation can be a frosty companion on a cold day. It can be a frosty companion on a warm day too, but the weather conditions don't really matter. Isolation radiates an iciness of its own that can permeate the fabric of the surroundings, rendering all opposing factors ineffective while transforming the rest into corrosive bandits. Warmth is obliterated and made irrelevant here, in the Highlands, like the sun shining through the glass pane of a high-arching ballroom of a Caledonian stone castle in mid-January winter. Light dispels the shadow and darkness erases brilliance while the cold expands in all directions without discretion or reprieve. The humidity turns to frost and eats away the surface of whatever it settles on. Even air isn't immune to this catalytic reaction. It becomes heavy and thwarted, crushing its own motion with its paralysed traction, and everything begins to stand worryingly still.

'The air sometimes rebels and tries to stir up breezes and gusts to protect itself, trying to shake away the consuming parasite that is eating away at its substance… In fact, this whole diluting plain is trying ever so desperately to reverberate back to life; it is struggling with all its might to remain intact and survive… But it fails. It fails and falls to isolation and torpor, two highly superior enemies that can advance ever so diligently upon every kind of surface at whatever pace seems most suitable to them; cold and very bitter, they encroach upon the Caledonian country, showing their multi-catalytic face and gnawing their way through the land. The wind bites in as hell freezes over, and it unleashes ice-fanged demons to haunt whatever life is unfortunate enough to be there. Animation is slowly being arrested. It begins to congeal. And it all takes place under that gloomy sun, now a reverie in a mid-winter day's nightmare…'

A chill raced through his spine and his teeth chattered like pebbles falling on a frozen lake as he turned his head around, trying to chase those images away.

He didn't like the cold. He didn't like it at all. It brought back very unpleasant memories. That's why he'd decided to move away, far away from Scotland, where he was from, and from Germany, where he had grown up, all the way to a new world… to a place where the sun's warmth existed in real-life three dimensions, and not in a flat and impotent fantasy.

At first he'd felt he had made the right decision, and now he was absolutely positive! He had fulfilled his dreams and changed his life, exchanging what he had with what he'd always wanted: a warm sun, a stable roof and a big garden, all under the care of GCC Home Providers and Co. What a wonderful place, what a wonderful service provider! What more could he ask for?

In fact, it all seemed too good to be true. Sometimes he had trouble believing that all these wonderful things had actually happened, and he would pinch his earlobes to make sure he wasn't dreaming. After all, he had lived in cold and barren plains for a very long time and had naturally grown accustomed to them; it wasn't easy to believe that he was no longer living there. But he wasn't! He was somewhere else, somewhere amazing. He knew it with every little pinch of his lobes.

What was that inspiring motto GCC were using? "Communicating liberates your soul." How wonderful, how true it was! It had touched his heart when he first heard it, so he went to GCC without second thought. He'd set up his account with them without further ado, and was almost swept off his feet by the unique way with which they'd processed his application. His contract felt more like a relationship, a relationship full of care and love that had sprung from the land of surrealism, flowing towards the realm of comfortable safety. "A contract you will never want to change." That was their other motto. How reassuring!

There was a pregnant pause across the line until the automated menu was activated. He waited patiently for the electronic combos that would be offered to him. He was hungry and eager to order but also unwearied and trusting. He lived by the virtue of patience and revered the old folk adagio, "Good things come to those who wait." Indeed, good food acquires its good essence when you wait for its preparation, smelling its tantalising odours from the kitchen. That's how good food becomes exquisite food. And it's the same with any kind of option available just as it is with food. Bon appetit.

'Welcome to the GCC general services automated menu,' said a female voice dripping with honey. 'You will now hear a list of options that might be relevant to your requirements. Please listen carefully, and choose the appropriate option by pressing promptly the corresponding number key on your telephone. If you do not own a digital phone device, then call the GCC equipment sales department at 1-800-555-5555 to buy one from our extensive inventory. This is necessary in order to enhance communications services and standards. Our prices begin as low as $59.99.'

'This is strange,' he thought. He didn't remember hearing this message the first time he'd called. It must have been added recently. No matter, he did have a digital phone so he didn't have to worry about that.

'If you are a potential subscriber and would like to initiate a service, press 1 now.' Yes, that was familiar. It was the option he had used when he had first called. Efficient and straight to the point, wasting no time. He hadn't had to go through the hassle of listening to a barrage of options before choosing. But he wasn't a first-time subscriber anymore, and he acknowledged that he would now have to go through more than one options, understandably. Yet, what mattered to him was the underlying approach; it was evident that the GCC system had been set up in such a way so as to serve their clients as efficiently and hassle-free as possible.

'If you are a current subscriber and would like another line service, you can now order one to be installed at half price. This offer is valid only till the end of January. To order a second installation, press 2 now.'

'A marvellous offer,' he admitted, 'but not right now. First thing's first. Let's clear up this misunderstanding now, and then why not?'

'To report a technical problem or discrepancy, press 3 now.'

Beep.

'You will now be connected to our Technical Support Department. Please stay on the line and the next available Benefactor will be with you shortly.'

He loved the terms they were using. The persons helping to set up a service were called "Advocates" and those helping to solve problems or discrepancies were called "Benefactors." How imaginative, how fresh!

'Hello, my name is Yeerd... I will be your GCC Benefactor today. How can I help you?'

'Hi, I'm calling to report a problem with my service.'

'What is the nature of your problem, sir?'

'I'm afraid there was some kind of mistake with my billing charges. I'm sure we'll clear it up right away.'

'I'm afraid that we can't assist you in this department sir. This is Technical Support. You need to negotiate with the Billing Department.'

'Oh, I'm sorry. I heard technical problems or discrepancies and I automatically thought that discrepancies included billing mistakes.'

'I'm sorry sir, I'm afraid it does not. All billing issues are covered by the Billing Department. Let me connect you back to the main menu right away.'

'Couldn't you connect me to the Billing Department directly...?' The last part of the question was already falling flat against a ring tone. He was already on his way back to the Main Menu. No matter, it wasn't as if he'd been disconnected; he had merely taken a detour and was now back on the right track via the long way. That Yeerd fellow was a tad too efficient to be honest! And what kind of a name was Yeerd anyway?

Irrelevant. The aim was to clear this misunderstanding up and get it out of the way.

'Welcome to the GCC general services automated menu...'

He wondered what number the Billing Department would be

on. He decided to place a bet with himself. '1 was for setting up a service, 2 for setting up a second service, 3 for technical support, so 4 must be for billing support,' he thought to himself, smiling. He wondered whether the billing persons would be called Benefactors too. They should. After all, they, too, were providing help and support.

'...If you are calling to set up payment using a check or credit card, press 4 now...'

Shit! He'd lost the bet! It made sense though. Bill mistakes are rare, so one should expect to first opt to pay his bill, as is the norm, and then go to the option of addressing a billing discrepancy. He hadn't thought of it that way. He reminded himself to be more logical and analytical in the future.

'We are currently experiencing an extremely high volume of calls and it will take a longer time than average to respond to your query. You can hang up and try later. If you wish to remain on the line, one of our representatives will be with you as soon as possible."

'Is that right?' he mumbled, looking at a photograph across the room.

A tune began playing. His thoughts strayed off the picture and went back to the bet. It still bothered him that he'd guessed wrong; he felt that he had taken things for granted. He hated doing that, taking things for granted. It was like wearing sunglasses in a cave. His uncle, a professional cave explorer, had once told him that the first thing cave explorers do when they go underground is take their sunglasses off. Then they bring out the apparatus, the instruments of aid that will help them find their way around. 'Life is like a dark cave we have to go through, my dear boy. The light at the end of the tunnel is hidden far away, and the only light that can actually guide you through the darkness is the one you yourself create. Use it well and illuminate your path with caution. You don't want to break a leg or fall in a pit. Watch your step and keep pushing on. When you reach a dead end, turn back and try again. Keep trying. If you navigate well and are lucky enough, you will one day reach the exit. Most people don't, but a few do, and that's what's important; it has been achieved. It most definitely has been achieved! Still, there are those who insist that it's impossible to reach, or that it's not worth seeking at all. And you know who these people are, right? Ay, my boy, they're those who have never reached it because they either failed midway or because they were simply too afraid to make the journey in the first place. They are the moles of the cave. They are the moles of comfort, of fear, and of failure. More Scotch, laddy?'

Beep.

'If you have questions about your billing statement, are uncertain or unclear about how the statement is set up, or would like more information regarding charges, we shall enlighten you if you press 5.'

Beep.

'This menu is getting stranger by the option,' he mumbled. Where was the "Press 5 now" prompt? Why did they change their format into "If you press 5?" And what was this "We shall enlighten you" thing?

'Hi, my name is Kanforn and I will be your GCC Enlightener today. How may I enlighten you?'

'Excuse me?'

'I'm sorry, this must be the first time you contact our Billing Enlightenment Department. Let me clarify in advance that we receive many grievances from people who try to trick their way through our system in order to deceive GCC and not pay what they owe. There are also many subscribers who simply don't pay the required attention to our Bill Decoding Instructions and call for explanations, thereby wasting their precious time. And then there are those who simply can't understand the instructions no matter what. GCC does not take such matters lightly and we are committed to rectifying these sources of inefficient behaviour in order to better serve our subscribers and the world they live in. Now, how may I enlighten you?'

A pang of frustration raced through his body as he felt for the first time since his relocation the unsettling touch of an imposing hand. It was a mild touch, and surely a necessary means of dealing with swindlers, but it nevertheless brought him great discomfort. This hand's skin was dead cold, as if a river of ice was flowing within it. Where was the trademark warm reception? Why wasn't it there? After all, this was a call to report a legitimate error, an error they had made, not he! And what about people's time? Isn't it theirs to waste if they choose to? GCC is perhaps a little too keen to help its customers!

These thoughts dashed through his mind as he tried to digest the new development and make the most sense of it. He felt he had been branded thief or fool by association, and this insulted him. On the other hand, he knew that ego and pride could blur one's view and destroy the moment. Time. Timeout.

'Fortunately for all of us my case is nothing of the sort. I am sure we will get it sorted out shortly, uh… I'm sorry, what was your name again?'

'My name is Kanforn sir, it rhymes with reborn.'

'Right… Kanforn…' Where were these people from, Tolkien's Middle Earth? Yeerd, Kanforn. Who's next? Saruman?! He sighed. 'Well, Kanforn… there seems to be an error in my bill.'

'Let's investigate the matter sir. What is your account number please?'

'Um, 480-464-0769/561123.'

'Address and date of birth please.'

'My address is 2012 E. Wake, Joyville. My date of birth is 20/10/74.'

'You mean 10/20/74 sir?'

Damn, he hated having to deal with numbers in ways that didn't make sense. Having grown up in Germany, away from his Scottish homeland, he'd learned to measure the world in metres, litres and kilograms, but now he'd have to rearrange all his previous knowledge and start measuring everything in feet, ounces and pounds. And on top of that he'd have to suspend his practice of sequencing things in ascending or descending order and start conceiving time in terms of 'first the month, then the date… and then the year!' What was that all about? He'd been born on the 20th day day of the 10th month of the 1,974th year following Christ's birth. Why would someone think that he was born on the 10th month, on the 20th day day of that month, in the year 1974? Wasn't that just confusing? And confused? Or how about just plain silly?

At least they counted time same as everywhere else. That was definitely something. He imagined counting time in cronkites, or something like that, instead of minutes. That would sum up the whole nine yards. 'Um, ok honey, I'll be there in 40 minutes… um, wait… let's convert that… 40 times 300, minus 10, divided by 13, plus 11… equals 933.31 cronkites… no, not minutes honey, cronkites… CRONKITES!' The thought amused him and he shook his head, squishing his nose.

'Yes, 10/20/74. Force of habit.'

'Don't worry sir, it will be corrected in time.'

There was a short moment of silence during which he could hear just the clicks of a keyboard across the line. 'I'll be damned if it will be corrected in any amount of time,' he grunted inside his head.

'Social security number and account password please.'

'Yeah, 993-87-9845. The password is 5dm90.' Silence and clicking once more. After 21.77 cronkites the Enlightener spoke. Enlightener! Talk about a wild imagination!

'Ok, I have pulled the data for the account 480-464-0769/561123, at 2012 E. Wake, Joyville. DOB 10/20/74, SSN 993-87-9845.' He thought he'd heard a small emphasis on the date of birth, but he disregarded it as the Enlightener continued.

'Am I speaking with Mr McAlister?'

'Yes indeed.'

'You are now free to negotiate your account details, Mr McAlister. What would you like to propose?'

All this funny talk had started to piss him off. It was the second time the word "negotiate" had crawled out from this conversation, and this time it had been preceded by "you are now free to" and followed by "propose." This prejudiced, imposing hand was not letting go and he felt the branding shift from "guilty by association" to "guilty by default." Did they cast the association away and decide to mingle the lambs with the goats? Are we all going to Hell? Maybe Kanforn is going through her PMS. Why, with a name like Kanforn she could very well have a chronic condition of shitty attitude. 'Hi, my name is Kanforn and I sound like a washing detergent. But I'm not full of bleach and I like colours a lot. Where do I apply for the Enlightener position?' The thought amused him but only for a short moment.

Kanforn was tapping away at her keyboard on the other side of the connection, waiting for his response. He could feel her breathing pattern seep through the phone, going right through his eardrum, on its way to his brain. There was something about it. He didn't like it – or her, for that matter; people like Kanforn were spoiling the image of companies like GCC, defeating the purpose of providing a good service in the first place and agitating customers without second thought. Had she been screened and trained for her position after all, or had she slipped through the cracks?

'Yes, well, there seems to be some mistake with my bill. Em…'

'Go on sir.'

'Well, I've been overcharged to be honest. I mean a lot of money! It's almost unbelievable. Like a movie scenario. No worries though. I'm sure we'll sort it out in no time.'

'We shall look into it right away, sir. On which items do you claim you have been overcharged?'

There was that patronising tone once again, mixed and served with a plateful of professionalism, ever so subtly present, yet, setting his judgement on fire like a well-blended spice – belatedly but with a vengeance. Or was he just overreacting?

'Well, I have been charged for many phone calls at extraordinary rates. And when I say extraordinary, I mean –'

'Hold on sir. Let's do things one at a time. Does your claim involve only phone calls?'

'Why... ye... what... what else would it involve?'

'Sir, are you claiming to have been overcharged only on phone calls, or do your claims also involve other items?'

'What other items?!'

'Sir, your bill includes a line rental fee, a maintenance fee, three tax fees, one of which is County and the other two State, a –'

'Yeah yeah, I am referring only to phone calls. Yeah.'

'Ok, that's good. Now sir, which phone calls are you referring to?'

'Well, most of them. I mean, if you look at the charges you'll see that I'm talking about a huge mistake...'

'These figures alone say nothing to me sir. You must be specific.'

'Jesus, you're so impersonal,' he blurted out. He just had to say it. Kanforn was really rubbing him the wrong way. 'Listen Kanforn, if you just take a moment and tune in with me I –'

'Sir, this is not the PR Department. This is the Billing Enlightenment Department where we deal with bill and charge discrepancies. In order to do so most efficiently and reliably I need you to tell me the exact phone calls on which you claim to have been overcharged so that I can look into the claim.'

A reasonable argument. Very reasonable indeed. So why did it have such a bad aftertaste?

'You want me to list all the calls?'

'That's right sir.'

'But there's hundreds of them!'

'Sir, I can only look into the ones on which you make an actual claim.'

Suddenly, life seemed so much more tedious and complicated. It wasn't as if Kanforn was wrong. She was certainly not going to surmise where the overcharging had taken place. Nor was it her job to look up the going rates, compare his calls to them, find out which calls had been overcharged, sum up the difference and send him a wax-sealed report with a credit slip, an apology note and a flower. Or was it?

'This is certainly not the kind of service GCC claims to be providing to its customers,' he retorted.

'Sir, we are of service to our subscribers. We provide services, not subservience. We handle claims and complaints for you, but not on your behalf. If there is something you do not agree with, you are free to propose it to us and we will do our best to handle your problem. Now sir, what can I do for you?'

Yep, life had certainly become much more tedious and complicated. Gone were the good old simple days where things just flowed. Back then, the phone bill was a simple payment that at least didn't cost time. Now he had to worry about a thousand little details, meandering through automated menus, negotiating with Enlighteners, seeking that elusive light at the end of the ever growing tunnel.

'Let me get the bill Kanforn... wait a minute... ok, here we go. I have here 337 calls in total, most of which are to London and Cyprus. I haven't counted the overcharged ones, but they certainly seem to make up the vast majority of the list here. So let's go through them one by one.'

'Sir, I suggest you hang up and go through them first, and then call us back if you like.'

'What?! No, no! I'm not going to go through all this procedure again. I have the itemised bill right here. I will identify each call to you, one by one. Now, on November 10, at 17:43, I made a 22-minute call to London, which was charged at $66. That's $3 per minute! My going rate for London is supposed to be 5 cents per minute. OK? Then I made a 10-minute call to Cyprus, which cost me $27, or $2.70 per minute, while my going rate was 18 cents –'

'The going rate for London Ontario is actually 3 cents, as it is for Cypress California…'

'What? No, not London Ontario and Cypress California! London. You know, London, the capital of England! And Cyprus. You know, Cyprus, the island state in the Mediterranean… the Mediterranean Sea? Europe…?'

'Sir, are you talking about international calls?'

'Yes, yes, I am talking about international calls!'

'I'm sorry, sir, this department deals only with local and national calls, including Canada. For all international billing discrepancies and claims you must hang up and try to connect to GCC Greater Services. Is there anything else I can assist you with today?'

His jaw dropped to the floor like a shot put.

'You must be joking!'

'No, sir. Is there anything else I can help you with today?'

'So I have to call another number and go through all this again?'

'I'm afraid so, sir.'

'Well, um… can you at least connect me through to GCC Greater Services, or whatever they are called, so that I can save some time?'

'I'm afraid I can't do that, sir. They are a different company, operating on a different system than ours. Is there anything else I can help you with today?'

'No… um… no… thank you.'

'Thank you for calling Global Communications Corporation. Have a nice day!'

Click.

Well… what the hell was that all about? Talk about severe reversals. He'd just been washed, bleached and thrown out to dry. And somehow, someway, he'd been left with the impression that he was the one to blame for the whole thing. As if he was unworthy.

The last time he'd experienced something similar was down in England, in London. He'd walked into a hotel somewhere in Mayfair, asking the going rates for a room…

'I'm afraid the cheapest room available here, sir, is £250 per night. I'm certain you'll find more appropriate prices south of the river.'

He put his hand in his combat trousers' side pockets and took out a roll of notes.

'I'm sure that these will cover your rates should I decide to stay here,' he said with a slight smile, fixing the desk clerk straight in the eye.

'I'm afraid we do not take Scottish Sterling, sir.'

'But you surely take Visa whether it is Scottish, English or Congolese, don't you?'

'We take all forms of plastic, sir.'

'Ay, I'm sure you do!'

'Excuse me sir?'

'I said I am glad that you are in the position to accept my plastic endorsement, should I wish to stay here.'

'Yes... oh, I am dreadfully sorry, sir. The last room on the cheap rate has just been given away. We have suites available though... £550 per night is the cheapest rate we have. Shall I make a booking for you?'

'No. Call the manager please.'

'Sir, I *am* the manager!'

Talk about being struck with a velvety-soft glove. He'd been made to look like the culprit! That's why he'd left the Old World. He'd had enough. It was time for something new, something fresh, something free from the cold and the damp. It was time to seek the light.

And now this! A condescending, arrogant, prickly phone clerk, wielding her authority like a mace, dispensing judgement and guilt to those that would not be enlightened, and doing it all as smooth as silk. She deserved to be fired. Definitely! It would save customers like himself a lot of grief. And it would benefit GCC greatly. Surely they did not condone such attitude. He would write a complaint letter and report her to the appropriate department. But now he had other work to do. He had to sort out what he'd started, that wretched phone bill.

He went online and looked up the number for GCC Greater Services. Ten minutes later, after two unsuccessful calls that had put him through to the Headquarters Front Desk and the Accounting Department, he was drilling his way through the automated menu to speak with the Greater Billing Enlightener.

'Hi, my name is Kaply and I will be your Greater GCC Enlightener today. How may I enlighten you?'

'Um, yeah... ok... what was your name again?'

'Kaply sir. It rhymes with "don't even ask why." He he.'

'I see,' he replied. He wasn't sure what to make of this guy.

'I'm sorry sir. Just a little joke to loosen up. No need in being stiff on this job. It's tough enough as it is. Now, how may I be of service to you?'

'Well… I seem to be having trouble with my bill.'

'What kind of trouble sir?'

'I have been overcharged for a great number of calls… international calls, that is! You do deal with international calls, right?'

'Sure we do! Now let's look into this. I'm sure we'll sort it out straight away. Can I have your details please?'

A few seconds later they were already all over the bill. That was more like it!

'Now, it seems to us that you are making a good number of calls to London Great Britain and Nicosia Cyprus. You also seem to be calling Hamburg, Germany quite a lot too.'

At last. Someone who knew a European city from a hole in their pants.

'Yes, I have family and friends in these places.'

'Great! Hold on a minute sir… ok! So tell me, what seems to be the problem?'

'Well, I have been charged a lot more than the rate I had been initially offered when I got this contract with your company.'

'I'm afraid you'll have to speak with your local service provider for this issue sir. From what I see here, it seems that these charges have come from them, not us.'

'What?! You must be fucking joking!'

'Sir, I must warn you that this call is currently being recorded and that we do not tolerate any verbal abuse. We understand that you may be frustrated, but there is no reason for you to be abusive. Now, because we want to provide our subscribers with the best possible service and understanding, we are always willing to overlook the first incidence of verbal violence towards our staff. So, coming back to our issue here, it seems that your international long distance contract was not put into effect until the end of November. This is standard procedure of course. As we have specified in the contract you have signed, it takes 1-3 weeks to enforce these connections. Sometimes it takes one week, but most of the times it takes longer. In your case it took 20 days, one day short of the maximum, which is not too bad if you want my opinion. 21 seems to be the magic number lately, so it looks like you caught a break. Now, any international calls made before the activation of your international calling contract were subject to random charging by your local provider, who, being your only communications service provider at the time, subcontracted the calls from a company able to provide international service, thereby charging higher rates.'

'But… the bill is in GCC's name damn it!'

Just then a little beep went off somewhere in the connection. What was that?

'Yes, the bill is in GCC's name, sir,' Kaply continued. "This is because we have a prearranged agreement with your local service provider to bill us. They bill us for your calls and we bill you in turn and collect the money. Nevertheless, any queries or discrepancies regarding those charges must go through your local service provider, coz they are the ones who set up the charges which you are now contesting.'

'But this is insane. I have just talked with your billing department that deals with local calls and they said no such thing.'

'Sir, I cannot account for Local Billing Enlightenment, or for what they told you. But what I can tell you with certainty is that we cannot deal with your claim here. You must call your local service provider, i.e. the company that installed your service in your residence. They are responsible for the charges incurred between the 10th and 30th of November.'

'This makes no goddamn sense, Kaply, or whatever the hell your name is!'

Another faint beep made its way through the crystal clear connection.

'I'm sorry sir. There's nothing I can do for you about this. Is there anything else I can help you with today?'

'Yeah, call Kanforn up at the Local Billing Enlightenment Department of Jargon and Ping Pong, and tell her you want to invite her to your house for a bit of invasive entertainment on a couple of gagged and bound strangers you kidnapped off the street. I'm sure she'll love it!' And he hung up. But not before hearing a faint beep once more. What the hell was that noise anyway?

He just sat there for a minute, trying to gather his thoughts. Everything had spiralled out of control. One hour ago he'd been immersed in a new and exciting life, enjoying his time in the fairytale land of his deliverance. Thirty minutes ago he'd been calling up one of the greatest contributors to his new life of pleasure and leisure, trying to sort out what seemed to be a glitch in the billing system. And now he was lost in a maze of infrastructure that had been decorated with poison ivy and laced with sticky webs. Have a nice day!

A nice day indeed! This was turning out to be a nightmare, the type he'd been experiencing throughout the winter of his early life.

He was going to put an end to this charade once and for all. He looked up his local service provider on the web and gave them a call. A few key selections later he was getting through to the billing department of Kwestion Communications. And not a moment too soon.

'Please wait while we connect you to our Billing Department of Corrections. Have a nice day!'

At least this company hadn't assumed a pompous title. No Enlightenment, no BS. Maybe they would own up to their name and correct their mistake.

'Hi there. How may I help you, sir?'

'Hi. I am calling about a billing discrepancy. I have been overcharged on a number of calls… In fact, I seem to have been randomly charged… Well, let me start from the beginning.'

'No need Mr McAlister. We are already aware of your problem and are working on it as we speak.'

'I see! But how… how did you know my name?'

'Oh, it's very simple. Kwestion Communications is a subsidiary of GCC. Your grievance has been relayed to us and we have red-flagged your account and your phone line. It is of top priority to us now. You shall be pleased to know that we have already dispatched our Emergency Team of Corrections, which is specifically trained to deal with cases such as yours. There is nothing to worry about Mr McAlister. We shall extinguish this problem in no time. Kwestion Communications and GCC value your business, and we will do everything we can in order to make sure that you remain with us. When we say that we offer "A contract you will never want to change," we mean it. This is not just a motto, sir. It is our creed.'

Well, finally! Service at last. Impeccably good service. Surprisingly good actually, even by his lofty expectations.

'So, you mean you know which calls have been overcharged?'

'Yes we do, sir.'

'And are you going to rectify those charges?'

'We are going to set everything straight, sir. You have my personal assurance.'

'I'm sorry, who am I speaking with?'

'My name is Kamanda, Mr McAlister. I am the director of this department.'

"Well, this is great news, Kamanda. I have been rebounding through various departments for almost 45 minutes now. I have to tell you that some of the employees I have spoken with have not been helpful at all. They have been abrupt and dismissive, or patronising and condescending. I don't think this type of attitude does a lot of good to your company. They don't fit the GCC image.'

'We are well aware of our employees' actions, Mr McAlister, and we are constantly making sure that they conform to our policies.'

'That's good to know, Kamanda. It would be a shame for you to lose customers on account of an unruly representative.'

'I assure you, unruliness and dissidence is something we take very seriously around here. We take every measure possible to make sure that unruly individuals comply with our regulations.'

'Excellent. Excellent. One can never yield to disorder, right?'

'You said it, Mr McAlister. One must be a strong commander, making sure that the disorderly ones yield, conform and comply.'

'You certainly mean business, man. These are very strong terms indeed. Yield, conform, comply…' He paused. Something started clicking. Things were beginning to assume a new sense in an alarming pace. The meaning of what had transpired over the last 45 minutes was being transfigured in a highly disturbing way.

Just then, there was a loud knock on the door. He hesitated for a moment, torn between his thoughts, his call and the forceful pounding on the door. Then a series of further knocks followed. The door started shaking in its hinges.

'I'm sorry… um… Kamanda… um, there's someone at the door. I better go see who it is…'

'Oh, don't bother, Mr McAlister. They'll be in before you manage to get up.'

Suddenly, the door burst wide open and a bunch of black uniforms stormed into his apartment. They were holding certain weird-looking instruments, and one of them was carrying a thick black briefcase. Before he could say anything they were all over him – something stung him in the forehead – he began drifting into a heavy slumber fast – there were voices all around him – he couldn't make out what they were saying – he was descending into a cold void fast, crashing through a series of flashing billboards… 'My name is Yield.' 'My name is Conform, sir, it rhymes with reborn.' 'Our subscribers.' 'For all international billing discrepancies and claims, you must hang up…' 'Comply sir, it rhymes with don't even ask why.' 'A contract you will never want to change.' 'A world where everyone is always connected.' 'Always connected.' 'Always connected.' 'If you say anything about this to anyone, we shall poison your food.' 'We shall mess with your car's brakes.' 'Your family will die in a freak accident.' 'Have a nice day!'

When he opened his eyes he was lying on the floor. There was no one in the apartment. He tried to move but a burning pain rushed through his head, pinning him down. He meekly turned his eyes towards the front door. It was closed. And intact.

He rolled over slowly and his whole body hurt, as if he'd been poisoned. All his internal organs ached and his skin burned. He tried to remember what had happened but his mind was as thick as mashed potatoes. All he could recollect was a feeling of panic cutting right through him, as if he had been threatened… as if he had been attacked… as if he had been thrown into a dark hole, where the only thing he could perceive were voices and apparitions that were terrorising his whole being. Had he been dreaming?

As he looked towards his left his eyes fell upon a phone device he'd never seen before; a shiny, slick, black device, covered in fancy buttons, its screen shining bright, mesmerising him, drawing his gaze upon it. A silver-blue display in the middle of the device indicated that the line was live. He picked up the receiver and brought it to his ear.

'Huh… hallo,' he garbled. A faint beep came across the connection.

'Your call will now be connected…'

He sat up and leaned on the wall, trying to get himself together. 'Hallo…? Hallo…'

'Mr McAlister, so good to hear your voice. My name is Grandemano. I have been assigned to monitor your account. I am extremely satisfied that we have dealt with your problem promptly and efficiently. Now, is there anything else we can help you with today?'

'No... I'm fine... Thank you. Thank you...' he mumbled.

'Always glad to be of service to our valued subscribers. If we all play our cards right we may enjoy a long life of cooperation together. Don't you agree?'

'Yes... yes indeed. A long life. A long life.'

'That is correct, sir. Now, are you sure there is nothing else I can help with today?'

'Yes... No... I mean yes... yes, I'm sure... no more help. Thank you.'

'Then let me hold you no longer than I have to and immediately connect you to our Contract Evaluators. We have observed that you have been calling Hamburg Germany and Madrid Spain a lot too, and we can set you up with a plan that will be beneficial to you.'

'That... that would be great. Great.'

'Oh, and one more thing, Mr McAlister. As you have already seen, we go to great lengths to ensure that all our problems are solved fully and permanently. We consider your case a fully and permanently solved problem, and we would like you to do the same. We have in fact taken the liberty to enrol you in our Preferred Subscriber Program and have provided you with our Exclusive Special Emergency Service, which is unfortunately not complimentary. Your bills shall therefore incur an additional special monthly charge for the benefit of enjoying our most immediate attention to any grievance you may have. Naturally, you shouldn't feel obliged to ask what the charge is about. Do you understand?'

'Yes... I understand.'

'Good. Have a nice day!'

And Mr McAlister lived happily ever after.

Victor Gente Delespejo

When Dreams Turn

He wondered how he got there. All alone, in the middle of somewhere, somewhere that could have been anywhere, anywhere in the wilderness…

It was a disconcertingly alien somewhere. He gazed at it in disbelief, totally unable to understand what was happening. It was just too much to take, too severe, too overbearing. Even purgatory has an end, an expiry date from which one can jump into the next level. But not this! This seemed to stretch into the cruel lengths of eternity, making the gravest statement of all; that of permanence… of permanent permanence, the kind from which there is no way out, no exit, no end. This was going to be a process that would perpetuate for all time. Stamina, tenacity and faith were totally irrelevant here. So were pain, surrender and repentance. Whatever the purpose of this process, it had a truly relentless nature. Nothing could stop it. Nothing. Not even death.

He looked around again, but his mind was hardly focusing on his new and frightful surroundings. His brain was unable to register the information sent to it by his frantic scanning eyes. Something else was overcoming him. He had already switched on the playback function, and the memory reel was well underway, spinning steadily, projecting its own stories, filling up his mind with old happenings and covering up everything else. He remembered how it used to be – so much warmer, so familiar, so convenient; everything making sense; every day a stroll down the neighbourhood, where everyone was where they were supposed to be, where they always were, in their own little niche. There they were, always there, doing what they always did, in the way they always did it, and he would walk on by and greet them with a big friendly smile. 'Hey there, neighbour! How are you doing today?' he would shout. 'Hey there, neighbour. I'm fine. How are you doing?' they would shout back. Some would crack a big smile too. Others would just wave and then get back to whatever they were doing. Some would start to gripe, letting loose the avalanche of events that had gone wrong in their lives during the last 24 hours, while others would just stand motionless, watching him go by. But they all had something to say – even when they never opened their mouths. They all responded, each in their own way, in the way they always responded.

It was all so great. His life was a veritable walk in the neighbourhood, in the good ole friendly neighbourhood, where everybody knew everyone else and no one was a stranger. Everyone fitted in. Even the misfits of the block. They were as much a part of the hamlet as anyone else. It was a great little community, and he felt blessed to be part of it. He could have asked for nothing more. In fact, he never did. He was so content with his life that he never doubted it or scrutinized it, not even for a second. He was blissfully happy there, and he could imagine nothing better than the life he had been blessed with.

'Hi there, my good friend! How are the kids?' he'd ask.

'Oh, they are just fine, buddy,' his neighbour would answer. Getting taller by the day. You know how kids are these days. In a hurry to grow up. Always in a hurry. They just can't take it easy.'

'Well, that's kids for you! Always so childish. Oh, I wish I were a kid again.'

'Yep, me too! But when I tell them this, they don't listen. They just wanna grow up. As if that will make them happier. "Just stay where you are," I tell them. "Stay where you are and enjoy it." But they don't listen. They just giggle and snort and start singing songs. "When I grow up what shall I do? I'll stay up late if I want to. When I grow up what shall I say? Well, anything I want to, so I can't wait…"'

'Hey, I remember that song! We used to sing it on our way to school and back. We used to sing it in the fields and the back alleys, coz back then, when the grownups heard this song, well, they gave us a piece of the ole boot and stick.'

'The ole swift 'n' caring kick in the ass!'

'So how'd it go? The song I mean. Um… "When I grow up what shall I do? I'll show the geezers a thing or two…" Yeah. That's how it went. And that's what we did, ain't that right, neighbour?'

'Sure is, neighbour. We sure showed them a thing or two. Got back at them for all those kicks in the ass.'

'Ah, but then what did we do?'

'You mean apart from realising that the geezers were right all along, and that the only reason they were kicking us in the ass was to keep us a little longer in childhood, where things are better than what they seem? Oh, nothing much!'

'But *then* what did we do? After we realised this I mean.'

'Ah, then, then we changed our tune! About time too! Remember how it went? "When I grew up what did I learn? That being a kid is what I yearn… I'm all grown up, what shall I do? I'll show those kids a thing or two… When you grow up what shall you do? You'll wish you didn't, kid, and you'll change your tune…"'

'We changed *ours*, that's for sure.'

'We sure did!'

'Well, my good neighbour, I gotta go. Have a nice day!'

'You too, neighbour. And God bless.'

'That's right! God bless this great neighbourhood. Life is just grand. So very grand… yep… yep… "When *I* grew up I told myself to be content with my own shelf…"'

'What did you say, neighbour?'

'Nothing neighbour, nothing. I was just humming our tune, thass'all. See you tomorrow.

'See you tomorrow! Dum *dum* dee dum, dum *dum* dee dum… dee-*dum* dee-*dum* dee-*dum* dum dum…'

And off he'd go, through the neighbourhood street, humming his song, strolling along, leaving behind a sing-along neighbour. And so it went, every day, day in day out. Nothing could be better than this. Nothing at all. With childhood on the other side of the rainbow, the magic had given way to a subtler kind of enchantment. The land of Oz had been long gone and another kind of world had surfaced, equally potent, equally mysterious, equally fulfilling: the Truman Show, where everything was working like clockwork, as if a great scriptwriter was creating and directing the whole affair, always on the lookout, always mindful of any changes, always ready to step in at the slightest sign of trouble in order to maintain the flawless perfection so diligently strived for. This was a world of orchestrated order – so well orchestrated in fact that it worked like magic – and it made him happy.

Perfect as it was, though, the script was not immune to the wear and tear of old age.

It was a day just like any other. He'd left the house in the morning to walk through the neighbourhood street, ready to greet the neighbours and kickstart another perfect day into life. He was strolling along, whistling on, dancing to the tunes of an age-old song, when he suddenly realised that his good friend was not in his garden raking the leaves as always.

'Hey, neighbour! Where are you?' he shouted. No reply. The door at the front porch was shut, and so were all the windows of the green house, as if no one was in. 'Hey, neighbour!' he shouted again. Nothing. The house stood there, perfectly still, and the wind rustled through the fallen leaves arrogantly, claiming its stake over the silent home. Just then a heavy branch broke off the oak and came crashing to the ground with a cracking thud, making him jump back with fright. Suddenly everything seemed worse. Now it felt as if someone actually was in the house, way in, locked inside, hiding, unwilling to be contacted and reluctant to be found.

He turned around, deeply disturbed, and walked on down the street. He walked on, eager to meet the rest of his neighbours, to meet them and greet them at their usual places doing their usual thing and speaking their usual lines, like they always did.

He saw no one. There was no one there. The street was empty. The neighbourhood appeared to be deserted. All the doors and windows were closed shut with their curtains drawn tightly. All the cars were gone too, and so were the animals. No dogs, no cats, nothing. Not even a single bird on the trees! Just the wind, blowing through the battered and balding branches, tearing away the yellow-orange leaves and blowing them all over the place.

He sat down on the kerb to think. What could have happened? Where could everyone be? Did they tell him that something was coming down that day? Had he heard but forgotten all about it? Or had this been an emergency, where something so appalling had come their way that they just had to disappear? Maybe. But what was it? What could it be? Everything seemed normal. The sky was blue, the sun was shining, the air was crisp, and his knee was hurting just like every October, right before the first snowfall. Everything seemed to be on track. So why had everybody gone? And where were they?

He started playing the previous day over in his head, trying to make better sense of things…

He had gotten up at 06:30 to the sound of his silver alarm clock. He kissed his wife – who was mumbling something incoherent – and got up. He went to the bathroom, brushed his teeth, went to the loo, had a shower, shaved and got dressed. Then he sauntered downstairs where he brewed some coffee, prepared a toast, opened the front door and got the newspaper, which had landed on the right part of the porch, and then sat in the kitchen to read it in the enjoyable company of a freshly made Brazilian Brew and a lightly buttered wholemeal toast.

Thirty minutes later, he folded his newspaper, placed his mug and plate in the sink, went upstairs to brush his teeth again, then gave another kiss to his wife on the forehead, making her sigh again – as she always did, in that so cutely grumbling way of hers – and went back downstairs. He got his keys, put on his anorak, got his mobile phone and walked out the door.

He began strolling towards the lake, which was about two miles down the street, all the way south.

He passed by the green house first, where a black Labrador was always chasing squirrels. 'You'll never catch them like that, you silly dog. I been telling you for years, but you never listen.' He turned his eyes away from the tenacious Labrador, who seemed to have a knack for disregarding all signs just as long as it was pleasing itself, and he looked for his good neighbour on the front lawn.

For a moment he couldn't see anyone or anything... then his neighbour materialised from behind a tall oak tree! That's what he always did. He'd be nowhere to be seen – the only resident on that front yard apparently being the thick-headed black Labrador, chasing after those squirrels with a most futile persistence – but suddenly, and as if by magic, his good neighbour would appear from behind the oak... Or he would just jump out of the driveway... Or sometimes he would materialise on the lawn as if he'd leapt through the porch door, or out of a hole in the ground... As if he'd been hiding in a place where he would have been found out within seconds, and the only thing to do was to blow his own cover and appear like Houdini rather than be hounded out like a hare in the ground. Good ole crazy neighbour. That's what he was.

'Hey there, neighbour,' he shouted at him. 'Good morning to you.'

'Good morning to you too,' said the neighbour with a big smile. He always smiled. Always. Whenever he talked. There wasn't a time when that man wouldn't smile at him.

'Your dog is still chasing shadows. He'll never catch anything like that,' he said, pointing at the bouncing Labrador.

'Yep, that's good ole Wonty for you,' replied the neighbour. 'He's as hard headed as they come. He seems to be always barking up the wrong tree, doin' his own thing no matter what and never paying attention to anything else. Silly dog.'

'I tell you, neighbour. I been trying to explain to this dog that he ain't gonna catch nothing like that. Not even his own tail. But he doesn't listen.'

'Yeah, he's just like my uncle Herman. Too far up his own mind's ass that he has to roll like a wheel to get to places. Ha… ha ha ha…'

'Ha ha ha! Good one, neighbour. Next time you speak to him, ask him if he can see shit! Ha! Ahem… Well… I'm off to the lake. Gonna feed the ducks and then have me a strawberry ice cream.'

'Good for you, neighbour.'

'Hey, want something from the store?'

'Nah… Got everything I want. But thanks anyway.'

'Suit yourself,' he said and began strolling down the street again.

He passed by a couple more houses, where no one was ever out and about that early. Their residents would always sleep in until 08:30. One could tell. At 08:29 the two houses were dead quiet. At 08:30 sharp, though, there'd be hollering, clanging, and all sorts of noises coming from inside, as if everyone had overslept, now in a terrible rush to get ready. By 09:00 they'd be out the door and into their cars.

Two cars, one for each house and family. They were always parked close, head to head, as if they, too, needed companionship during the long nights when the streets were cold and empty and the living rooms warm and cosy. Parked up front, on the kerb, they would keep each other company until morning, when their owners would crash out of sleep. Then, at 08:35, two people would rush out, one from each house, turn their engines on and rush back inside. Then the cats would come out of the woods and sit on the hoods of the cars, sprawled out like royalty and scanning the area like miniature lions. At 09:00 sharp, though, their breather would be cut short by two wild bunches of humans rushing out their homes and into their cars, on their way to the diner they all owned and run together. "The Flapjack on Rowdy Shore." What a name for a diner! What a crazy bunch of people!

He chuckled as he passed by the now silent houses and the

kissing cars, enjoying the serenity and imagining the mayhem that would start in about 90 minutes. He stopped for a second, waving hi to the two houses first, then to the two cars, then to the cats hiding in the woods, and walked on down the road.

A few seconds later, he brought his left hand up to his face, shielding his eyes from the rays of a warm fiery sun. Rising from the southeast, it was shooting its rays sideways across the land, rending the thick foliage and shedding light on the west side of the street.

The rays were strong, warming up the left part of his body in an instant. He walked through them for a little while, immersed in their energy, sucking it up and charging his batteries, preparing for what lay ahead. His brow started sweating and his heartbeat picked it up a notch. Suddenly, he stepped into the cool embrace of a big shade. The warmness was gone, cut like a cord. He brought his hand back down and turned to his left, where the grey brick-and-stone house that stood taller than every other building on the street lay, looming above him like a gargoyle and obscuring the faraway yellow nuclear giant behind its massive structure.

It was a truly massive building, a mansion. Its huge latch windows were open, and its extremely high ceilings made it look even bigger. The curtains were hanging over the shelves, waving in the morning breeze like gigantic banners, and on the far side – at the second-floor window – a woman was standing firm, looking out onto the street. She looked microscopic, like a chess piece on a great mantle, and the only clue that she was a living human being – and not a piece of sculpture – was her long red hair, hanging over her right shoulder and dangling in the morning breeze against the grey stone and brick.

'Good morning, Mrs Jona,' he cried, waving at her, trying to swallow through his cottoned up mouth. She didn't move. She never moved. She just stood there, watching him go by without turning her head an inch.

As he walked by, he took another couple of looks at her, like always – one when he was directly in front of her window, and one when he was about 50 yards further down – and saw that she was still facing straight ahead. Yet, he had the eeriest of feelings that she had been following him with her eyes all along, from the moment he had stepped into the mansion's sight and for the duration of the next two minutes, up until the moment when he would soon disappear behind the tree line that lay just ahead… where he would enter the vicinity of the giant willow, the good giant willow! A truly spectacular specimen of natural grandeur, it overshadowed all other trees, even the black oaks! The birds used to flock on its branches and the squirrels used to play hide and seek all over it. Children of all ages used to gather underneath it and have fun all day long. It was a haven of joy, where life would just gather for an unknown reason and let loose. The birds did not seem to be scared of the loud kids there, and neither did the squirrels. As for the children, they were only too delighted to be flanked by carefree animals. It was an experience unlike any other, and they enjoyed playing among these critters – and sharing space as if they had all grown up together – more than they enjoyed playing in any other field and fairground.

'Good morning, kids,' he said, but his voice was lost in the happy commotion. They'd never hear him from the first go, but he didn't mind. He would rather greet them softly first and then speak a little louder rather than greet them with a booming voice and startle the joy out of them.

'Good morning, kids!' he shouted softly.

'Good morning, Mister,' they all shouted back, like a chorus, some joining in a few moments later than others, and so it took a few seconds to complete. It sounded something like, 'Goooood mooooooorniiiiiinnng Mmmiiiiisteeeeerr…' and it came with a host of little hands waving 'hello.'

'Goooood moooorniiinng kiiiiiiiidsss…' he sung back, laughing. 'What are you doing today, kids?'

'We are playing, Mister,' some of them responded excitedly.

'I can see that. And what are you playing?'

'We are playing Cowboys and Indians!'

'What a great game. We used to play it too when we were kids. So how does the game go today?'

'The Injuns attacked Lakeside Ranch, and they took Red Eye Jim's wife prisoner. The Cowboys are getting ready to attack their reservation and bring the lady back.'

'Damsel in distress… Defending great love… Some of the best scenarios ever! We used to play them out a great deal. They were some of our favourites.'

'What else did you play, Mister?'

'Well, "Triumphing over Evil" was also one of our favourites. And we couldn't say no to "Being Strong and Rich" either.' He noticed that this was not the answer they were looking for. 'Ahem,' he said, clearing his throat. 'Cops and Robbers was a good game. Patriots and Redcoats was a good one too. What else, what else…? Um… ah! Romans and Christians!'

'What?' said some of the kids, looking at him cluelessly.

'Yeah, Romans and Christians, which then turned into Christians and Pagans… and then into Christians and Atheists…?' He paused for a moment. 'You have no idea what I'm talking about, right?' he said, looking at their blank faces.

'No, Mister,' said one of the younger kids. 'But we know Patriots and Redcoats! And we sure know Cops and Robbers. When I grow up I'm gonna be a cop and get all those bad guys.'

'And *I'm* gonna be a gangster, and I'm gonna shoot you every day. Bang bang!'

'No you won't. I'm gonna get you first.'

'Alright kids, settle down now,' he said, relieved at their narrow attention span. Childhood was just great; so spontaneous, so careless, so promising. And free, free from the straits of analysis and the burdens of the past! The faults of the grownups had not yet been inherited in full by their offspring. There was still a large part of these children that was still untouched by the jaded blade of its predecessors, untouched and untarnished. For how long though? Not very. Time was running out.

'When *I* grow up,' shouted another kid, 'I will be like my dad.'

'And *I* will be like *mine*,' said another. 'And *my* dad is better than *your* dad.'

"No, he's not. My dad can kick your dad's ass any time."

'I said settle down now, ok?' he said in a calm but firm voice. Time was indeed running out. Society was catching up with the innocent souls of these young kids. It was catching up fast. Some of them were no longer kids; they were already young adults in the making, developing and revealing various aspects of adulthood timidly but, nevertheless, unequivocally. Always in a hurry. Always eager to grow up. Always eager to become adults.

'Now, who knows the name of the horse rider who galloped across the land to warn everyone that the British were coming?' he asked with excitement.

'Revere, Revere...' they shouted eagerly. 'Paul Revere... Paul Revere...'

'That's right! Paul Revere. And who wants to be like Paul Revere?' he asked, lifting his arms up and holding his breath, waiting for the imminent answer.

'Me, me, me me me...' they shouted together. Each in their own way.

'That's right!' he said, releasing his breath and letting his hands come down a notch. 'That's right. And you know why? Because Paul Revere was a good and brave man who put the interests of his fellow men and women before his own. Now that's a good person, a good man, a good dad, and don't you forget it!'

'Did he bring ice cream when he came back?' asked a little girl in the back, leaning against the willow bark.

'No,' he answered chuckling. 'But he made sure that you and your friends and me, all of us, can get all the ice cream we want.'

'Did he make the ice cream for us?' she asked again.

'Well, sort of. He made sure that we could do whatever we wanted in our lives, whatever we chose. So if it's ice cream we want, then ice cream we get!' He stopped for a moment and looked towards the lake. He could not see its waters from where he was standing, but he could surely smell them. He took a whiff and then turned back to the kids. 'But you know what comes before ice cream?' he asked, looking at all the kids at once. Then he paused again.

'No...' mumbled some of the kids, while the others were waiting with open mouths, their eyes drenched in a glare of eager anticipation, sparkling like jewels.

'The bogeymaaaaan...' he screamed, and started chasing after the kids, pretending to be nasty and mean.

'Aaaaaa...' the kids yelled back, scattering in all directions and running around the willow, screaming and laughing as he chased them around.

'It's the bogeyman. Aaaah... Run away, run away,' shouted some of them.

'No it's not. Can't you see who it is?" shouted the older ones while still running away from him, all giggling and excited.

'Look at his beard,' one of the kids shouted. 'It's so thick. He's like the Caveman of Bear Canyon. Look at the beard. Look at the beard!'

Beard? What beard? What were they talking about? He had shaved off his beard thirty years ago, shortly after he had first arrived at Lakeside. And he'd never grown it since. So, what were they talking about?

He looked around. The sun was ready to rise above the trees, eager to shed its warmth on the whole street. But how could that be? This was October. The sun was supposed to be lower in the horizon and not near the top of the tree line! It was very strange!

He looked around again. Most trees should have shed their leaves by now. But the foliage was as thick as cotton. Why was that? And why was the day so warm?

He turned to the kids, who were still running underneath the good giant willow, screaming and laughing around him, playing tag with the bogeyman.

'What's the matter, Mister?' asked one kid.

'Have you forgotten where you are?'

'You seem confused.'

He jumped back, startled and wary, unable to comprehend what was happening. Everything was breaking down. Nothing was making sense.

'What's the matter, Mister? Can't understand what's going on?'

'Everything seem strange?'

'Strange but familiar?'

It was the eeriest of feelings. Everything did seem totally strange, yet, strangely familiar, as if he'd been there before. His heart began to pound. What was going on? He felt close to an answer, and yet very far away, as if he were looking into the muddy lake through the glass bottom of a boat; things would swish through the silt rapidly, flashing in and out of sight so fast that he could not identify anything with certainty. For a brief moment he would know what he saw, and then he would just be in doubt again.

'Don't be afraid, Mister. You have been asleep for a very long time. It's time to wake up, time to see what has happened.'

'Think, Mister. Think. Think! Why are things not making sense? How long before things that make sense begin to break down?'

'What did you wanna be when you grew up, Mister? What did you wanna say? What did you wanna do? What did you wanna do when the truth passed through...?'

Ravaged by sudden waves of terror, he yelled and backed away. With every breath, with every thought and every word out of the kids' mouths he felt the picture being shaved, losing one more layer of meaning each time, drawing closer to the bare and naked truth that lay beneath all the coats of colour that had been diligently applied over the years onto the canvas of his life. Was it finally time to face the sketch of his being? Had the fateful moment arrived when he would compare this sketch to the painting that had sprung from it, assessing whether the two had any connection at all?

'Don't look away, Mister. Look at us. Come on, look at us. Then look at everything else. Look very carefully...'

He turned towards the kids for a moment, then towards the grey mansion behind the tree line. Something was sucking his attention towards it. His eyes fell upon the trees, trying to drill through them and peer onto the building. The kids were still running around him, underneath the good giant willow, but he wasn't paying attention to them anymore. He couldn't hear them at all. A muffled buzz had begun to fill his ears, and the grey stone-and-brick house started materialising before his eyes. It was becoming clearer with every passing second. Yet, the seconds could have been hours, or days, or years. He couldn't tell. He couldn't have known. Time had ceased to exist. All that mattered now was the image of that house slowly taking shape before his eyes, getting clearer and crisper and more and more solid. There it was, taking form in front of the tree line, obscuring everything in sight – the trees, the sun, the mountains in the distance – throwing a great cold shadow over the land. Then an image flashed through his mind, sucking his breath away and making him squirm with fear. It was the image of Mrs Jona looking at him, staring at him through a pair of grey eyes, grey like the stone-and-brick structure of the house. But that was not what had terrorised him. It was something else. Her hair. The colour of her hair, shiny silver, dangling in the morning breeze... dangling shiny silver, not red. And she? She looked fainter, greyer, older.

He began to understand. Everything started making sense. A lucid and disturbing sense.

He focused his attention on the mansion. There was danger there; he could sense it very vividly. It was creeping from the mansion's bowels right into the sinews of his composure, splitting his internal bonds. He turned his head away and took a few deep breaths, trying to remain calm. But the mansion was calling him. He turned his head back towards it and stared at it intently.

He shouldn't have done so. The image of Mrs Jona blasted through him without warning once again, dashing through his mind and shattering his mental screens to jagged shards and smithereens. And his biography began to bleed while a whole new set of memories were carving another past in his mind, a whole new history and story.

He concentrated on Mrs Jona's red hair and watched it fade to shiny silver, and his eyes began to burn as he realised that thirty whole years had passed since he'd actually seen that red hair, thirty whole years in which he hadn't lived at all. He just hadn't been present in his own life. Every day that had gone by had simply not been registered. He'd been absent from the workings of his own existence, as if his mind had decided to detach itself from what was going on and focus on that perfect summer day instead, when he had taken a stroll down the street, latching onto the fleeting perfection he had experienced, trying to preserve it forever. The black Labrador, the good ole friendly neighbour, the kissing cars in front of the silent houses, the warm sun, the thick foliage, the fiery red hair dangling against the grey stone-and-brick wall of mystery, the kids playing underneath the good giant willow… they were all playbacks from the reel of his memories – authentic playbacks, but in the past, the distant past – not yesterday's but yesteryear's – thirty whole yesteryears lumped together, all piled up one after another, until his life became one long thread of mindfully crafted and compressed déjà vus.

He had finally found the thread! Now, it was time to follow it. But it seemed to lead to a very frightening place, a terrible, devastating place. Could he handle it?

He could always turn back and pretend he had never seen this. Immerse himself in the warm comfort of familiarity and live his life as he had been living it all these years.

But what if the pane of familiarity could never be fully mended? What if the cracks were there to stay, making him go through this all over again at another time, when he would least expect it, like today? Could he go through all this again? Could he make this choice one more time? Or was this the fateful kind of moment that had to be seized swiftly and without second thought? Was this it, the time to face the truth, to stare through the lies, to see behind the mirror?

He looked around perplexed. The children had formed a circle around him and were doing a merry-go round, singing in harmony.

'When you grow up what shall you do? You'll face the truth… You'll face the truth… You'll face the errors of your youth…'

He tried to walk away but the children were all around him. They would not break the circle. Round and round and round they went, singing to an eerie tune.

'Face the errors of your youth… Face the errors of your youth…'

He jerked around in a desperate attempt to break away but they clamped their little hands together and stood their ground.

'Let me out,' he began to shout. 'Let me go.'

'No, Mister, no. No! Face the errors of your youth… Face the errors of your youth…'

'Who are you? What is happening here?' he shouted.

'When you grew up what did you do? You lost perspective of the truth…'

'I did not lose perspective. I did what I had to do,' he stated desperately.

'When you grew up what did you shout? I've got the answers figured out…'

'But I did. I did! Things were finally making sense. I just followed my path,' he cried.

'When you grew up what did you say? Listen kids, I've got it made…'

'But I was only trying to help. How could I offer anything to anyone without being sure of what I was offering?' he pleaded.

'When you grew up what did you do? You lost perspective… You took your life for granted… Ceased to question what was given and you slowly died inside… You slowly died inside… You slowly died inside…'

He let out a horrified scream and decided to run. He wanted to break out of there at any cost. Their song was scraping against his reality, tearing away whatever colour it had, leaving behind patches of painful uncertainty. Whatever picture was being revealed from underneath the countless layers of wishful thinking that had adorned his life was not a pleasant one to stare at; chaffed and grated by every word and every note, his reality was becoming unbearable to watch and was closing in on him. He just had to turn away and get out before it would engulf him completely.

He screamed again and charged at the kids, trying to swipe them out of his way, only to feel a huge impact, as if he'd hit a brick wall. Then he opened his eyes and found himself lying flat on the ground. What had just happened? What the hell was going on?

He squinted and began to mumble, now staring into the hanging branches of the good giant willow through a circular frame of children's faces spinning around in a merry-go round and singing at the top of their voices.

'When you grew up what did you do? You tried to run away, you fool,' shouted a little girl.

'There's no running away from yourself, Mister,' cried another girl.

'You will face what you've done. It's inevitable,' said an older boy. 'At some point in time, someplace, somehow, you will have to deal with your choices. Until then, your life will be an elaborate lie. You will be living in a fake fantasy. You will be living in an excuse made out of your precious weaknesses. And no matter how hard you try to safeguard it, Mister, and regardless how much fun you may have while living it out, it will always be only as real and meaningful as an amusement park.'

He closed his eyes and tried to ignore everything, pretending that all this was not happening. Perhaps this was just a bad dream, a nightmare rising from the forgotten clefts of his mind, where he had buried his most disturbing childhood insecurities. All he had to do was close his eyes and sleep it through. Then he would wake up and everything would be normal again.

He began to breathe slowly and more deeply, and it made him feel better. A certain wave of calm was starting to flow through him. The panic was receding, giving way to a thickening sense of assuredness. Everything was coalescing back into form. The children's voices sounded more and more distant, fading away in the background. A formidable silence was making its way through, spreading everywhere, covering everything with its motionless veils... setting all around... slowly... gradually... until there was no sound at all. Nothing. Perfect silence.

He just lay there for what seemed to be an eternity. Time had ceased to exist. It was no longer a concept at all, never had been. He just lay there totally still, as if floating in outer space, asleep, yet, fully aware. This was a strange kind of awareness though. There was no internal dialogue or distracting chitter-chatter. It was just an awareness, a presence, a perceiving presence floating through perfect silence, so perfect and still... that it almost resonated. It felt as if everything was just a membrane away from bursting into a loud symphony but unwilling to do so because the pregnant silence would then cease to be. Its perfection stood on a razor's edge, and he found himself gliding through that finest of lines, resonating in the space between boundaries, gliding through them, listening deeply.

There, in the midst of perfect silence and on the cusp of an exalted harmony, he had a revelation. He appreciated the real nature of sound for the very first time, and he felt at peace. At long awaited peace.

Then he began to see images from his childhood. He saw himself playing in the neighbourhood streets with the other kids, going to school for the first time, going on summer vacation, meeting his friends and playing ball... He saw it all. He saw his first kiss with a girl, his first real fight, his first A in class. He saw himself dreaming of being a doctor, a lawyer and a football player. He saw himself dreaming of being an astronaut, wondering what it would be like to float in space, looking at the earth and the stars from his spaceship. He saw himself wondering whether it was possible for him to do that, whether it was realistic. He watched himself think it through. Everyone had told him that being an astronaut was just not possible. He would have to become a realist and choose something else. He would have to grow up and take a proper decision. He saw himself think these things.

And then he began to hear creaks. He heard them coming from the depths of somewhere far away. The perfect silence was cracking all around. Something was breaking apart. Perhaps his dreams.

A thought rushed through him on why his vision of being an astronaut was not a realistic one. There were very few astronauts in the world indeed. The chances of becoming one were very few. They were just not worth considering. He should wish for something else. Perhaps it was for the best. He liked being on earth anyway, near his home, where he could hear the familiar tunes that used to bring such joy to him. He liked to sing them out. He enjoyed singing. Perhaps he could become a good singer.

Then he heard another series of thoughts crash through his mind. Singing was not a serious profession. It was not respectable enough. It didn't carry the same clout as a judge or a surgeon or a certified accountant. There were a thousand small reasons to not become a singer, and they all lunged at him together, tapping away at his mind, making their case heard. And they were getting louder and stronger, pushing away at his dreams, banging against his wishes, pounding on his convictions relentlessly until his peace of mind was shattered to splinters, giving way to a barrage of thoughts and reasons and expectations that had been conjured up from the depths of compulsion to pummel him for the rest of his life.

He lashed out against them, trying to drive them away, seeking out the perfect silence that had nurtured his dreams, but they were unstoppable. The more he pushed them back, the harder they came at him, hollering and demanding and analysing the proper move for him to make, the reasonable way to go, the grownup way of dealing with things. The more he pushed them the stronger they became. He began to buckle down, curl up, give in. And they began to feast on his weaknesses, driving him insane. Nothing could stop them. Nothing. Not even death. Whatever the purpose of this process, it had a truly relentless nature. Stamina, tenacity and faith were totally irrelevant here. So were pain, surrender and repentance. This process seemed poised to perpetuate for all time, stretching into the cruel lengths of eternity, making the gravest statement of all; no exit, no end.

What was this place? Gazing around in disbelief, he tried to make sense of it. Then the barrage stopped and there was silence once again, but not the serene kind. No, this was a different kind of silence.

He was standing on a long and straight road – straight and silver as a narrow moonbeam – facing ahead, into the faraway distance. Mirrors were mounted all along the road's length, on either side, framing it all the way through, up to the point where it seemed to converge into a tiny spot of light.

He traced the road with his eyes, all the way to its source, mirrors condensing into the distance until they became a glossy strand. Then he traced the road back, all the way to himself, mirrors and road resolving back into their separate forms, standing firm and separate before him. He sighed and stepped forward, and the road suddenly stretched all the way behind him too, all the way into infinity, narrowing into the distance gradually, mirrors and road merging into one glossy, yet, darkened sliver once again.

He brought his gaze back from the rear distance slowly, wondering. Then he looked around him, into the mirrors enframing him. Each of them was playing a different episode of his childhood – episodes which he recognised, all of them, without exception. His whole childhood was being played over in those mirrors – everything, from his birth onwards – for him to see once again.

He walked down the road for a while, watching himself in the mirrors in total silence. For how long, he didn't know. It could have been a day, a year, a century, or a second. He just walked on down the road, looking at his life unfolding before his eyes silently.

Suddenly, without warning, the mirrors blacked out. He stopped. Everything was dark. Then the mirrors zapped back on, blinding him. He lifted his hands up, shielding his eyes, and fell to his knees. Gradually, his vision returned, but when it cleared up completely, his heart shrivelled painfully. All the mirrors were showing the same thing; they were playing that first day at Lakeside, that perfect first day… over and over and over again. He got up and walked on down the road, eager to see something else in the mirrors ahead. But the mirrors kept playing that same day over and over again, each a different episode, all at once.

On his right he could see himself making breakfast and sipping on the Brazilian Brew. In front of that he could see himself passing by the two kissing cars and waving at them. On his left he was saying hi to the kids under the good giant willow. Behind that he was speaking to Wonty, the black Labrador, telling him to stop barking up the wrong tree… Every single episode of that day was being played over in those mirrors, all muddled up and mixed together, projected in a cacophony of recollection.

He turned back and began running back towards the direction he'd come from, back towards those mirrors which had been playing his life in proper sequence, from birth onwards. But those episodes had been erased. Every single mirror along the road was now playing that perfect first day at Lakeside, all at once and in one great big assault on his mind. He began to shout, asking for something more, something other than that hauntingly beautiful day to be revealed to him. And then some of the mirrors began to play all the things that had led him to Lakeside, every single detail that had influenced him to move there.

And then there was sound. All the mirrors suddenly erupted into sound, playing the episodes of that perfect day loud and clear. The experience became dense, real, overwhelming. A waft of smells began to sift from the mirrors, penetrating every single cell of his body, inundating him, taking him places, tearing him apart.

He fell to his knees and asked for the future, for everything that had happened after that perfect day. And the mirrors turned matte. Impenetrably matte. There was something going on inside them, something vivid – he was sure – but he could not see through the lacklustre coating.

He lunged at the closest mirror and stuck his head against its surface. It burned like ice. He jumped back startled and in pain, and then lunged at it again, kicking it in as hard as he could. It shattered without a sound, and in its place stood a wide gaping hole, a void so cold and impossible that his mind cracked inside his head upon seeing it. Or was that just the delayed sound of the mirror being shattered?

He tried to squeeze between the mirrors and get off that road, but he couldn't. The slits between them were just too narrow. His legs began to wobble, the bones inside them turning as soft as the flesh that enveloped them. A pang of exasperation cut through him, foreboding the torment of an eternity spent in déjà vu – not as a participant this time, but as an outside observer, awake and aware that he is watching himself living in a dream that had turned into a nightmare.

He began to run, stumbling along the endless road – the mirrors playing that perfect day over and over again, then going out behind dark and matte veils – and he started screaming, begging to be released from the hell of his own doing. The more he screamed the louder the mirrors played his life over, growing bigger and louder, towering over him, closing in. How much longer could he take this? How much longer would he have to endure it?

He prayed for absolution and cursed his endurance away,

inviting surrender and wishing to be annihilated. But to no avail. He could not surrender there, not even if he wanted to. Deep down, he knew it. This was the time when he would simply have to endure the hell of his familiarity in the prison of his entrenched habits. This was the eternal moment of reflection.

He collapsed and curled up against the towering mirror pillars. He closed his eyes and began to mumble, trying to drown out the racket of his petrified life. Amidst the growing commotion, he began to wonder if this was his first time through there or whether he had gone through this ordeal before. If he had, then it must have an end to it, surely. But if he kept coming back, then that meant that he could not remember going through it and that he was repeating his mistakes in life over and over and over again, eventually ending up back in that same place. And round and round and round he went. How many times had he gone through all this? How many times more would he have to go through it before breaking out of the loop? Could he break out of it, or was this what life was all about, an endless rollercoaster ride around the complacencies of one's actions?

Perhaps this was not life at all. Perhaps it was hell, where he'd been damned to spend eternity for what he had done. Taking life for granted now certainly seemed an abominable act, fit for the harshest punishment there was. And there was no harsher punishment than to be forced to go through the motions of his complacent life perpetually and without reprieve, reliving that which he had taken for granted over and over and over again while being awakened every now and again in order to become aware of his fallacy and folly – doomed to watch it for an eternity and fully aware that he is going to be sent back into it without any recollection of what he had gone through, bound to repeat the process one more time.

He just lay there, curled up. For how long he did not know. He just lay there wondering whether there was any way out of this loop, some kind of possibility to break the process and move on with his life, do new things, open new doors, grow a bit more... develop himself and grow stronger and wiser rather than ossify and rot in the false sense of security that a hurriedly claimed adulthood brings. Could he actually do that? Could he actually change? Or was he addicted beyond repair to a specific way of doing things?

When he opened his eyes he saw his wife's beautiful face on the pillow next to him, sleeping like an angel. He switched off the silver alarm clock and began getting up. He stopped. His eyes froze.

Had something happened? It surely felt like it. But he couldn't place his finger on it.

He shook his head. Then he turned around and kissed his wife, and got up.

A little more than thirty minutes later, he was out the door, keys and mobile phone in hand, zipping up his anorak and making his way towards the lake. And there was ole Wonty, the big black Labrador, chasing squirrels on the front lawn of the green house just like always. 'You'll never catch them like that, you silly dog,' he said out loud. 'I been telling you for years, but you never listen. If you wanna catch something, you gotta wait for the right moment and strike just once.' The dog turned and looked at him, then jumped back and began bouncing around the lawn.

He turned his eyes away from the dog and looked for his good neighbour. For a moment he couldn't see him anywhere. He stood and waited for him to materialise out of thin air, but nothing was happening. There was no one there. He began to wonder. Had something happened? It surely felt like it.

Worried, he began to walk towards the house. Then he heard a twig snap. He stopped and turned towards the tall oak tree growing on the front lawn. Another twig snapped. Then his crazy neighbour appeared from behind the oak trunk.

'Ah, there you are! Good morning to you, neighbour,' he shouted at him relieved.

'Good morning, neighbour,' smiled the neighbour back. 'A good morning indeed.'

It truly was. The sun was rising into a crystal blue sky, the breeze was pleasant, and the birds were chirping in the thick green branches. He looked around and thanked the Lord for another perfect day.

'Your dog ain't gonna catch any squirrels if he continues like that. I been telling him so every day but he doesn't listen,' he said with a smile.

'Yep, I know. But that's ole Wonty for you. Hard headed as they come,' the neighbour replied, smiling back. 'Can't teach an ole dog new tricks.'

'Well, I'll keep telling him what to do and how to catch them anyway. I'll be telling him every day! Who knows? Something may stick after all. You never know.'

'Be my guest, neighbour. Keep trying. It's good for the soul.'

'Sure is, neighbour. See you later.'

'As always. G'bye, neighbour. God be with ye.'

He turned his eyes back on the street and began to walk down. Just then, the dog lunged towards him like black lightning and bit him on the ankle.

'WONTY!' yelled the neighbour. 'NO! Get back. Back!' he commanded the dog, which had already jumped back to the lawn, sitting comfortably on its hind legs, staring down the empty road. 'I'm sorry, neighbour. This is very unusual. Wonty has never bitten anyone in his life.'

'Don't worry about it neighbour, it's nothing, it's nothing,' he said hurriedly, trying to hide the pain. It hurt a lot, but he didn't want to show it. He turned down and looked at his bleeding leg, the blood trickling silently onto the dry ground, then swung his head towards Wonty. The dog was still looking down the road, its tongue sticking out of its mouth as if nothing had happened. Then it turned its head around and faced him, panting happily. He chuckled faintly, squinting his eyes and tilting his head a little to the side; he could have sworn the dog was smiling at him! He turned around and looked down the street, then at his leg again. Everything was very unusual indeed. To his great surprise, though, this didn't disturb him at all. In fact, deep down, it kind of made him feel good. Real good! Perhaps this was going to be an unusual day after all, the kind of which he'd never gone through before, the kind of day he hadn't dreamed of in ages – all exciting and fresh and full of crazy surprises. Perhaps this was going to be the first day of the rest of his life.

Xavier Thorntrail

∞ ...Will They Finally Get It?
(They're On the Same Road!) ∞

Somewhere deep in unknown territory, two strange figures are cutting through the barren wasteland. They are communicating in the sweltering heat through strange tongues and mannerisms.

Niet: Move to the right. No, not THAT right (*slaps Snie on the left cheek first*)... THIS right! (*slaps him on the right one*). How much more cliché can we get?

Snie: Don't know.

Niet: Don't start with that again!

Snie: Why not? Um... start with what?

Niet: O brother! (*He pulls his hat down and covers his whole head in it*). Good thing for you I am a cripple, or I'd show you a thing or two (*quickly tries to lift the hat, which is stuck. He pulls harder and his head is freed with a pop*). Yeah, I know you are blind and can't see. So, how would I show you? Well, if I weren't a cripple, you'd feel the kick of my foot. No matter though. I still have my wonderfully mobile hands. A bit to the left (*slap!*).

Snie: How are we doing?

Niet: Good, really good. Right! (*slap*). Left! (*slap*). Good! You're getting it. Soon I won't need to slap you. (*left slap, right slap...*). Yeah, good! You are beautiful!

Snie: All this sense of direction is making me hurt.

Niet: Is that so? Well, when you develop an awareness for the difference between right and left, I will start directing you with words only. Pit hole ahead. Right...(*slap*). So pay attention. Left! (*slap*)...

Snie: There are little colourful spots jumping around my head.

Niet: Really? What colour?

Snie: Yellow.

Niet: Maybe it's the Great Yeller, offering you an omen!

Snie: What kind of omen?

Niet: That if you don't learn right from left really quick, you're gonna pass out. Right! I said right... The other way you moron! (*slap... slap, slap, slap...*).

Snie: Ok, I got it.

Niet: Oh yeah? Let me see... Left. Good! Ok... Right! Goood! One more... Lllll... Right! Perfect, you got it! Ok, now we can relax. Go straight for a while... No, not that way! Straight damn it! STRAIGHT! O brother... *(he sighs and then lifts both his hands. He releases them and they come down swiftly. They land with force on either side of Snie's face at the same time. Crack!).* Aha, there we go... Straight!

They walk for a little while longer under the beat of Niet's hands. Their journey has been uneventful all day long. They are both exhausted and agitated. Ten days in the barren wasteland and still no sign of the Black Box. Only a few skeletons under the burning sun, picked clean by the roaming vultures. And a morphing horizon, which seems to be dancing.

Snie: I have a question.

Niet: Fire ahead. I mean... ask!

Snie: Until I learn right from left and straight, can you direct me by my ears?

Niet: No, I can't. That's precisely the point of this exercise... Learn the difference the hard way so that you can eventually understand the directions verbally.

Snie: What are you talking about? I just want you to grab me by the ears and steer me. I will hurt less that way.

Niet: This person never ceases to surprise me. Ok partner, let's ride!

They go on for a little while longer. Their journey is quieter now. Nothing can be heard. Nothing can be seen for miles and miles. Only blue refreshing pools.

Snie: Water water everywhere, but it disappears when we get close to it.

Niet: It's not water, you fool. I told you already, it's the sky being reflected off the warm rising air. We are in the Mirror Plains. There's no water down here.

Snie: I'd love to drink the sky.

Niet: So did many poets. But they knew that it wasn't made of water.

Snie: Oh yeah? And where does rain come from?

Niet: Nowhere. It hardly ever rains. Or haven't you noticed?

Snie: I know. But where does rain come from when it *does* rain?

Niet: From the vaporised droplets of water.

Snie: What are those?

Niet: Water that evaporates from the earth and rises to the sky. Then it falls back down again.

Snie: Where does the water from the earth come from?

Niet: I told you already. It falls like rain from the sky.

Snie: I'd love to drink the sky.

Niet: Em... shut up! Always confusing me with your gibber-jabber. Pay attention to your ears now and move on.

...

Snie: Um... Niet?

Niet: Yeah?

Snie: Have you ever seen a Black Patrol?

Niet: No.

Snie: Do you know someone who did?

Niet: I told you, no one's ever seen a Black Patrol.

Snie: How do you know what it looks like?

Niet: I don't.

Snie: How will you recognise it from something else?

Niet: By its colour, birdbrain. It's the Black Patrol! Does the word "black" mean anything to you?

Snie: Yeah but... How do you know it's black if no one's seen it?

Niet: Well... I guess someone saw it, a long time ago. The word got passed on. We just don't know who it was.

...

Snie: Um, Niet?

Niet: Yeah Snie?

Snie: Why do the Black Patrols have the same colour as the Black Box?

Niet: Why are you asking me all these stupid questions?

Snie: Well, I thought...

Niet: Oh, you thought! Congratulations.

Snie: No, I meant...

Niet: Shut up! You thought... You meant... What else? An opinion on colours? Since when did you become the colour enthusiast? Apart from a few yellow spots, you can't even remember what colours are like!

Snie: But black is not really a colour...

Niet: Yeah, yeah. It's the absence of all colours. You get an A, as they used to say. Now, let me interpret the visible world and you... You just move along and follow my lead. Giddy up!

Snie: (whispers to himself) But black is when all colours are absorbed, and nothing is reflected back. Black is the presence of all colours. We just can't see them! Right? They are trapped inside.

Niet: What are you muttering to yourself? Go on, move. We have a long way ahead of us. The Great Yeller never stopped riding. Gnikwah said that he was tireless. He wouldn't sleep for days, maybe weeks. One time, the Great Yeller stopped in a small town. Everyone fell to their knees upon seeing him and the sky lit up even brighter for a while... This is one of Gnikwah's favourite stories. Mine too... So, the Great Yeller asked for the mayor. Are you listening? Pay attention! Now, the mayor came to greet him...

> They frolicked along – the talking Niet riding the listening Snie, telling him stories of the Great Yeller – into the barren wasteland.
>
> Suddenly, a gust of wind swept across them, clearing the air. The horizon cleared up from the morphing reflections, and there it was. A Black Box in the far away distance. Niet caught a fleeting glance. Then it was lost behind the dust. Funny! It looked just like Ecosystem 9...
>
> He didn't have time to assess what he'd seen. A deafening buzz sent them both crashing to the ground with hands glued on their ears. The gust of wind grew stronger, lifting a panel of dust around them and hiding the surroundings from Niet's eyes completely. But Snie could sense the change. Unfamiliar vibrations all around. Maliciously unfamiliar vibrations.
>
> The panel of dust circulated around the two fallen explorers, closing in on them slowly, disturbingly slowly. They felt an overwhelming presence bearing in on them. Then... Nothing. Only the faint dreamlike memory of passing through a colossal gate, followed by a surge, an almost triumphant cheer, and a resounding clang.

∞ ∞ ∞

In The Dark

"The whole purpose of education is to turn mirrors into windows"
–Sydney J. Harris

Sunset

I am sitting in a café in the middle of somewhere, watching the world go by. The sun is going down and the butterflies are looking for a place to perch on and sleep. They are gliding through the air, silently, like dreams looking for sanctuary in the darkening wilderness. And as the darkness begins to settle, I can't help but wonder how long this night will be.

Victor Gente Delespejo

Metamorphosis

Night. When it falls the butterflies seek refuge. And while some of them die in the darkness, others are born from it. They emerge tenaciously from their cocoon and stand steady on their legs, stretching their wings for the first time, scanning the new and awesome world that is unfolding before them. They wait, ready to jump into it in the company of their kind, young and old, ready to fly under the sun like dreams fluttered up from the depths of sleep by a passing inspiration. And just like that, in the whisk of a moment, they hop into the air and begin to billow around with courage and grace.

Butterflies... Warrior Butterflies, Defenders of the Faith, Dwellers of the Hidden World, making sure that when the sun rises the following day it shall shine upon an inspiring reality. For what would the fields be without Warrior Butterflies? Mere plains crawling with rudimentary caterpillars, busy bees, lemmings, rats and birds of prey! Not a promising place to wake up in – and hardly inspirational at all – it would be like a conflict without grace... like a breath without oxygen... like a relationship without love... senseless and terminal. Just plain terminal.

But thankfully this is not so. With every cocoon broken a new world is born and another sun rises. The wonder of seeing new landscapes is replaced by the magic of seeing with new eyes, and reality is transfigured in ways that tickle the imagination. And as the spirit soars high above the coarse and harsh surface, there, in the midst of a sunlit day, it gives everyone something to look up to, drawing the vision out of the cell of habit and into the great wide open, where our ongoing transformation has been flourishing for millions of years in the greater ebb and flow.

Xavier Thorntrail

Reflections

As I look in the mirror I realise that you and I are aspects of the same coin, different denominations of a new currency that has begun to circulate around the Globe.

There are many out there, just like you and me, eager to put this currency to good use. They are waiting, looking for others like them, individuals to share their thoughts with in order to create a new paradigm together, a new world. They are out there, lost amidst the Cynics and hunted by the Gurus and the Takers, trying to survive. They are wandering the land, trying to find each other and stand together. They are looking for each other and looking out for their children. Their time has come. And they know it.

As I look in the mirror I see the gloomy reflections of this world begin to transmute into something new, yet, familiar, something good, aspiring and fresh. The dull shades of grey begin to recede, pushed away by an eruption of life and colour, and the wilderness turns into Eden – a haven and sanctuary for the centuries to come. Or is this but a wishful dream that shall go up in flames before it ever sets firm root? Is that what will happen? Will it be consumed by a great inferno? Or will it manage to survive and flourish?

Perhaps both. Perhaps it can only flourish on the ashes of a lost world, just like a forest grows out of its own remains... just like the Modern World rose from the ashes of the Mediaeval, out of the shadow of the Dark Ages and into the modern light. Such a wonderful dream, rebirth. Some call it Phoenix, Phoenix rising. Just like the sun. Just like a diamond.

As I look in the mirror, I see myself in you... Yourself in me... And I wonder whether you really exist. For I think I have made you up. Xavier Thorntrail, a figment of my imagination... A person to talk to in the wilderness, a friend to envision a new reality with. A fellow Warrior Butterfly who will touch the right nerves and ask the burning questions, fighting for a return to substance and to a world based on dreams and principles, not gold dust and glitter. Xavier Thorntrail, my alter ego... The foremost person to turn to... My own dear self!

As I look in the mirror I begin to wonder… Am I looking into it, or am I looking out? It's getting darker. I wonder. I wonder…

∞

"And there, behind the mirror, I saw the truth"
                                                        –Unknown

Printed in the United Kingdom
by Lightning Source UK Ltd.
126540UK00002B/58-273/A